A SMALL TALE OF

UNCOMMON GRACE

Carrie Birde

Blydyn Square Books

Kenilworth, New Jersey

CIP available upon request.
Cover design by: Lisa Schroeder, Di'studio
Interior design by: Gram Telen
Interior illustrations done by the author

DEDICATION

This book is dedicated to Adam & Aaron, to Catbird,
& to anyone and everyone who feels
as if they don't quite "fit"...

CHAPTER ONE

Grace stood in the open doorway, in a spill of clear, mid-morning light. Though the air warmed, the cast-iron door latch beneath her fingers retained its memory of the prior evening's chill and sent a cascade of prickles marching up her arm.

"I really don't like you wandering around the Wood. . . ." Her mother's voice sailed over Grace's shoulder.

"I know, Mom," Grace sighed. The conversation, like migratory birds, returned each spring. Grace understood. Her mother, like many who lived on the fern-lipped edges of the Bright Wood, felt strong reluctance to tarry within its gold- and green-flecked shimmering for long stretches of time. Something about the Wood—how it yielded itself to any who sipped its ligneous beauty through eyes, nose, skin—recalled the latent touch of some deeper, antique intelligence, some memory of primordial magic.

"You remember Aunt Livinia's Uncle Talbin?"

"Yes, Mom," Grace said. "You've told me. . . ." She curled her bare toes over the worn threshold and looked out over the insistent greening of the world—the swaying fields and dormant, stretching landscape; the Bright Wood's shadow-drenched fringes.

"He was lost in the Wood for three days."

Absently, Grace nodded. The air smelled of damp earth and snow melt, loamy and metallic. A corner of her mouth crooked up at one side.

"Are you laughing?"

"No," Grace replied.

Somehow, regardless of season, the Wood possessed a suggestion of green. Even at this distance, seeing it fueled her heart's tempo. Turning on her heel, she crossed the broad-planked wooden floor, left the door flung wide to spring's slow unfolding. When she reached her mother's side, she wrapped her arms about the elder woman's waist. They were of a similar height, and she easily nested her chin into the bare slope of her mother's neck and shoulder.

"You shouldn't laugh," Grace's mother scolded. She measured flour and sugar and salt into a wide wooden bowl, perfectly at ease, draped in her daughter's embrace.

"I'm not laughing, I promise." Grace turned her head slightly, so her right cheek kissed her mother's collarbone. "Am I laughing, Father?"

Across the open room, her father sat on a stool with a pipe clamped between his teeth. He worked steadily, weaving new strips of cane into the damaged seat of an old chair. Glancing over his spectacles at his wife and daughter, he spoke around his pipe's stump: "She's not laughing, Lettie." At the sound of his voice, the brown dog stretched out on the hearthrug near his feet thumped his tail and disturbed a neat stack of slim reeds. This, in turn, drew the attention of a sleek, black-and-tan tabby cat. Pouncing, the cat scattered the pile, slapped at reeds with deft paws.

Lettie sniffed. "You always take her side, Gaven."

"Mom!" Now, Grace laughed in earnest. "There's no side to take!"

"She's right," Gaven agreed, aware of his assertion's irony. He bent to collect and neaten his materials, allowed the cat a length to swipe at.

Lettie gave them each a sideways glance, one brow arched, alert to mischief. "Well." She whisked the bowl's contents, shifted Grace's cheek and chin. "You might not laugh if it had been *you*."

"Mother, I love you dearly." Displaced, Grace crossed the floor between her parents, her bare feet sticking slightly to polished floorboards, until she stood in the honeyed rectangle of light the open door allowed. "But I don't recall that great-grand-uncle. . . ." She paused. "Is that twice removed, or three times?" Scrunching her brow, she ran her index finger along her lower lip and shook her head. "I don't recall any stories of Talbin *complaining*. . . ."

"True," Gaven said. Resuming his task, he wove—in careful, over-under fashion—a slim length of reed into place. "*But*," he continued before his wife could protest or his daughter exult, "those who lived with him had enough to grumble about."

Lettie waved her whisk in triumph, sent a pale dust of flour to glitter and wink in angled light. "His poor wife! She never got another wink of sleep! He shone so, even piled under sheets and blankets!"

"Mom!" Exasperation got the better of Grace. "Everyone claims to have a *distant relation* who returned from some prolonged 'venture through the Wood' *changed* or *altered* or *gifted* somehow, but it's never any intimate friend or family member!"

Lettie, lips pressed into a thin line, cracked eggs into the wide bowl and kept silence. Gaven puffed sweet blue smoke from his pipe, and the dog—unaccustomed to anything vaguely argumentative—roused itself to sitting and whined.

"I'm sorry, Mom." Grace hastened to her mother's side, dismayed. "But you shouldn't worry. It hardly ever happens, if it happens at all. Doesn't that make you *wonder* . . . ?"

Her mother wiped her hands clean on a crisp linen towel. "I love you, Grace, dear, but some things are better left *unwondered*." She brushed Grace's hair back from her face, kissed her cheek. "Now, help me make this cake, or we'll be celebrating your birthday tomorrow." She paused, fixed her daughter with a meaningful glance. "You *did* remember to invite Thaniel for cake, didn't you?"

Grace positioned herself beside her mother, their shoulders brushing, and handed her butter, milk, rosewater. "Hmmm?" A quizzical note issued from her throat, and she nodded vaguely. "Oh, yes, I remembered."

As her mother mixed and stirred, Grace prepared a pan for baking, held it secure as her mother scraped the batter from the bowl into it and smoothed the top.

Though anchored here in the cottage, Grace's thoughts wandered elsewhere, tiptoed quietly out the open door and beyond, toward the Bright Wood. There, she wandered among its great, cathedralled trees, through panes of light framed by branch and bough, over plush carpets of moss and toothy thickets of fern. When the dog leaned against her skirt, his tail sweeping the floor, Grace leaned down and splayed her fingers so he might lick them clean.

"Such a good boy, Murl," Grace said. Smiling, she stroked the dog's head.

Keeping her thoughts to herself, she said nothing of how frequently she wondered what gift or mark or token the Wood might give her, how much she secretly wished to know, and how disappointed she was each year that she remained, simply, Grace.

CHAPTER TWO

She rose early the next morning, long fingers of sunlight tapping at her bedroom window. A gap between the window's sash and frame permitted the sweet, dew-damp breeze to pluck at white cotton curtains. Grace sat on the bed's edge amid the snarl of bedclothes still warm with her body's heat. After exchanging nightclothes for blouse and knit top, thick socks and green woolen skirts with deep pockets, she rose, set feet to floorboards.

"Hello, little ones," she said, greeting the small birds gathered on the windowsill.

The birds scattered at her approach, their plump, energetic forms distorted by the window's rippled glass as they winged off. Always, their rapid departure surprised and disappointed. A long sigh escaped her.

Before slipping down the narrow staircase, she paused at her parents' room, pressed her ear to the closed door. Beyond the oak's grained partition, she heard the soft hum of their contented slumber. Rarely did they sleep past the sun's climb over the distant Wood's crown, but they had all leaned deep into the previous evening, toasting Grace's health with song and story, tea and cake, and a thumb or two of plum cordial. Her mouth curved in smile. *Let them sleep*, she thought.

Lightly, her hand grazed the banister as she slipped, skirts shushing, down the stairs. Evidence of celebration remained—used dishes stacked on the pie safe; bone-dry washbasin upon the worktable; stubbed candles; crumpled linens; and, on a large, round platter, a sizeable portion of cake—a rough semicircle of yellow, top and sides frosted white and adorned with a ring of dried rose petals and three tender fiddleheads, their crowns tightly curled. Given her mother's habits, it was a rare and disorderly sight.

Beside the cake stood a tall earthenware vase, filled with pale gray pussy willows—Thaniel's gift. Walking her fingers over the small, tight catkins, she recalled the previous evening, gathered round the table as her parents regaled Thaniel with the story of her name's origin.

"Our Grace was born on a Tuesday, of the Vernal Equinox," Lettie had said, patting her daughter's hand and intertwining their fingers.

"A day of twofold and perfect balance," Gaven had chimed in, raising his glass of cordial so that it winked rosy-purple in the pulse of candlelight. He had met his wife's eyes. "And what name do you think we would have given our girl, Lettie," he had paused to sip his cordial, "if she'd been born on a Thursday of the Winter Solstice, or a Sunday at summer's height?"

"Oh, I don't know," her mother had mused. With her head tilted to one side, her expression dreamy, she had considered Grace, given her hand a squeeze. "Constance, perhaps. Or Bliss."

After nineteen years, Grace knew the narrative by heart, felt a deep sense of gratification to share in a ritual that brought her parents such pleasure. She recalled, too, the new addition to the annual event, both curious and welcome: Thaniel.

"No other name would do," Thaniel had said. The quiet timbre of his voice had matched his gaze. "*Grace* suits you." In response, Gaven and Lettie had lifted their cups in unison.

Then, as now, thinking of Thaniel, of his clear, brown-eyed regard, raised a small, insistent flutter in the pit of Grace's stomach. She sliced herself a slim wedge of yellow cake to occupy it. Thaniel, Edgewoode's veterinarian, had ever been part of the tapestry of their lives, her life. But lately . . .

Grace broke a morsel of cake with her fingers and popped the bit into her mouth, tasting sweet butter and egg, the floral trace of rosewater. She heard, from the hearth across the room, the soft click and pad of approaching feet, instinctively dropped her left hand to receive the dog's damp nose. Murl licked stray cake crumbs from Grace's fingertips, his brown brush tail thumping a steady beat against her skirts.

"Let's go for a walk," Grace said. She reached down to scratch Murl's brown-and-white head, his feathery ears, and the wagging increased. "Just a short walk, just you and me, before everyone wakes up." She crossed the room to the cottage's door, the dog at her heels, and stuffed her stockinged feet into a pair of well-scuffed boots. She took her new green knit shawl from a peg, swirled it about her shoulders, and together, young woman and dog stepped outside to greet the rosy morning.

A haphazard path of bricks charted a course past a neat kitchen garden, beneath a willow arch knotted with vines. Murl dashed ahead, and Grace followed, pausing to touch the small green nubs tucked, like secrets, within the vine's snarled skein of growth.

Their cottage lay at the eastern fringe of Edgewoode, a small town snugged just outside the Bright Wood's green, northwestern fringes. Grace knew every stitch of the town—every tree, creek bed, and dirt path; every meadow, farm, and inhabitant. Edgewoode resided, with all its memory of fact, fable, and folklore, in her blood.

Overhead, the wide, slow-bluing sky yawned, full of pewter-edged clouds that hinted at rain. She stepped over and around small puddles strewn and collected across the dirt track, while Murl, heedless of such obstacles, dashed forward and back; upon each return, he sent up spatters of mud to speckle Grace's skirts. Ahead, and to the right, the omnipresent green of the Bright Wood burgeoned in silent invitation. To her mother's distress, Grace knew much of the nearby Bright Wood, as well; rather than fearing it, she felt an unspecified comfort in its presence.

In truth, she often felt more at ease amid the Wood's bounds than she did with the small town's folk. After nineteen years, the people of Edgewoode knew her as a girl unchanged and affectionately teased for walking barefoot in the rain or wearing flowers tucked behind her ears. And it remained true that she collected stones and feathers and discarded nests, and that she always carried a bit of biscuit or an apple or a scattering of seed in her pocket to toss to any creature she came across. She wondered, as she walked, if, after nineteen years of being so, this must now change. The mere thought sent a splinter through her core.

Motion caught her gaze, the abrupt smear of iridescent wings. Starlings. The flock of birds lifted, as one, from a straw-pale field and moved through the air as if they were a single creature constructed of a hundred pairs of wings. She waved in greeting, as she always greeted everyone, *everyone*—man, woman, or child; furred, feathered, scaled, antennaed; leafed or petalled; ligneous or moss-coated—with whom she crossed paths. Must this, too, change?

"Good morning!" She called aloud to that shared, wind-born body. A small act of defiance. The starlings moved overhead, undulating, their wings at once a single vibration of sound comprised of many.

Grace let her gaze fall away from the flock, resettled now at a safer distance. Though she relished this cool air—damp, not dry; a breath of green life stirring—she curled her shoulders beneath her shawl and increased her gait. Her skirts, dampening, slapped about her legs, her boots. For the moment, Murl trotted along beside her, flop-ears pricked and nose twitching, ever alert, when, with a sudden bark, he dashed off. A cascade of mud marked the dog's progress. Keeping her feet on the track, Grace traced his progress, curious as to whom or what had caught the dog's interest.

Slowing to stop in the grass-fringed track, Grace shielded her eyes beneath the blade of her hand. She watched Murl lope along a low, wooden fence through a neighboring field and stop, tail sweeping, to greet Thaniel. Catching her hair in one hand and weaving her fingers through to keep the wind from thoroughly tangling it, Grace watched the veterinarian stoop to draw his hand over Murl's marbled brown fur in long, even strokes. She wondered what domestic ailment called Thaniel to her neighbor's door and quietly, in her heart, wished them ease.

The morning sun climbed and collected about Grace's shoulders. She could think of nothing more she might want than these moments, assembled and woven into the warp and weft of her contented life; their slow unfolding, one into the next. With the breeze curling through her hair, laced with the fragrant promise of spring; with tree shadow lengthening over tussled grasses beneath the sun's measured arc. It seemed implausible to want or wish for more. Ever.

And yet . . .

And yet. She felt a tug. Small. Coy. Insistent.

Grace glanced left, past fallow growth, greening and eager to cast off winter; past the familiar shapes of Murl and Thaniel, bound in friendly communion. She stood—here and now—feet planted amid the well-trodden hip and sway of packed earth that connected all the villagers of Edgewoode. Yet, she was ever aware that beyond the track's bend, just ahead, the Bright Wood swelled. She heard its rustle and song, felt her skin prickle in response.

"Murl!" Grace called. She rubbed her arms to kindle warmth, snugged her shawl about herself into a tight knot. The dog turned and pelted back along the fence and arrived, panting and grinning, at Grace's side.

"Such a good boy," she said. Knees pressed to earth, Grace scratched the ruff of Murl's neck with both her hands. The dog's tail swept with renewed vigor. Grace stood and smiled at Thaniel as he moved toward her, a large satchel slung over one shoulder and one broad palm lifted in greeting.

"What brings you this way?" Grace called as he approached. "Anything amiss at the Steffords'?"

Thaniel shook his head. A strip of leather bound his hair at the nape of his neck, but here and there, a dark wave or curl escaped. "All is well," he said. He shifted the satchel and bent to pat Murl's head again, received a thorough licking. "It's lambing season. A busy time." Standing, straightening, he smiled at her. "Thank you for inviting me to dinner last night. The stories your parents shared . . . were entertaining!"

"After you've heard them a dozen years or so, you might change your mind."

"Is that a promise of future invitations?" Thaniel waggled his eyebrows at her.

Grace laughed and considered the toes of her boots. She could not quite convince herself it was the wind that warmed her cheeks.

"Did your neighbors truly consult sages and midwives, and have star charts drawn in hopes of having a child like you?" Amusement lit his brown eyes, his mouth's curve.

"I only know what I've been told." She looked at him sideways, smiled through the veil of her hair. "I was too young to observe, personally."

"Yes, of course." Thaniel nodded, grin broadening. "So. How does it feel, one day into your personal new year?"

Shrugging beneath her shawl, Grace met his eyes, returned a fraction of his smile. "Should it feel different?" Murl leaned contentedly against her right leg. She skritched the dog's domed skull, appreciative of his warmth.

"That depends on your expectations," he said.

"I guess I was expecting . . . I was hoping that . . ." The words tumbled out of her in a rush before she caught herself. Murl whined as, absently, she straightened and withdrew her hand from behind his left ear. She saw, beyond Thaniel's shoulder, that the dark, glittering flock of starlings and blackbirds had settled again among the field's weave and stir of grasses.

"Grace?" Her name on Thaniel's tongue held a particular warmth.

She smiled with more certainty than she felt. "It's nothing," she began. "Only . . . It's just that . . ." She searched his face, as if the answer lay in the stroke of his jaw, the plane of his cheek or brow.

"What?"

One of the qualities she appreciated about Thaniel—he asked; he never demanded. The flutter in her stomach returned, and she slid her gaze sideways, down. "It feels like something's ending. . . ." No sooner had she named the nascent impression, than it took on a firmer aspect, like a kernel or nut or seed, full of its own purpose and dimension.

Thaniel's lips pursed as he considered. "Sometimes," he said slowly, "endings are beginnings in disguise." His brows rose, hopeful, encouraging.

"I like that." Grace smiled. Murl thumped his tail.

"Good. Now, I've got to go. The Steffords are expecting me." He adjusted the satchel against his back and shoulder. "There, see? Lambing is the perfect example of endings as beginnings."

Grace considered this with an admiring glance. "I suppose it is."

"Well, then, my work here is done." Thaniel grinned. "On to the day's tasks!" Flashing his palm in salutation, he turned back along the earthen track from the direction he had come.

"Thaniel!" Grace called to his quick-departing form. "There's still cake—you should help us with it, when you have time!"

"Happy to," he called back. Distance softened and reshaped his voice's tone.

Grace watched Thaniel as he made his way through the field along the long, low wooden fence, up and over a rough stile toward a huddled fieldstone farmhouse. In unison, the starlings and blackbirds lifted—pulsing and trilling—once more at his approach. Beneath the edge of her hand, Grace followed their rippling pattern scrawled across the sky. Dropping her arm, she looked at Murl, who wagged and grinned doggily up at her. "Everyone must be up by now," she said to him. "I guess we should go home."

As if he understood, Murl turned and sped in that direction, tail streaming behind him. Grace followed, less fleet of foot. As she trod the earthen track back toward the cottage, she heard, at first faintly, a rushing sound, as of wind or wings. She glanced over her shoulder, expecting to see the flock curled and extended against the firmament, but a quick scan revealed only a cloud-brushed sky, the field full of abstract, strutting motion.

She continued walking, and the morning elongated and expanded all around her, like a sigh.

The faint sound of rushing, rustling, susurrating persisted inexplicably, grew.

CHAPTER THREE

Spring advanced, and the regularity of Grace's excursions to the Bright Wood increased. The Wood contained a bounty of resources—food, herbs, firewood; one needed only to know when and where to look. And Grace knew all the local niches and small nooks and ledges where things grew and thrived. Pockets filled with wild ramps and watercress and a small bouquet of primrose, Grace returned along the packed-earth track that hugged the Wood's edge toward home. Though her mother fussed, she appreciated the replenishments to her pantry.

Today, the Bright Wood threw light and shadow against Grace's cheek. Wind plucked at her skirts, at the tasseled edge of her green shawl and the hair tucked behind her left ear. All the while, the Wood breathed, in leaf and fern and wildflower. Grace's gaze slipped over the forest as she passed, over moss-stroked trunks and tree limbs, over the thickening swaths of green undergrowth. The Wood invited her. Deep within, she felt its sly wink and gentle tug; its tendrilled reach, in flora and fauna, in the shift and change of its seasons. A call. A toll of something greater that echoed in her flesh.

Underfoot, the path she walked both described and divided—a ribboned line drawn of earth. To her right, bicolored goats and sleek auburn horses mingled in sun-warmed pastures; sheep drifted like earthbound clouds. To her left, the light-spangled embrace of the Bright Wood soared skyward. All her morning chores lay behind her: chickens fed, coop raked out, water fetched from the well. She would tend the family's small kitchen garden and its tender, greenling plants this afternoon, then sort, clean, and store her foraged edibles.

Skirts whispering about her legs and ankles, boot laces trailing, she walked alone, thoughts free to drift. The night had released its burden of rain, and the Bright Wood dripped and pattered—each leaf and grass blade gleamed, brightly beaded. Pausing, she bent to pick a moss pink from a blushing patch of growth at the track's edge.

Tilting her head to one side, she wove the flower behind her left ear. Her hair curled with moisture, and it seemed the forest's subtle pull intensified. She dismissed the notion as imagination.

For a moment, she lingered at the understory's edge, hoping to hear spring's true herald: the wood thrush. Each season, at winter's end, she heard the thrush in this vicinity, where tended land pressed up against the Bright Wood's flank, his song a flutter of light-dappled melody stroked over every branch and bough and leaf bud. She would stand on the verge, on that unseen divide, with her face angled slightly upward. As if to catch the fall of dappled light on her cheeks would allow her to absorb the song itself through her flesh and impress it, note by rolling note, into memory. As if the liquid song stitched upon the air might imbue her with . . . *something*. She knew not what.

Today, though, among the chatter and call of songbirds, the thrush's song remained absent.

Resuming her walk, she measured the tramp of her footsteps along the muddied track against the silent-yet-not Wood, listened to the staccato rustle and slap of her dampened skirts against her boots and calves. With a sideways glance, she sought to peel back the layers of green-soaked light and invoke that small, rust-brown bird into being, but resigned herself to patience.

She slipped her hand into her skirt's deep pocket and drew out a cloth napkin, and unfolded a domed, palm-sized mound—a biscuit, snatched from the cooling rack when her mother's back was turned. Breaking a piece from the whole, she popped it into her mouth. Light in texture, the biscuit melted, sweet and buttery, over her tongue. Her mother was an exceptional baker; the biscuit, proof.

Sweeping her hand along the front of her dress, she brushed away a veil of ivory crumbs, breaking off another piece of biscuit, when a sharp, sudden noise drew her attention: a loud, scolding chatter. Her steps slowed, and she turned in place, squinted through bands of fluid light. The scolding grew—louder, more insistent. She craned her neck and peered beyond a slip of tree, tried to penetrate the deep, wayward tangle of scrub and thicket. The underbrush stirred and rustled. She knew the noises of the Wood, knew they often sounded larger and louder than their makers. All the same, she halted, her heart hiccupping beneath her sternum.

A sleek, gray squirrel darted forward. Front paws clasped and folded over its white-furred chest, the creature sat up and curled its long, gray-brush tail over its back. It eyed her seriously with bright, black eyes.

Grace grinned. "Hello," she said.

The Bright Wood sheltered a wide variety of flora and fauna; squirrels were among the most common. She considered the creature: the compact, oblong head balanced on narrow shoulders; overlarge eyes and furred, thumbnail-sized ears; the wizened fingers, so suggestive of a human's, curled against its breast. The squirrel twitched beneath her gaze, increasing the impression of a nervous, skittish being.

"It's okay." She spoke in a modulated voice, broke off a corner of the biscuit. "Have some."

The creature dropped one front paw, flashed its tail against its smooth back, and chattered sharply. Grace took this as consent. She knelt in the muddied track, knees pressed to earth and moss and stones. Her woolen skirts pooled about her, green lapping brown.

"Here . . ."

Leaning forward over her knees, she extended her arm and flung the biscuit with a flick of her wrist. The piece bumped and rolled along the track, crumbled as it traveled. Darting forward, the squirrel deftly claimed the largest portion. It eyed her cagily as it rolled the bit between its paws and teeth, scattering crumbs.

"It's good, isn't it? Want some more?" Grace flicked another piece toward the creature, which the squirrel immediately snatched up.

After a moment's observation, Grace gathered her skirts in fistfuls. Though she rose slowly, smoothly, the squirrel reacted in frenzied fashion. It dashed left, then right, backward and forward, and finally froze at the Wood's edge. Four paws spread, it pressed its white belly to the earth and fixed her with a wild eye. Quickly, it stuffed the remaining crumbs of biscuit into its mouth.

"*NoNoNo! Mine! Not yours mine!*"

A torrent of words, nearly unintelligible, found Grace's ear. Breathless, she rose and remained very still. Twining fingers through the folds of her skirts, she cocked her head slightly.

"What?" The word sat on her tongue, feeble in its uncertainty.

"*Not mine not yours! MineYoursNot!*"

Heart thumping, Grace watched the squirrel turn, scramble, and dash back into the underbrush. She remained rooted. Staring fixedly at the point of the squirrel's departure, she forced herself to swallow several deep, even breaths, and strove to comprehend, to separate fact from fancy.

"Squirrels." Another voice, a sigh—from above, behind, everywhere and nowhere.

"What?" Again, that insufficient word! Grace pushed her hair back and behind her ear, loosening the carefully placed moss pink. In a five-petalled flutter, the small pink flower spiraled, unnoticed, to the forest floor.

"Truly pitiful . . ."

Lightheaded, Grace pivoted in place; or perhaps, the world itself spun. It seemed as though the Bright Wood were speaking.

"They *try*, but one can't expect too much from them. . . ."

Grace lifted her gaze. The voice held a fluttering quality, and drifted down like rain, like sunlight through the gilt-leafed canopy.

"They lack etiquette . . . conversational skills . . ." The voice paused, dropped in tone and volume, then added: "A bit addled, you could say."

In spite of herself and the extraordinary situation, Grace laughed. The word *addled* seemed curiously appropriate and might apply as easily to herself as well as squirrels.

"I, though," the voice continued, "possess many of the very qualities that squirrels, in general, lack."

Chin lifted, neck arched, Grace turned a near half circle before she found the speaker's source: a bird—chestnut and ivory, bright-eyed and speckle-breasted. Wood thrush. It mused aloud, perched on a slender beech limb. The thrush tilted his head and asked: "Is there any biscuit left?"

"Yes." Somewhat giddily, Grace nodded—room for a moment's hesitation, a moment's disbelief, did not exist.

"Is it currant?"

"It is." She broke off yet another piece of her dwindling supply and poked at the dark, wrinkled fruit strewn against her palm. "See?" She raised her hand up for the bird's inspection.

"My favorite," he chirruped brightly. "May I?"

"Oh, yes, of course," she answered. Her head swam with confused delight.

"Thank you."

The thrush spread cinnamon wings, lifted from his perch, and settled slim, salmon-pink talons on Grace's outstretched wrist. Folding wings, flicking his tail, he picked at her palm, his slender beak carefully collecting currants first, then crumbs. Each time he swallowed, a small lump moved down his throat, raising pale feathers.

"Very good." He stood in her palm, cocked his head, peered at her with bright eyes. "Did you make it?"

"No." The implausibility of the situation vied with all reason, yet she responded calmly, judiciously. "My mother did. She's an excellent baker." Thrush's slim legs were lightly scaled, and the feather-light touch of his claws pricked and tickled.

"Well." Thrush bobbed his head in appreciation. "I should be off. Work to do, grounds to establish."

"Of course," Grace said with a reasonable shrug. Chores awaited her at home, also.

"Thank you."

"You're welcome," she said.

"Never mind the squirrels," he told her; "they can't help themselves."

"Oh . . ." She didn't know what to say, though Thrush's comment made curious, intuitive sense.

With a tilt of his head and a slight hop, Thrush unfurled his wings and spiraled effortlessly into the air.

"Wait," Grace called. She turned in place to follow the lift and glide of his flight, reluctant to allow the exceptional moment to end. "Will I see you again?"

"Most likely," he chirped. Tipping a wing, he circled overhead. "I sing this territory spring through summer."

"I'll listen for you." She raised her voice to call after him: "I'm Grace."

"I know who you are. We all do." Thrush's flutelike song chimed down as he departed. "We've been waiting for you. . . ."

Grace stood, rooted, face lifted. She watched, vision narrowing, as the thrush winged away and into the Bright Wood, beyond her line of sight—a fleet, bright ember flaring against oak and maple, beech and spruce. Heart racing, breath tight against her ribs, she nonetheless clung to her connection to him, to that moment. She stared hard at the slim gap in the branches through which he slipped. Motionless. Considering. Simultaneously confused, elated, stunned.

Eventually, she remembered herself. Ramps and cress in her apron pockets, feet stuffed in heavy boots; earthbound, yet soaring. She reoriented herself and picked her way reflexively along the dirt track. As she walked, she ate the biscuit's remainder without realizing she did so.

To Grace's left, the Bright Wood glittered and hummed.

CHAPTER FOUR

Dr. Endrue snapped his medical bag shut. Despite age and wear, the bag's brass clasps and stiff leather shone with a warm patina. His bearing expressed a similar august maturity as he directed a mild yet steady gaze over Grace's head at her parents and pronounced: "There is nothing physically wrong with your daughter."

"Nothing wrong?" Grace's mother's voice held an uncharacteristic edge.

"Now, Lettie . . ." Gaven, recognizing the look in his wife's eye, stopped mid-speech.

"Don't take that tone with me!" The edge of Lettie's voice sharpened. "Our daughter is *hearing* things!"

Grace, three days after her nineteenth birthday, found herself relegated once more to childhood. In the newly re-caned chair, she sat surrounded—her parents arranged to either side, the doctor before her. "Mom," she turned her head, looked up into her mother's concern. "I feel fine, really."

"No." Lettie gestured, fingers spread, palms wide. "You are not *fine*!"

Grace shifted in her chair; rigid reeds rubbed against one another in subtle protest. The cottage was filled to brimming with golden light; floors, cabinetry, and table were burnished to warmth with the sun's westering path. At the table's center, the haloed pussy willows shone in their vase. Grace had been poked, prodded, and palpated. Dr. Endrue's uncalloused hands belied practical strength and tactile knowledge. When he had leaned close, Grace detected traces of camphor and lanolin and aniseed. With the examination concluded, she looked past the doctor's tweed-clad shoulder, out the window. She had managed to keep her secret for three days only.

"Grace is in perfect health," Dr. Endrue confirmed, his voice at once calm and authoritative. Removing his spectacles, he held them up for inspection, frowned as afternoon light glanced off their lenses. He procured a crisp white handkerchief from his vest pocket and proceeded to carefully clean the lenses.

Exasperated, Lettie clucked her tongue and folded her arms beneath her breast.

A new voice, previously unheard, whined a soft inquiry: "Why is everyone angry?"

Grace looked down at Murl, who pressed against her leg and settled on the hem of her skirt. The dog gazed up at her with a doleful expression, silky flop-ears flattened against his skull.

Another voice, a honeyed reverberation: "This has nothing to do with you, dog. This is a human issue."

Grace slid her gaze sideways toward the hearthrug, where Sylvie lay stretched in graceful feline arch, striped head resting on her crossed front paws. The tabby's tail tip twitched to its own rhythm.

"Did I do something wrong?" Murl set his long jaw against Grace's thigh.

"No." Grace shook her head, unable to hold her tongue when faced with the dog's worry. "You didn't do a thing." She smiled, smoothed her hand over Murl's brindled head.

"There, you see?" The swift sweep of her mother's hand indicated Grace.

Dr. Endrue replaced his spectacles on the bridge of his nose and, nodding in a pacifying manner, stroked his trim, silvered beard. "I see nothing," he said, "but a young woman in full health." He held up his index finger to indicate he had not finished. "What Grace does or does not hear, only she can say."

A stricken look moved over Lettie's features. Her eyes shone. "But . . ."

"Lettie," Gaven said, approaching his wife and slipping his arm around her waist in a consoling half-embrace. "It will be all right." He glanced at the doctor for affirmation.

"Almost certainly." The doctor ducked his chin. Light glinted, flashed off the wire and glass of his spectacles, concealing his eyes.

"Every year," Lettie said, "every year, I caution her against spending time in the Wood." Though she directed her statement toward the doctor, she stared fixedly at Grace.

Again, the doggie voice interposed itself upon Grace's aural faculties and her thoughts: "I like the Wood."

With effort, Grace kept her gaze level with her parents and the doctor. Dropping her hand, she scratched Murl behind the ears.

"On that point, dog, we agree," Sylvie's voice insinuated, smooth as a whisker.

"There are *so many good smells* in the Wood!" Murl's tongue lolled as he grinned and panted.

The tabby cat yawned wide exaggeration: "And . . . we revert to form." Sylvie spread and extended her front claws, sank them into the hearthrug, and elongated her spine.

"Grace! Are you even listening?"

Grace startled, opened her mouth to respond, found herself speechless. She blinked at her mother in silent apology.

"To be fair, Lettie," Dr. Endrue soothed. "The Wood itself may not be entirely to blame." He paused, stroked trim chin whiskers, lifted his gaze and studied the plaster ceiling. "I know of one particular case—a village not far west of here—over a period of time, this particular individual developed the knack of seeing in utter darkness." The doctor shrugged, met Lettie's gaze. "They had never set foot in the Wood."

"Never, you say?" Gaven hugged his wife to him, gently, held her hand.

"Nor even laid eyes upon it," the doctor affirmed.

"But . . ." Lettie clutched Gaven, as if the contact tethered her to firm ground. "What do we *do*?"

"*Do*?" Dr. Endrue lifted his silver brush brow—the only untamed detail of his demeanor. "Why, you live! *She* lives! You find your way forward—together, gratefully. You thank your lucky stars Grace was born to *this* time, to this place."

Sylvie leapt into Grace's lap, thrust her small, hard skull into Grace's ribs. "What other time or place is there?" the cat drawled. "It is always *now*." Curling herself atop Grace's thighs, she let her striped tail dangle and switch against Murl's nose.

"I'm glad it's now." Murl whuffled the cat's tail, sneezed.

Grace laughed, then felt the weight of her parents' and Dr. Endrue's attentive stares.

Dr. Endrue gripped his medical bag and saw himself to the door, where he donned his coat and hat. "As astonishing and uncommon as it may be, these things happen." With a thoughtful expression, he reached down to pat Murl, who had followed him across the floor to snuffle his pant leg.

Straightening, the doctor drew the door open and spring spilled in. Framed in gold-washed light, he tipped his hat to Lettie and Gaven. Addressing Grace, he said: "This will be what you make of it—gift or burden. The choice is yours and yours alone."

CHAPTER FIVE

As the days followed one after another, Grace found herself in the new and unexpected role of eavesdropper—from the distant cries of a lone, mournful wolf, to the small and dusty sparrows that huddled on her window's ledge each morning, to this very moment. Here, in the chicken coop, the hens frothed about her, darting and scuttling in and out. Slowly, Grace drew the rake over the coop's crooked wooden boards, collected soiled straw and scattered fresh. No longer were the hens' soft clucks and mutters the simple sounds of previous days.

"She always gets the center nest box," one buff hen squawked.

A speckled hen, pecking at Grace's bootlace, jerked her head up and asked, tartly: "What's so special about the center nest box?"

"That's what I'd like to know," said the buff. She cocked her head to one side and stared up and down at once. "Not that I've ever had the chance."

"You're never happy unless you've got something to complain about," said the speckled hen.

"Who's not happy?" A red hen ducked into the coop.

"Who else?"

The red hen stretched her wings and flapped in the doorway. "Still on about the center box, is she?"

"*What* else?" The speckled hen jabbed at Grace's bootlace.

"It isn't *fair*!" Fluffing with indignance, the buff hen sent several pale feathers drifting.

"Would you *mind*?" A plump russet hen squawked from the contested box. "I'm trying to *lay* here."

Another voice—clipped with authority—rose above the fracas: "What's all the fuss about in here, ladies?"

Grace turned toward the coop's door as the resident rooster pushed past the hens. Strutting down the aisle, he eyed each hen from beneath the scallop-edged curl of his comb. They scurried from his path and considered their scaled feet to avoid his yellow eye, mumbled a low chorus of negation among themselves.

"This wouldn't have anything to do with nest boxes, would it?" the rooster demanded. He crowed sharply, turned and dodged back down the aisle with his head lowered. Glossy green-black feathers stood out off his stretched neck. Again, the hens clucked and stammered.

"Good," the rooster said. Satisfied, he drew himself up to his full height and, with several strong thrusts of his wings, beat the air. Briefly, he paused to glare up at Grace. "Useless. Utterly useless."

Uncertain whether she, too, had been chastised, Grace observed the rooster as he stalked down the wooden ramp and out into the yard, where he continued scolding without pause. She resumed raking up soiled straw, and the hens' discourse continued around her ankles.

"Who does he think he is, anyway?" Buff clucked.

"As if he could tell the difference between a good nest box and a fat grub," Russet, from the center box, agreed.

"I wouldn't let him talk to *me* that way. . . ." Speckled tugged at Grace's bootlace, untied the whole.

"I think he's dreamy," said Red. "Do you see how his tail feathers curl and shine?"

"You would," remarked Speckled. "He sets one spur on me, and I'll pluck him featherless." Dropping Grace's bootlace, she delivered a sharp peck to Red's combless head.

Grace stepped back as Red squawked and flounced from harm's way, then resumed working. With several strong strokes, she raked the last of the soiled straw out into the chicken yard and, hens scattering before her, behind the coop. Through the coop's slat wooden walls, she heard the nesting hen's wails: "Can't I have some *peace*? I'm trying to *lay*!"

After breakfast, with Murl at her side, Grace headed out again. A basket of brown and white eggs swung from her forearm.

"Where are we going?" The dog grinned a broad, doggie grin as he looked up at her. His tongue lolled over pink gums and time-blunted teeth.

"To Kenston's farm, to trade eggs for cheese," she said. Murl had specifically asked to join her, and she wondered if this had always been the case.

"I like cheese." If possible, the dog's grin increased.

Grace laughed. "So do I."

Gradually, the sloping pastures widened into uninterrupted meadowland, and Murl darted ahead, white-tipped tail held high. Over bristled grass heads, drifting like song, Grace heard cows lowing, goats bleating. The sounds, random and lovely, took slow shape in her mind, became recognizable patterns.

"I wish he would take more care," a brown cow said softly to her companion between mouthfuls of new grass. Her large dark eyes, fringed with thick lashes, shone soulful and dewy.

"Your dewlap to bliss's ear," replied the cow's friend. She switched her long, tassel-tipped tail and chewed contemplatively. "As if a full udder isn't its own discomfort."

Grace's step slowed. Pushing her hair back from her face, she considered the cows—soft and brown and placid—just beyond a plain, timber fence. After a moment's hesitation, she spoke: "I could speak to him . . . the farmer, if you like . . ."

Both cows—still chewing—swung their heavy heads, their large-eyed gazes toward Grace.

"Would you?" the first asked.

"It's just that his hands are so . . . *rough*. . . ." said the second.

"And cold."

"We really don't like to complain. . . ."

"I'm headed to see him now." Grace lifted the eggs in explanation, then, uncertain of interspecies etiquette, clasped the basket behind her back. "I'll speak with him," she promised.

"Thank you, dear," the cows lowed in unison.

Continuing along the fence, Grace soon lost the cows' conversation. Interspersed among the docile, bovine herd, an energetic and loose-knit flock of goats romped and frisked. One of these, a white kid, tussled with a slightly older black-and-white goat.

"I'll bet I can jump clear over!" the kid proclaimed. She stood erect on her small pointed hooves, tail flicking, ready to spring. The object of her attention dozed in the sun a mere dash away—an elderly nanny goat.

The black-and-white rolled his eyes. "You couldn't even." His lower teeth extended slightly forward of his upper jaw.

"I can so too," the kid protested. It butted its small head into the black-and-white's hindquarters.

"Not in a crow's age," the black-and-white goaded. "Not in a *mule's* age." Disengaging the smaller goat, he arched his head backward and scratched his neck experimentally with the tips of new-grown horns. His pupil shone, a dark bar amid an iris of gold. Unblinking, he stared at the kid with teeth bared. "Not ever."

"Crows' and mules' and *all ages*!" The kid frisked and stamped. Without visible effort, she pushed herself skyward several inches into the air, hooves free of damp turf. With a snort and a bleat and a kick of stiff legs, she lowered her head and dashed toward the bearded nanny. She dashed and leapt—and landed squarely on the nanny's broad back.

"Off off *off*!" The nanny bleated fury, flashed her tail back and forth in vexation.

"See?!" the kid called from her perch. She danced in place, triumphant, tapping small cloven hooves along the nanny's spine. "I told you I could so too!"

"Off!" The nanny shook herself, levered her back end skyward. "Now!"

The black-and-white goat chewed, unimpressed. "You said you could get clear *over*." His jaw slid from side to side.

"I *am* over. . . ." She adjusted her footing as the nanny creaked beneath her.

"*Off*!" Nanny ratcheted her front end up.

"That's not over," the black-and-white said. "That's atop."

"Same difference."

"Just different," the black-and-white said. "Not the same."

The nanny twitched the flesh and muscles along her torso like a wave, from withers to flanks. She cursed—pointedly and inventively.

Delighted, the kid disembarked. She pranced in circles through new grass and clover, over stone and stump, toward her friend. "Bet I can jump clear over *him*. . . ."

"You don't know what *over* means."

"I do so *too* know," the kid insisted.

Grace realized, as she walked along the fence, the basket of eggs swaying against her arm, that she was laughing aloud.

She departed Kenston's with the farmer's somewhat bewildered promise to warm his hands before milking his cows, as well as her basket filled. Rounds and wedges of cloth-wrapped cheeses tucked within the woven hollow hung from her arm. At the lowest point of the basket's arching swing, Murl snuffled and licked.

Approaching from the opposite direction, Grace glimpsed Obie, the shepherd boy, and waved. He walked behind a bawling wooly tide, guided his flock along the Bright Wood's flank with a long crook. A sleek black and white dog darted along the flock's fluid edges, in response to Obie's short calls and whistles.

Grace stepped off the track and allowed the sheep room to pass, and Obie waved appreciation from the back of the flock. Compressed into a dense knot—agitated and prattling; necks arching and straining—the sheep hurried past Grace, past Murl at her side. From the sheep's collective monologue, formed like a chant on their tongues, she plucked a single word: *wolf*.

Eyes rolling, the flock huddled and pressed, rushed past like a frothing river. "*Wolf wolf wolf!*"

At Grace's side, Murl met the sheep's anxious moaning with a volley of sudden barks: "I am *dog*, not wolf," he yelped. "Dog! *Dog!*"

"Hush, Murl." Grace ran her hand over the ridge of fur raised along Murl's brown and white splotched back. "It's all right."

"I'm a *good dog*."

"The *best*," Grace affirmed. Smiling, she met his brown-eyed concern.

The flock jogged by, encouraged along by Obie's black and white dog. "Pay them no heed, friend," the dog said, addressing Murl as he whisked past. "We're all wolves to this lot." With a wink, he nipped a ewe's backward bent knee and set the flock to wailing.

Murl thumped his tail—once, twice—but without enthusiasm. Lifting his graying muzzle so his ears fell back against his ruff, he sought Grace's eye. "They always accuse," he whined. "They never *listen*."

"*I'm* listening," she said.

Hand cupped to his ear, Obie called to Grace as he strode amid his flock, corralling stragglers. "What's that, Miss Grace?"

"Good day," she said, with a smile and a wave.

Obie grinned and tipped his hat, drove his flock off down the earthen track.

Murl cocked his head to regard Grace. "You said you were listening," he woofed.

"And I am." Grace looked down and met Murl's open gaze.

"That's not what you *said* you said." Murl glanced backward over his torso and brush tail after Obie and his sheep, then swept his attention up to Grace once more. "To *him*."

Grace considered for a moment. "I don't think he'd understand."

"Oh." Murl grumbled softly to himself. "Like his *sheep*."

"Something like that," Grace said. She reached down, scratched Murl's ruff and shoulder. The dog's tongue lolled; his tail wagged in response.

She tumbled through the days that followed—greeting, listening, mediating, advising. Grace held each new experience, each new exchange like a dislodged nestling—wondrous and delicate. Time unspooled, day into day, week after week. More and more often, she found herself sought out to settle disputes, smooth complicated treaties. Chipmunks and mice each thought the other hoarded more seeds and nuts and grass heads than their fair share; a rabbit, having lost one of its kits to a fox, required consolation; the fox, aware she had caused a fellow mother grief, would not allow her guilt to be assuaged. Grace assured the small, lumpy toad that cowered beneath a clutch of ferns near the well that he was, indeed, handsome, his croaking robust, and he would surely attract a worthy mate.

When she was not arbitrating debates, she offered crusts of bread and meal scraps to jays and crows and teeming flocks of blackbirds. In exchange, the birds shared news and gossip from the towns and villages surrounding the Bright Wood and beyond. Despite the decidedly avian slant of the details—predators sighted, an orchard's ripening, thermals and approaching weather systems—Grace cherished the exchanges. She grew accustomed to sifting for context.

But for all her burgeoning aptitude, regardless of her comfort with hearing and understanding the scope and reach of her emerging talent, the squirrels' chatter remained out of reach and maddeningly indecipherable.

When night fell—dark and full and velvet—Grace found herself worn thin. This evening was no exception. Seated in the newly caned chair, her attention strayed from the small book spread open in her lap—a book of magic and faraway lands, of fabled folk and a young woman cursed to sleep behind a wall of thorns for a century. But she could not read. Before her, the hearth fire's mutable mock-tongues sparked and leapt, and she wondered: Did she imagine she heard the crackle and pop of voices in those bright embers? Did wood speak, or fire? Or the heated air itself? Did she hear words where there were none to hear? Would she know the difference?

Hands splayed over the pages of her book, Grace clamped her eyes shut. To her left, her mother hummed softly while she folded linens, patched clothes, and kept a sharp eye pinned to her daughter. Her father mended household items, oiled and sharpened various tools. Murl, stretched along the hearthrug, belly warming, twitched in his dream. Night crowded the windows.

When Grace opened her eyes again, Sylvie materialized near her slippered feet. She pulled her arms wide to accept the tabby's leap. The cat padded back and forth over Grace's lap, over her open book, and settled lengthwise in the fissure between the book's yellowed pages.

"Let it rest," Sylvie said. "Yesterday, last season, last year—the world spoke. It has always spoken." The cat paused to smooth her whiskers. "Nothing has changed."

"It seems, though," Grace said softly, "that *I* have." She rubbed the cat's cheek with her thumb, feeling the weight of her mother's attention.

"So it seems." With a twitch of whiskers, Sylvie agreed, seemingly unconcerned by the contradiction.

"But . . ." Grace's hand stilled on the cat's striped form. "But *why*?"

White-tipped tail curled over her front paws, the cat leaned into Grace's hand. "The world is its own secret," she rumbled. "It is not your mystery to solve."

Grace stroked Sylvie's black and tan fur, felt the curve of the cat's strung-bead spine beneath her palm. Her head buzzed with a riot of disordered thoughts, and she felt the sudden, unreasonable urge to weep.

"Change is growth." Sylvie, purring, looked up at Grace through slit-pupiled eyes. "Growth can be painful."

Nodding, Grace swiped a tear from her cheek and hoped it escaped her mother's notice.

"But you endure." Sylvie sat up, creasing the book's splayed pages, and thrust her head up against Grace's chin. "Your strength will be your protection."

Murl chose that moment to rouse himself from the hearthrug. Ambling over, he sat, panting, at Grace's knee. "I'll protect you," he said.

Breath catching in her throat somewhere between relief and laughter, Grace leaned forward. She hugged Sylvie to her ribs and pressed her lips to Murl's sweet, domed skull.

CHAPTER SIX

With saw-toothed grasses and bright-eyed wildflowers snagging and swooning against her green skirts, Grace strolled the short distance to the well. Her fringed shawl, her fluid shadow, trailed behind her. On her right hip, she balanced an empty earthen jug, index and middle fingers hooked through the glazed loop handle.

"Why?" This had become Grace's persistent question. The jug's slight bulge rocked against her ribs and bicep.

"Does a gift require a reason?" Wood Thrush countered.

Grace glanced left, caught the small, sprightly bird's dip-and-glide flight—an agile cinnamon shadow brushed with dappled light. He had found Grace when she passed beneath the smooth-trunked, silvered beech.

"Then, why *now*?" Grace molded her bare feet over pebbles and soft hummocks of moss. Her boots waited at home, in a patch of curling onion grass near the garden gate.

"All things in their own season," Thrush sang. He seemed to enjoy the riposte, and this, like so much recently, surprised her.

Grace changed the manner of her questions. "I hear more each day." She shook her head, as if to dislodge a voice or two.

Thrush's flight possessed an undulating pattern, similar to his song. Spring passed beneath the upward curl of his wingtips in a whisper. With a burst of speed, he darted ahead and alit on the slim bough of a dogwood. The forked branch bobbed as he waited for her to catch up. "Mayhap," he said, "you weren't fully fledged."

Grinning at Thrush's prim phrasing, Grace shifted the jug to her left hip and fingers, considered his suggestion.

"Or perhaps you listened with your ears," he said, "not your heart. Each translates in its own fashion."

She shook loose hair back from her face and neck, brushed the fingertips of her right hand along her sternum. It had never occurred to her that her heart might hear. "It's a little . . . overwhelming."

"Undoubtedly," Thrush said. He spread his wings, lifting easily from the dogwood as she drew near. "You have tumbled from the nest and found the world far larger than you expected."

Together, they arrived at the well. Thrush curled his feet along the edge of the well's small, shingled roof, and Grace set her jug on the grass, near unraveling ferns. She wondered where the toad had gone.

A length of rope lay coiled near the well's fieldstone sides. Grace fed this through a series of pulleys, lowered the attached bucket down the well's throat. "Sometimes . . ." She paused, listened for the bucket's splash as it broke the skin of dark water below. "I think I hear the wildflowers, whispering. . . ."

"No doubt, no doubt," Thrush said. Judiciously, he preened, pulled each speckled breast feather, one by one, through his beak. "Their travel is limited to airborne and digested seeds, rootlings, random passersby—but they have extensive networks. Their observations may be rather specified, but they have a valid perspective to offer. Hawkweeds are particularly skilled at parsing fact from fiction."

"So, trees must also speak. . . ." Grace's hands stilled upon the coarse rope, and the wooden bucket hung suspended, midway in its upward journey. It clattered against the well's stone sides, dropped a gradual diminishment of echoes.

"Oh, naturally, indeed," Thrush said. His manner was patient, matter-of-fact, as if he addressed a fledgling.

"I hadn't considered. . . ." It made easy sense to her that any creature in possession of a tongue—birds and foxes, cats and dogs, snakes and bees and toads—should speak. But extending this trait to those that lacked throats and tongues . . . She swayed a little where she stood, then took firm grasp of the rope and hauled the bucket up. Leaning against the well's rim, hipbones pressed to stone, she grabbed the bucket by the handle, set it down with a slight thump. A tongue of water splashed her bare feet. It seemed the trees crowded closer: maple, oak, linden, beech. White pine and hickory. She strained to hear their leaf-born, full-throated shouts; singular, collective.

"Trees are . . . challenging to converse with," Thrush said. He pitched his fluted voice low, a midtone of light and shadow. "They choose their words with care and speak rather . . . deliberately."

Grace shifted her gaze toward the Bright Wood, the haphazard and specific expanse that lived and breathed and waited. Her own breath caught.

"They are hardly the most complicated, though; that distinction belongs to the earth itself. My great-great-great-great-grandfather began a conversation, in a meadow not far from here, with a large, venerable stone upon which he would eat black cherries. My ancestors, his descendants, and I have been collecting the response a generation at a time."

Pulling her gaze from the Wood, Grace angled her head slightly, focused on Thrush in an attempt to ground herself. She concentrated on his chestnut wings and tail; his streaked and speckled breast; the bold, white ring that encircled his glittering dark eye. She laughed.

With a sharp flick of his tail, Thrush puffed out his feathers, cocked his head to one side, and stared at her with vague avian pique.

"Oh, no, I'm sorry," Grace said. "I believe you. I just wondered what I would say to a stone."

Smoothing his feathers against himself, Thrush flared his wings slightly at the shoulder in a minute shrug. "From what I have gathered thus far, the stone objects . . ."

"The stone objects?" Grace echoed softly.

". . . to pits and stains and repetitious knocks," Thrush concluded.

"The stone *objects* . . ." Grace considered the small stones pressed against the soles of her feet, wondered if they objected to the burden of *her* upon them. Gathering up lengths of rope, she returned those coarse coils to their neat pile, then tipped the bucket into her blue, earthenware jug. No longer a careless weight, the jug now brimmed with clear water—much as her mind brimmed with thought and voices, her own and others'. She shook her head, furrowing her brow as she hefted the jug. She clasped it close, and the jug rocked against and bruised her hip.

Thrush continued, wistfully: "Perhaps the chicks of my chicks' chicks will hatch the full answer."

Grace hugged the cool earthen jug to herself as ballast, a firm anchor. "Everything has changed," she said, and felt herself coming unmoored, her thoughts spiraling out, away. Collecting wood. Preparing fields. Harvesting apples, peaches, honey, wheat . . .

Deliberately, firmly, she cut short that line of rationale, before it rubbed too closely against more visceral subjects.

The whole vast world rocked and swam about her, and she felt suddenly lightheaded.

"Everything is as it is, and has always been so," Thrush piped gently.

"Is it?" she asked. It seemed a small, distant quirk of irony that his words rang similarly to Sylvie's—bird and cat in agreement. A small lump—laughter, protest, disbelief—formed in her throat. Palm up, she extended her hand. Thrush flew to her, and the slight tickle and scratch of his pale feet against her skin offered curious reassurance. "This feels like drowning. Or dreaming."

"You," Thrush said, "are most certainly wide awake."

Grace looked at him, at the small chestnut bird in her hand, his cream-pale breast and belly stroked with smoky spots, and his bright, dark, intelligent eye. Did she see or imagine, in Thrush's pert beak, the trace of a canny smile?

"We each have our own nest and flight," Thrush said. "All that lives has its own wisdom, its own voice, its own song to share."

Grace angled her head toward Thrush; she attempted, again, to open her heart to hear with that muscled, rhythmic organ and encourage its expansion. It seemed as though her heart's beat—that firm, steady affirmation—registered through every cell in her body, foot's sole to crown of head.

"Like an egg, a tadpole, or a caterpillar," Thrush said. "You begin again."

"I . . . don't know anymore. . . ." Grace said.

"Then simply listen." Once more, it seemed Thrush shrugged, with a tilt of his head and a small lift of scapula. He rose from her hand on spread wings and flew toward the Bright Wood's musing, green-leafed fringe. "And keep listening," he called.

Grace followed the sinuous line of his departure. Out of habit, she raised her hand, waved. For a moment, she stared at that spot where Thrush had vanished from view, then turned to walk home. She listened: to the jug sloshing against her hip. To her barefooted step upon grass and earth. To her breath's motion and the thump of her heart as she wove her own rhythm into the surrounding world's.

CHAPTER SEVEN

With the clothespins clamped between her teeth, Grace wondered: Did she taste poplar, ash, or sycamore against her tongue? She pulled a pin from between her lips, secured another of her father's homespun shirts to the line. To her left, a pace away, her mother added socks to the cord, and a damp tangle of lisle stockings. Grace watched her mother's fingers—far more skilled than her own—easily manipulate the wooden pins over the freshly washed clothing.

"Excuse me," Grace said, addressing an assemblage of doves to her right. Wing to wing, they perched and bobbed on the clothesline. She took an apologetic step in that direction. "Would you mind . . . ?"

"As if we *wouldn't*!" The nearest dove puffed its dust-brown breast feathers.

"Being dashed off," a second intoned, blinking.

A third finished: "Like common *sparrows*!"

On blurred and creaking wings, the half-dozen doves took sudden flight, then resettled a short distance away on the cottage's spine. Tucking their coral-pink feet beneath themselves, the collective stared at Grace, offended. Cooing and muttering, they consoled one another, ducked delicate heads against their soft breasts.

"They . . . understand you?" Grace's mother squinted against lush sunlight. She glanced at her only child, the familiar reshaped as mystery.

Grace returned her mother's gaze, hitched one shoulder and offered an oblique smile. The day bloomed too fine to quarrel or placate. Securing a storm-colored shirt to the line, she noted, from the corner of her eye, her father's attempts at casual disinterest—with one knee pressed to fresh-turned soil of their small garden, he tied young, curling tomato plants to wooden stakes. Grace found her parents' attempts to address the subject of her newfound talent curious. They approached worriedly, indirectly, in the same way they might approach a skittish horse, a wild hare, or a river swollen with snowmelt.

"And you . . ." Grace's mother shifted her gaze, now, to the displaced doves. "You understand *them*."

Grace shrugged, reached into her skirt pocket for another clothespin. Theirs had ever been a close family—remained so—but had, recently, taken on an aura of fragility. Poised on the threshold of maturity, Grace's childhood was fresh and untarnished in her mind, easily accessible. Unwittingly, she had crossed some dividing line, some unseen rift; she missed the ease with which her parents previously encouraged her curiosity and growth. Until recently, they had indulged her barefooted wandering, her tree climbing. With good humor, they had tolerated her tendency to speak to each and every creature whose path she crossed—furred or feathered, scaled, or otherwise.

Grace glanced toward the cottage, toward the arc of doves preening and murmuring along the roofline. Bright avian eyes, darkly aglitter with undisclosed knowledge, returned her stare. Mere weeks ago, by way of a random squirrel, monologue had transformed into dialogue. She had crossed thresholds. A lever had been shifted in her mind. A sluiceway opened. A candle lit. The words, those voices had rearranged themselves and become discernable to her ear. Now, she understood.

"Are they . . . still talking?" Lettie deftly framed her query.

The doves tutted in offense: "*Still?*"

"In*deed!*"

"As if we'd *stopped!*"

"In*cred*ible."

"Yes," Grace said. "They're in a bit of a snit."

She caught her mother's eye, then slid her glance away. Pulling a sheet from the knot of laundry, she secured one corner to the sagging line, feeling a swift swell of relief when her mother picked up the sheet's other end. As, between them, they pulled the length of cloth over the clothesline, Grace considered the abrupt erasure of old barriers, the creation of new; how the map of her being had been redrawn and left her parents shaken.

"I've always liked the sound of doves." Lettie plucked a clothespin from between her teeth. "They're such placid creatures."

"Isn't that just like a *human*," huffed a dove. "To reduce an entire *species* to a single trait."

Grace covered her mouth with her hand, swallowed a laugh. She wondered if the bird understood the irony of its statement.

Lettie's fingers paused in their work. "What is it?"

"Nothing," Grace said, with a shake of her head.

Lettie arched a single brow, then bent and picked up the empty willow basket.

Grace swallowed the laughter still caught in her throat and watched her mother walk the curving path back toward the cottage, where she paused to exchange a knowing glance with Grace's father as he inched—slow, meticulous—down his row of young plants.

The sheet on the line, stretched taut between Grace and her parents, reminded her of the intangible barrier she perceived. Bright with sun and snapping in random breeze, the line dripped over green-clovered grass. Standing quite still, Grace turned her attention toward the roof. There, beneath the curl of the doves' coral pink toes, beneath the eaves, lay her room. A narrow shelf within those walls bore evidence of her connection to the natural world. Half-cups of pearled birds' eggs, a snake's shed skin, the papery hull of a wasp's nest. Each was arranged along a crowded bookshelf, carefully placed between slim, cloth-bound volumes. Each, a touchstone of Edgewoode's meadows, fields, streams, and copses; of the Bright Wood's call.

She thought, again, of her conversation with Sylvie: *Change is growth. Growth can be painful.*

Though this change had come swiftly, abruptly; though, at times, it jarred and confused; in moments of distraction, Grace found it far more curious that she had not *always* understood.

CHAPTER EIGHT

Grace leaned against an old timber fence of silvered wood. A large burlap sack of flour lay across the rail, cushioning her hips and elbows from the timber's toothless bite. Fog curled over slow-warming earth, bestowed an ethereal quality to the morning. Edges and distance blurred, softened at its touch. Pearl-gray, the mist pooled about the fence's leaning posts and rails, prowled over Grace's boots; doubtless would retreat beneath the sun's ascendant path. For the moment, she enjoyed its soft-furred trace against her exposed skin—cheek and throat, the backs of her hands; its discreet silence. A rare thing, and soon to be interrupted. She heard, from behind her, the telltale scuff and stroke of approaching steps.

Straightening unconsciously, Grace shifted her stance against the sack of flour, lifted from elbows to forearms.

The damp-muffled steps neared. With her gaze fixed on the middle distance, she trained her eye upon the slow progress of a team of draft horses. The great creatures pulled a plow through earth and mist. As she watched, she hoped, perhaps the passerby would do just that, pass by and continue on their way.

"Are you coming or going?"

All tension slipped away at the sound of Thaniel's voice. Relaxed, Grace turned to smile at him. "Both," she said. Then, with a shake of her head added: "Neither."

Thaniel stepped off the rutted, muddied road and approached through the lash of dewy grass. "Can I wait with you while you decide?"

Grace made room for him on the fence, and Thaniel dropped his medical bag, leaned over the rail beside her. Every inch of him seemed coated in mud, from caked boots to stippled shirt, pants, face and hands.

"You smell like a barn." Grace laughed.

He gave her a wry smile: "A privilege of the trade." Bending forward over the rail, he lightly shook his head, raked his scalp with long fingers.

"And," she said, drawing a length of straw from his dark hair, "you look tired."

"Between lambing and hoof rot . . ." He dragged a mud-spattered sleeve across his forehead, sighed.

They leaned in silence, arms brushing, eyes fixed on the distant team. The plow trailed a cloud of blackbirds in its wake, coursing, diving after the insects raised. Somewhere, not far, a vernal pool within the Bright Wood's skirts chirred with frog song.

"More cake?"

Grace looked at him askance, her brow furrowed in unspoken question. Thaniel inclined his head toward the burlap sack dimpling beneath her forearms.

"Ah, no." Grace patted the coarse burlap. "My errand. My means of escape."

Thaniel turned the line of his body to face her, adjusting his right hand and elbow against the rail. "From?"

She took a deep breath and expelled a name: "Adelaide." In the distance, Grace heard the farmer encourage his team into a gentle turn.

"Adelaide?" Thaniel repeated, curious. "Little Adelaide? The lacemaker?"

"The very one." Grace avoided his eye, her attention fastened upon the two bay draft horses. Their low voices carried over the field to her ear—Conrad, with the mane and tail that flowed in the breeze like cream, admired Henri's straw hat.

"But . . ." Thaniel scratched grit from the stubble along his jaw.

"Adelaide, you see . . ." Despite herself, her own deep well of frustration, Grace composed herself. Casting a glance at Thaniel, she continued smoothly: ". . . has a son, Sturn."

"Ah." Slowly, Thaniel slid his brown-eyed gaze away, considered each of his broad palms in turn.

"This is her third visit in a week." An uncharacteristic frown flitted over Grace's features. "It seems that now, I have . . ." She half-shrugged, and her shawl caught—a dark green wing—beneath the weight of hair. "Certain 'marriageable' qualities."

Thaniel dropped his hands, intercepted her gaze with his own. "I could have told her so last winter."

Grace felt her cheeks heat, wished she could swallow back her words. She opened her mouth to clarify, pacify, reframe.

"I'm sorry," Thaniel said. "I shouldn't have said that."

She shook her head, further tangling her hair within the shawl's weave. She had asked for time, and he had granted it. "You, of all people, have the right. You know—I'll wed whom, and when, I want, and not because I'm suddenly 'useful.'" This time, she met his steady gaze. "And it won't be Sturn."

A small smile reworked Thaniel's mouth, the set of his jaw.

From the field beyond, the bay team's deep voices caught Grace's ear. Despite yoke and heavy plow, she heard no friction between the horses, but rather, the continuous, amiable banter of old friends. The great creatures' voices traveled in a low burr, like the distant thunder of a summer storm. Of all creatures, horses seemed a particularly contented group.

"So," Thaniel said, "to avoid Adelaide, you escaped to the mill?"

"Where, naturally, I ran into Sem." With a long sigh, she shook her head. "By the time I'd gotten the flour and was on my way, he'd introduced me to every creature at the mill—dog and cat, barn swallows, two goats, and the donkey." She thought now of Sem's donkey, harnessed to the millstone and walking an endless circle. The creature lamented his shaggy coat and rangy limbs, that he had not been born sleek and smooth like his equine cousins. Despite her efforts to comfort, he remained disconsolate. Her heart constricted with recollection.

"Sem let you talk?" Thaniel could not hide his amusement.

"There's a first time for everything," she answered.

Thaniel laughed under his breath.

"He also informed everyone who happened by the mill of my 'aptitude.'" She bit her lower lip in exasperation. It did not sit well to be annoyed with the miller's son, a genuinely warm and affable fellow.

"That sounds like Sem."

"Yes," Grace agreed. "But . . ." She picked at a stitch in the burlap's seam.

"But if anyone in Edgewoode was still unaware of your new 'aptitude,'" Thaniel completed her thought, "they'll know by nightfall."

She nodded. Already, word had spread throughout Edgewoode—fleet as flight or fire, swift as illness. Overnight, she was transformed into a source of curiosity and local pride, her insight sought on various domestic fronts. Could she persuade the oxen to pull the plow?

Encourage the hens to lay more consistently? Convince the spotted gelding to cease extending his great belly when his saddle's girth wanted tightening? All this and more, without Sem's unwitting help.

"I wish I had more time. To get used to it. But always, neighbors and strangers are at our door, asking for interpretations and negotiations and propositions." She paused for a breath, heard Henri and Conrad discussing the finer qualities of sweet grass and clover over winter hay and oats. Shaking her head, she added, "I'm happy to help. I *want* to help. But . . ." She paused again. "Now, thanks to Sem, there will be *more*. . . ."

"It must be overwhelming," Thaniel said.

Grace held onto his calm presence as an anchor. "It *is*." She swept her hair up in her hands and twisted it into a thick coil below her left ear. "Overwhelming and wonderful and what I've always dreamed of." She felt slightly giddy, wondered if she heard chatter drifting from the swirl of distant blackbirds, or merely the beaten wind sliding beneath their wings. Dropping the rope of her hair, she ran her hands over her face, her forehead. "I'm tired," she sighed. "I want to go home."

"I'll walk with you." His statement sounded like a request.

"Do you think it's safe? Adelaide may still be there." Grace arched her eyebrow at him. "She considers you Sturn's *rival*."

"I'm not afraid of little Adelaide." Thaniel grinned at her, swung his medical satchel over one shoulder and, wresting the sack of flour from the fence rail, slung it over his other. He matched his stride to hers, and they left fence and field, horses and blackbirds behind.

"Mom will ask you to join us later for dinner." Grace looked up at him from the corner of her eye.

"That should put a kink in any of Adelaide's plans." Thaniel winked at her.

"Should I set a place for you?"

He tilted his head, considered the sun's angle. "I should have time enough to get cleaned up." He met Grace's eye. "Someone told me I smell like a barn."

CHAPTER NINE

In light-lashed, dusted bands, the sweet scents of hay and oats and equine sweat enveloped Grace. She stood in a wooden stall amid a drift of fresh straw, smoothing her hands over a chestnut mare's curved jaw. Muscle and sinew bunched and quivered beneath her palms; the mare's mane spilled over her hands and fingers. Thaniel had requested that she join him.

"How long?" Thaniel turned from the mare's hugely swollen abdomen, addressing the woman standing just beyond the stall's gate.

"Since daybreak," the woman answered. She was blade-thin and clutched at her apron with knuckled fists. "She seemed to be progressing well, and then . . . Oh, my poor Tilli."

Thaniel shrugged out of his vest, suspenders, and work shirt, bent over a waiting tub of hot water, while Grace ran her hands along Tilli's neck, from jaw to withers. The mare stomped and blew and slashed her honey-colored tail back and forth, but otherwise endured Thaniel's examination.

"Her foal is backwards, Mrs. Meeks." He looked expectantly at the woman as he re-soaped his hands and arms. "I need to turn it."

Rubbing at her upper lip with one knotted hand, Mrs. Meeks agreed with a slight, downward jerk of her graying head. She increased her grip on her apron with the other hand.

Again, Thaniel scrubbed himself clean, then snapped his gaze up to Grace. "You can explain?"

Grace, her heartbeat ratcheting beneath her ribs, nodded. Shifting her stance slightly within the straw-strewn stall, she stood directly before Tilli's head, placed her hands to either side of the mare's long face. "Help is here," she said.

Tilli lowered her head, touched her white-starred forehead to Grace's starless brow. "Please," she whinnied, "my little one . . . the pain . . ."

"Try to relax." Grace pitched her voice low, spoke to the large, tufted and twitching ears. "All will be well."

The mare kept her head pressed to Grace's, whickered softly, and Grace heard in that sound, comprehension, acceptance. Trust. She planted her boots firmly against the stall's warped boards, braced herself, leaned into Tilli's thrust.

It seemed to Grace that, beneath the currents of external sound—the barn's creaking, the arhythmic thump of hooves, the animal and human chatter—another voice reached her. Faint, elusive; distant, yet near. Lifting her gaze, Grace peered around the mare's shoulder, down that length of gleaming, heaving side. She cupped Tilli's jaw in her hands. "I hear it," she said. "I hear your foal."

Thaniel, in cotton undershirt, suspenders hanging past his hips, paused and studied Grace intently. "Incredible," he said, and flashed a broad grin. "Just . . . wonderful." He shook his head and laid his hand on Tilli's sleek flank. Then, his expression sobered: "Tell me anything you hear. Anything I should know."

Intent, unblinking, Grace met Thaniel's eye. She swept her hair back from her face and nodded.

Of the recent flush of visitors to Grace's home; of all the folk who knocked on her parents' door, at all hours of the day, with all manner of requests and overtures—many accepted, some considered, others rejected outright and flatly—Thaniel stood apart. His proposal, dropped casually during dinner, was unique.

Would she assist him in his work?

She had immediately accepted.

More and more frequently, she joined Thaniel on his visits to farms and crofts and smallholdings, within and occasionally outside of Edgewoode. Over recent weeks, a network of sorts had sprung up, and Grace found herself sought by creatures as well as humans—mice and crickets, swifts and crows and gossiping sparrows bore messages of those in need. Often, it was she who stood on Thaniel's doorstep, urging him to get his medical kit.

Tilli stamped and snorted. "I'm too tired," the mare lamented. "I can't do this. . . ."

"We're here for you." Her arms circling the mare's broad neck and stroking the sweat-dampened coat, Grace bore the weight of the horse's head against her shoulder. "We won't leave you."

"Oh, Tilli," Mrs. Meeks moaned, "my poor, poor Tilli."

Thaniel spoke, his voice strained: "I've found the head."

The whites of the mare's eyes showed as Tilli tossed her head free of Grace's arms and whinnied distress. "I can't anymore," she bayed. "I just can't. . . ."

"Tell her we're almost there." Thaniel's voice was muffled.

Reaching up, Grace trapped the mare's stiff-bristled muzzle in her cupped hands. "Only a little longer," she said.

While her own heart thumped and her mind crowded with Tilli's desperate thoughts, Grace listened—to mare and foal. She spoke soft reassurance to Tilli, translated for Thaniel; she kept the flow of communication between beast and man open, holding fast to her own tremulous calm.

Again, the mare whinnied sharply, stomped an iron-shod hoof. Grace's hands crept up Tilli's chestnut neck and knotted in thick bristled mane. Flashing her gaze down the mare's sweating length revealed Thaniel, stooped and bowed, all but hidden from view.

"It's done," Thaniel called. A note of satisfaction rang in his voice. He mopped a cloth over his face, withdrew several paces to tub and soap and sponge, began rescrubbing himself. "It's her turn, now."

Mrs. Meeks sobbed with soft gratitude, covered her face with both of her stiff, chapped hands.

An undefined lightness of spirit settled over Grace, and she considered Thaniel as he washed. Redirecting her attention to the mare, she said: "Try again, *now*."

"I just need to rest. . . ." Tilli dropped her chestnut head to her boot-black front hooves, expelling a great breath. She whickered long and low in her throat.

"I know," Grace said. She wove her arms around the mare's neck, pressed her cheek to Tilli's musky, sweat-curled coat. "But first, try again, just once more."

With a great shake of her head, Tilli pulled free of Grace's grasp. She blew again, with more force; the swollen barrel of her torso heaved. The mare snorted and stamped and whickered.

"Right," Thaniel said, quickly toweling off. "Back to work, then."

The colt arrived soon after—glossy bay, with three white socks and a blaze beneath its damp forelock. Tilli licked and nudged and nuzzled it. Within minutes, it stood on knobby-kneed legs and thrust its forehead into her side. It suckled loudly.

While Mrs. Meeks rushed from the barn to share the good news, Grace shadowed Thaniel, observed his careful re-examination of Tilli and her colt, placed ointments and implements in his outstretched hand, returned each to his kit when it was no longer needed. Despite the recent novelty of their working association, they moved with practiced ease—quietly, easily.

At such moments, Grace's mind stilled. The voices lapping against her ear dipped to a hush and rustle, as a wind curling through autumn trees. A small respite. Those voices amused, intrigued, enlightened—sheep, constantly perplexed by nearly all things; wren's judgment of where, with what, and how many nests to build. Even Murl, her own sweet-tempered dog, fretted over wolves and foxes, for whom he held a not-so-secret jealous admiration.

Regardless, the voices never ceased. Grace strove to allow them to wash over her mind's ear, like soft music, unless she was directly addressed, a skill she had yet to master. They called her She and Her and Female and Woman. They called her Voice and Listener and The-One-Who-Hears. Sometimes, they simply called her The One. Always, she answered.

"We're a good team, you and I."

Thaniel's voice, here beside her, grounded.

"It seems so." She handed him his work shirt, the linen crisp and cool against her fingertips.

"And you could hear the foal?" Thaniel asked. He buttoned up the shirt and tucked it in, shrugged into his suspenders.

"He didn't *speak*, really." Grace passed Thaniel his canvas vest. "It was more . . . an intense feeling of restriction, an undeniable need for more room . . . for change."

"Incredible," Thaniel said. He tugged his vest into place, grabbed his kit, and held the stall door open for Grace.

"Goodbye, Tilli." Grace touched the mare's jaw.

"Thank you, miss," the mare whickered. "You saved us. *My boy*."

"He's strong," Grace said. "Like his mother."

She and Thaniel left the barn, exchanged dusted light and air for clear, and found Mrs. Meeks crossing the wide yard to meet them. She bore tokens of gratitude—a still-warm pie placed in Grace's hands, and a sack of grain that Thaniel slung over one shoulder. The day had passed, and, with the sun at their backs, they followed their own shadows home. Mrs. Meeks's praise trailed behind them.

Thaniel smiled down at Grace. "Your help is . . . beyond measure."

"I'm happy to," Grace said, and meant it. The rhubarb pie blushed through its latticework crust; the plate warmed her palms.

Grace heard spring yawning inside her, with each day's new minute of additional light. She listened to the murmur and snap of new growth, to the throb of her footsteps and the gentle thump of the grain sack as it struck Thaniel's back. Though he could easily outpace her, he matched his stride to hers.

"Half this grain is yours." Thaniel said.

"Not really." Grace stole a sideways glance at him. "You did *most* of the work."

Thaniel laughed. He seemed to consider the trees' pattern of arching limbs overhead.

"Wait." Grace stopped walking, mid-stride. "Are you angling for dinner? Again?"

He shrugged, offered her a lopsided smile. "I don't like to eat alone."

"And you know there's *pie* for dessert." She lifted the tin plate, inhaled the sweet, spicy scents of cinnamon and tart rhubarb.

"I thought that was *mine*." He grinned.

"In that case," Grace said, "we should take the long way home. To make sure our timing's right."

Turning off the wider track, she chose a footpath that dipped into the Bright Wood and ran alongside a small creek swollen with snowmelt. Maroon-beaked skunk cabbages flowered in a riot at the creek's edges, alongside the slender whips of pussy willows studded with gray catkins.

Balancing the pie between her hands, Grace glanced over her shoulder to see if Thaniel followed. There, she saw him—kit in hand, grain sack swaying—a mere stride behind her.

CHAPTER TEN

Seated between her father and Sem, Grace heard everything and nothing, near and far. The landscape jostled by, subject to the rutted road that grabbed at the wagon's rough, wooden wheels and tugged at the teamed horses' rhythmic gait. She had never traveled beyond Edgewoode's borders, and now, she found herself en route to the town of Aldermere. She felt the slow, quiet, exhilarated expanse of her own smile, her head a riot of thought and expectation.

"We're obliged to you, Sem, for making room for us, aren't we, Grace?"

Grace responded to the elbow her father thrust against her ribs. "Oh, yes, very," she said.

"Not at all, sir," Sem replied with typical good cheer. "To be honest, I'm happy of the company. The ride'll pass more quickly with conversation! It's not a *long* ride to Aldermere—only a few hours, depending on the weather, and luckily, we've got a nice, clear day ahead of us; but in truth, it can feel *a lot longer* on my own, with no one to talk to but the horses. And, unlike your daughter, sir—gifted as she is—my conversations with them are distinctly one-sided!" He laughed and, to prove his point, called to his team, who whickered and blew and twitched their ears.

"He does prattle on, doesn't he?" The lean sorrel gelding jerked his head, tongued the bit in his mouth.

The dappled mare replied: "I prefer it to his *singing*."

Grace cupped her hands over her mouth, hid laughter beneath a cough.

Sem turned toward her, his eyes a shade paler than his oak-brown hair. "Are you all right?"

"I'm fine." Grace cleared her throat. "Really."

"I imagine," Gaven said, eyeing his daughter cannily and diverting the conversation, "the journey would pass much more . . . quietly . . . on your own, Sem."

"'Tis true, sir, 'tis quite true." Holding the reins lightly in both hands, Sem grinned and nodded, encouraging his team with a curl of wrist and snick of braided leather.

The sorrel twitched an ear and blew loudly through flared nostrils. "Why *does* he do that?"

"He thinks we've forgotten him," his dappled partner drawled.

The two horses chortled deep in their chests, until harness and bridles jangled and shook. To contain herself,

Grace looked past her father, jostling in the seat beside her, and out over the swimming landscape.

Low hills and shallow glades leapt past, thickly stippled with trees and variable green growth licked with deep violet shadow. The horses clopped through a modest valley along a cleared, earthen track, easily the breadth of two wagons. Tilting her head, Grace squinted up at a band of blue sky that expanded and shrank according to the reach and spread of beech and maple, oak and hickory. Surely, the Bright Wood stood watch as they orbited its distant flanks. Sunlight and leaf-shadow flickered from all angles in disorienting fashion, and she wondered where, in relation to their rootless, roving presence, the Wood flourished and breathed.

Again, Sem's voice intruded, rose and fell against her ear like wave, like wind, like memory. "Is it true the magistrate himself requested your visit?"

"Grace's, yes." Gaven considered his daughter.

Sem whistled, a low, thoughtful sound. "That's quite an honor."

"An honor." Gaven allowed his gaze to wander over thickets of foliage, then shrugged. "An inconvenience."

Laughing, Sem adjusted a dusty blue cap over his brown thatch of hair and nudged Grace, shoulder to shoulder. "But *you* must be excited, yes?"

She hesitated, met Sem's gaze, his cheerful, guileless expression. The letter, written in the firm hand of Bertren, magistrate of Aldermere, lay snug within its pale envelope, tucked inside her vest's pocket. "I'm . . . nervous."

"Oh, there's no need for that." Sem grinned broad reassurance. "Aldermere's a fair-sized town. Bigger than our own, to be sure, and busy as an anthill, but friendly enough. You'll be fine."

Ignoring the hiccup in her belly, she asked: "Have you met the magistrate?" Her mind conjured up a stern image, grim, frowning.

"Not me," Sem laughed. "Not important enough! Not like *some* folk!" He leaned briefly against her and waggled his eyebrows.

"*No* one is more important than *you*, Sem."

He hooted. "I'll be sure to tell him you said so—when *my* invitation comes!"

"More a 'summons' than an invitation." Gaven grumbled under his breath, attempted to find comfort on the narrow plank bench the three shared.

"Dad!"

"What? We couldn't very well decline, could we? That's a 'summons.'"

"They're our neighbors. I *want* to help, if I can."

"And how are you to know what's wrong with their lake?" Gaven crossed his arms over his belly. "Or any other body of water, for that matter."

"I don't know," she said, and wondered about those three small words, how their combined meaning shifted, dependent on each word's emphasis.

For over an hour, they had traveled this bone-rattling, rutted road, as the sun chased alongside and skimmed a brilliant curve above the trees. For Grace, this journey sang of opportunity—an expansion of her small world, of her place within it; of how, with her nascent and unanticipated gift, she might contribute to its whole. Yet, keen awareness of her father's discontent blunted her joy, increased her own unspoken anxiety. She had no inkling how she might communicate with Aldermere's lake, nor any other elemental expression of life; nor how she might determine the source of the lake's ailing. The scope and extent of her talents remained untried beyond the boundaries of her own village. Settling her hands in her lap—loosely, finger pads lightly touching—she turned her thoughts, hopes, and ears toward the animate world, in hopes of catching any snatch of speech. A flock of dark-glittering starlings coursed among the canopy, shrilling of crusts and cores and other scraps associated with humans. She admired their resourceful nature, and hearing their calls, understanding them, provoked a deep sense of relief.

Again, Sem's voice diverted attention, as he plied Gaven with conversation. "You'll be staying the night in Aldermere?"

"I suspect so," Gaven said. In one hand, he held his pipe, with the other, he pulled a small pouch from inside his coat pocket. Tapping tobacco into the pipe's bowl, the stem between his teeth, he lit a match, drew breath. "The sooner I'm back at my own hearth, the better." Pale smoke wreathed each word he spoke.

"May I suggest, sir, that you seek lodging at the Alder's Bough?" Sem clicked his tongue at the horses, discouraged the sorrel from nipping the dappled. "It's family-run, clean and snug and quiet, and you can get a good, hot meal at a fair cost."

"Much appreciated, Sem."

Grace felt, sitting between the two men, reduced to childhood again—despite her recent birthday and the fact that a mere season lay between her and Sem, and she the elder of the two. They spoke around her, over her, through her. Grace had imagined her first venture beyond Edgewoode somewhat differently. She stared ahead and quietly considered the dimensions of her discontent.

"Ah, here we are!" Sem said.

Grace sat up, expectant, and scanned the ragged road, the trees surrounding. Her brow creased in confusion. "We're *where*, exactly?"

"See that?" Sem indicated a large old oak, its trunk a thick column of grooved and patchwork bark. "We're about an hour away. It's time for a snack. Here, take these." He handed Grace the reins, stood, and climbed over the seat into the wagon's open bed. "Just follow the road," he called.

"I'll take them." Her father spread his hand, expelled a long, pent breath.

"That's all right," she said. "I'd like to try."

Gaven nodded, refolded his hands over his stomach, and winked at her.

She felt a subtle shift of posture as she held the reins—a lengthening of spine, a forward inclination of shoulders, hips, and torso. With both feet squarely planted against the floorboards and the reins lightly in hand, Grace felt inexplicably taller. She grinned. "What are their names, Sem? Your horses?" She heard the bump and scrape of baggage as he rummaged.

"Morris and Juelz."

"I'm Juelz," the sorrel said, with a flick of his long, ivory tail. "She's Morris."

The dappled mare snorted: "Like she'll believe *that* . . . !"

"Juelz is a strong name. A stallion's name." The sorrel lifted his head high, tugged against the reins.

"Wow. Thanks, *Morris*," the dappled mare said pointedly. "You managed to insult us both with *that* sugar cube."

"What?" Morris stretched his great, glossy neck and shook his pale mane. He tongued his bit again.

"Let's just say it's a good thing you're not driving," Juelz chuffed. She turned her head, looked directly at Grace with one large, dark eye. "Don't worry. I know the way. I've been this way so many times, I could trot it in my sleep. But I won't. Not like *some*." She rolled her eye toward Morris, then skyward, so the white showed.

"Well, I'm glad of that," Grace said. "I've never been outside Edgewoode."

"Few travel as much as we do," she said. "Many lack interest or opportunity to leave their own pastures. But it's good to explore new meadows, meet new folk. Good for the soul."

Morris lifted his head high and added: "Good for the appetite!"

Juelz snorted. "Morris is ruled by his stomach."

"And I'm a contented subject!" Morris whinnied agreement.

Nickering with laughter, Juelz shook her gray brush mane.

Sem clattered into the seat beside Grace. "What've I missed?" Eyes wide, he steadied a large, woven hamper on his knees.

"She's been conversing with your team," Gaven replied. He observed Grace with a mixture of pride and paternal worry.

"Really!" Sem parceled out bread and dried fruit and hard cheese the color of parchment between them. "What'd they say?"

"Well," Grace paused, considered. "They enjoy travel." She watched Sem make a rough sandwich of torn bread, dried plums, and cheese. "I think you and Morris may have a lot in common."

She said nothing of her relief and growing confidence that her newfound talent exceeded the limits of her village, nor her curiosity as to how far it might extend.

The Alder's Bough smelled of plaster, warm bread, and dried lavender, of old, oiled oak soaked in sunlight. Grace stood with her father at the bar—a curl-edged slab of scrubbed chestnut, nicked and notched and grooved along its uninterrupted length. The room, though sparsely populated at this hour, recalled multitudes in its vacant chairs, stools, benches cloistered about sturdy trestle tables of varied accommodations. Across the room, from the sill of a deep-set window, a large calico cat surveyed them, plumed tail twitching.

"Sem recommended us, you say?" The woman behind the bar slid a chipped amber jug into a pool of sunlight; the spray of forsythia contained within flared, lambent. "I guess all his chatter has an upside, after all!"

Gaven exhaled slowly, adopted a neutral tone. "So it seems," he agreed. He glanced around the open room, unaware that he nodded approvingly to himself.

"Well, as I know most folk in town worth knowing, but I don't know you," the woman said, her pale blue gaze stealing from Gaven to Grace, "I presume you must be the girl the magistrate sent for. Who speaks to animals and such." She leaned forward, forearms folded against the bar, shirtsleeves rolled to elbows, and searched Grace's features. "You've come to help us with our lake."

Grace met that blue-eyed gaze—the color of periwinkles, of summer chicory—and noted the fine lines stitched at their corners, about her mouth. Nodding, hands clasped tightly together out of sight, she said, "I hope so."

"Well, there's little to be lost in trying, and much to regain." The woman pushed off the bar, walked its length toward a pair of saloon doors. Gesturing, she said, "This way. I've set aside rooms for you, at the magistrate's request. That'd be Bertren," she elaborated. "He's a good sort."

Grace fell into step behind her father. They followed the woman up a set of well-used stairs—treads thinned at the middles, edges sloped—along a wide gallery. Hips buttressed against the rail, hands gripping wood, Grace lingered, peering down at the common room below. From this vantage point, the tables and chairs constellated an arrangement imperceptible at ground level. Heels lifting, she leaned further but could not find the calico.

"Grace?"

"Coming . . ."

Turning, she followed her father's voice down a short hall, its oiled panels inset with carved floral motifs. She traced fingers over violets, roses, tight-curled fiddlehead ferns that flourished, heedless of the semi-dark.

Gaven stood outside an open door, similarly carved, shaking his head. "This is too much." He touched the coin purse that hung from his belt. "Maybe something smaller, something less . . ."

"That wouldn't do." The woman made an amused sound as they entered the small suite of airy rooms. "You're the magistrate's guests. He's seen to everything." She smoothed the bed's lake-blue cover, needlessly straightened a pillow. Steps muffled by a thick carpet, she crossed the room and drew open the heavy drapes folded against two deep-set casement windows to either side of the bed. A flood of watery light quivered on floors, walls, ceiling. Next, she opened a smaller door tucked under the eaves of the interior wall. "And here's the miss's room."

Leaning against the door, fingers plucking its wooden blooms, Grace allowed the woman space to exit.

"I'll have your bags sent up. I trust you'll be comfortable, but if you need anything, just ask—I'm Vida." She gave Grace an appraising look as she passed, eyes searching, intent. "You can sort yourselves out. I'll send a courier to let the magistrate know you've arrived."

Grace watched Vida march down the hall, her gait precise, the sway of gray wool-skirted hips efficient. Her apron's ties, knotted in a neat bow at her back, kept tempo, rose and fell with her stride as she rounded the corner and swept out of sight.

"Fish."

Grace's gaze fell. A pace away from her sat the calico cat, its tail a froth curled over its toes. "Fish?" Grace echoed.

"Fishing." The calico fixed her with clear, amber eyes. "The lake is necessary." Without going into further detail, she picked herself up and flowed through the open doorway and into the room.

Tracking the cat's progress, Grace's attention swiveled, settled upon her father who stood, alone at the room's center—a room large enough to contain the footprint of their cottage.

"I don't know what to expect next." Gaven wore a bewildered expression. He watched as the calico leapt onto the bed and made herself comfortable.

Seeing her father there, so obviously lost and ill at ease, provoked a curious feeling within Grace. The urge to *protect* him, as he had always done for her. She wondered when her hands had crept from the door's carved surface and clasped themselves together at her sternum. When she reached his side, she tucked her head beneath his chin, wrapped her arms around his waist. He returned her embrace, the weight of his arms a comfort about her shoulders.

"Don't worry," she said, assuring him as he had her countless times. "It will all be all right."

CHAPTER ELEVEN

She understood now, standing on the lake's scrubbed shore, why their rooms at the inn swam with light. Reflections bowed off the water's surface, caught and slanted and replicated at random angles. Yet, despite the echoes of scattered light, a peculiar stillness prevailed.

Magistrate Bertren had allowed just enough time for her and her father to settle into their rooms and shake the dust from their clothes before coming to introduce himself and collect them. Grace found him neither stern nor grim, though he could be forgiven the despondent expression that pinched the bridge of his nose and drew his gray moustache over the downstroke of his mouth. He seemed, as Vida described him, a "decent sort" and stood, now, several paces behind her at the head of a small crowd. He allowed none to approach Grace, or interfere, and kept bustle and chatter to a minimum. He managed this with soft-spoken words, pacifying gestures. Her father stood at the magistrate's right hand, visibly uncomfortable with the position.

Lake Aldermere defied its designation. An asymmetric plate of deep blue water, it stretched within its stony shoreline farther than possibility. Grace's thoughts swam with descriptions she had read of the sea, and marveled that it could be larger.

To the east, a wooden dock extended out over the water's surface, an array of small craft nosing against its length. Farther out on the lake, a skein of boats drifted, white sails limp. Grace stepped closer to the water's edge; reeds and rushes and cattails stroked her skirts. Her steps crunched softly against the silence. Nothing spoke to her—neither fish nor plant, neither insect nor bird.

The silence unsettled. Tucked beneath the cool spring air, an odor: sour, unpleasant. Looking down, where the water's edge foamed near her boots, she spied a small crab. Green-gray, its shell rimmed in ivory, jointed legs orange and butter yellow—it lay still, blunt-toothed claws slack. Grace squatted, touched the unblemished carapace. The creature's mouth bubbled; it waved a listless antenna.

Looking out over the water, its mirrored surface skinned in rainbow hues, she felt the full burden of Aldermere's hopeful expectations. She closed her eyes, strained to hear anything beyond the townsfolk's murmurings. Ribs pressed to knees, skirts lapping the shore's damp stones, she stretched her palm out over the water. Her ears filled with nothing and nothing and . . . something. A gurgle. A faint ripple of sound. She strove to listen further, beyond, *into* the depth of water. To find that distant voice. To connect.

Blinking her eyes open, Grace stood. She did not stop to think, to *over*think; instinct propelled her to action. She unlaced her boots, tugged socks free; she unbuttoned her woolen overskirt and stepped out of it. Green wool bloomed upon the gray pebble shore. She cast her shawl onto the pile, green on green. Did they whisper, draw a collective breath of shock, of dismay as she stepped into their lake, their livelihood? Did her father frown and thrust his empty hands into his trouser pockets? She did not know. She knew nothing beyond the grip of icy water that closed over her ankles, calves, knees as she eased herself into the silenced lake.

Step by slow, steady step, the cold crept up over her thighs, her hips. Her petticoats—white as summer cloud, as snowfall—drifted atop the water's skin, saturated, sank. Soft mud beneath her heels, her toes. Trailing fingers along the water's surface, she ruptured a skim of clouded opalescence, and saw, among the thicket of lofty rushes, the half-submerged shapes of fish. Mouths gaping, gills working, they struggled, trapped in shallow water. On the western shore, an egret waded. Spreading white wings, he lifted into the air, beak and talons empty.

Grace lowered herself fully, and the lake's cold claimed her, clambered up over her belly, her ribs. She leaned back into its rainbowed shadows. Her hair—a honeyed nimbus—swam about her, where schools of fish and water striders did not. She curled fingers around the hollow throats of reeds and cattails. Water lapped against her cheeks, her ears. With the spring sun swimming in the sky overhead, she closed her eyes. Floating, she sought that distant voice. Listened.

Wavelets rippled, uncurled. Listless. An unintelligible, liquid slur. A hollow depth, muffled. Grace lay in water, a singular form made flesh, buoyed by formless fluidity, contained by earth. She frowned, uncertain what she listened for—one voice, a multitude? Sending her thoughts out, she felt into deep, blue-green eddies, into the gyre and motion.

"Are you there?"

The words thrummed against her ear. Her words. Her voice. Like an echo. Sounding distant, distorted, curiously dislocated. Internalizing the question, shaping the thought's dimensions, she had verbalized it, spoken it aloud. This surprised her. Patiently, she considered this. Gliding her fingers' grip up algaed reeds, she listened.

Grace tried again: "Will you—"

Almost immediately, found herself interrupted.

"I . . .

. . . a▾m . . .

W▾e . . .

. . . a▾r▾e . . ."

Grace's eyes flashed open, and daylight blinded. Sealing her lids again, tightly, she returned her attention to the water surrounding, supporting. To a depth of voice and voices—distant, blurred, softly rippled.

"Tell me," she said.

Images washed over her mind's eye. Whirls and currents angled against her hearing. Thought swam with internal vision. The lake's choked, liquid voice arranged, rearranged slurred images until, at last, Grace understood. Her mind's eye brimmed. She heard, she saw. The lake showed her.

A foreign substance. Dark. Oily. Metal-flecked. Seeping. Spreading. Thickening and congealing. Oxygen, depleted. Algae mats clotting, expanding. Fish, suffocating. Pale, scaled bellies, cast over the water's surface like phantom waterlilies. Crayfish, crabs, mussels dying in their beds.

"L▾e▾a▾v▾e . . .

. . . n▾o▾w . . ."

"T▾o▾o . . .

. . . c▾o▾l▾d . . ."

Grace stood, streaming water, and covered her face with her hands. She wept—tears and lake's water—and stumbled through the reeds, up the shore. Voices in her ears—human voices, brusque and sharp and questioning. Hands upon her. Someone wrapped her in warmth, in coat and heavy blanket. Parted the throng and led her through. And still, she wept.

CHAPTER TWELVE

With her back curved against the tub's sloped sides, Grace braced her feet against its curved seam and drew her knees up. They broke the water's surface, small islands visible amid the lift and stir of steam. Her hair skimmed her shoulders, clung to her cheeks, her throat. She felt the lap of water, scented with lavender oil, against the soft underside of her chin. Though nearly submerged, she shuddered with cold. Memory of Aldermere's waters lived in the marrow of her bones. She wished the tub were closer to the fireplace. Only clenching her teeth kept them from chattering.

She barely recalled returning to the inn, that short stumbling distance from the lake's stubbled shore, swaddled in a coarse blanket and the magistrate's heavy coat. The gathered crowd—surrounding, parting, closing about them as Bertren ushered her through. Questions, demands, concerns, accusations, all borne on a score of human tongues like barbs, like birds, flung and flown.

All she had wanted was the certainty of her father. Of Thaniel.

But she had, instead, sat in a corner of the Alder's Bough, its common room cleared of curious onlookers, and answered the magistrate's questions as best she could:

Please, tell me what you've learned—what is happening to our lake?

A foreign substance—oil and metal—is spreading through the waters, allowing algae to grow, depleting oxygen.

Were you able to learn the origins of this contamination?

The farther side, where a stream empties into the lake.

Might this be a natural event?

No.

And, do you—does the lake—know who is committing this deed?

I don't know.

Is it a citizen of Aldermere?

I don't know.

Is it one or many?

I don't know.

She had sat, wrapped in sodden chemise and petticoats, blanket and Bertren's heavy coat, in a hoop-backed chair, shaking her head again and again. Streaming from her hair and clothes, lake water had seeped an oily path down the chair's seat and legs to pool in strange iridescence upon the wide planked floor. The brackish, pungent scent, laced with decay, had roiled her stomach.

Your lake is dying. Desperation had sounded in her voice. *You must save it.*

Grace's breath caught, a small, wracked sound. She rested the back of her head against the tub's rolled rim; the tub tolled with contact—deep, dull, low. Light streamed through the peaked, dormered window of her snug room, shivered over the bath's surface. The ceiling eddied with reflection. She had scrubbed herself pink, from toes to collarbones—scrubbed, with guilt, to remove the odor of decay—and wrung out the soft washcloth, hanging it over the tub's side. The cloth drip-plip-dripped its own rhythm, a counterpoint to the pop and hiss of flames confined to the fireplace tucked into the room's corner. All within this room contained heat and light, yet she doubted she would ever be warm again.

The lake's voice spilled through her thoughts, and she blinked against the urge to weep.

A soft knock interrupted the tidal pull of recent memory. Grace brushed her damp hands over her cheeks, her eyes, and sank a little deeper into the tub. Warm water lapped, splashed. She tasted the sharp, bright tang of lavender. Behind her, she heard the narrow door scrape open beneath the angled eaves, the floorboards creak with soft steps, a hushed voice speak.

"Miss? It's me, Dessa?" The statement held the quality of a question.

"Hello, Dessa." Grace tilted her head, caught the girl's fleet movements. "Please, come in."

The door clicked shut, and a petite young woman, about Grace's own age, entered. Clad in slate-blue cotton and a crisp white pinafore, her dark hair shone, coiled loosely at the base of her neck. She approached the tub as if on tiptoe, her arms laden with thick, pale blue cloth and a parcel wrapped in ochre paper, tied with string. "I've brought fresh towels, and a gift from the magistrate." She set it all on the bed.

"He's very generous, your magistrate," Grace said, uncertain which caused more discomfort—unexpected gifts, or having her bath attended to by this seemingly kind-hearted yet utter stranger.

"He hopes you'll wear them to dinner this evening?" The upward lilt of Dessa's words floated in the air, dissipated. "I've washed your travel clothes myself; they're in the kitchen, hanging near the baking oven."

"I can't think of a better place to dry them." Grace saw no point in sharing that her travel clothes, as Dessa termed them, bore no such distinction.

"Can I add more hot water to your bath?"

"Please, thank you." Grace tracked the young woman's movements. She seemed at once skittish and adept, like a deer.

"I heard what happened, what you did earlier. All of Aldermere's talking about it." Wrapping her hand in a cloth, Dessa lifted a pail from its place above the fire and tipped it slowly into the tub. Water sluiced over the curled lip, glittering and streaming like spun glass, and raised a veil of steam, soft-edged as Dessa's voice. Wide-eyed, she asked, "Did you really speak to our lake? I wish I could have been there."

Slowly, the heated water curled over Grace's body, insinuated itself around her legs, hips, torso. For a moment, she allowed her eyes to close. Yes. She had spoken with the lake, with its ailing yet animate waters—so unlike these mute, heated waters in which she was immersed now. Everything, *everything* brought up more questions.

"Oh, I'm so sorry, is it too hot?" The stream of water abruptly ceased.

With a flash, Grace opened her eyes. Had she sobbed aloud?

"No, it's wonderful."

She smiled reassurance, relieved when Dessa continued to pour. Hearing, again, the flow's purl and splash, she wondered if this was a tamed, aqueous voice.

"Dessa," she asked, "have you seen my father?"

"Not myself, but I believe he's with the magistrate." She dropped the sodden washcloth into the emptied pail, bent to spread a mat on the floor between tub and fireplace. "Once the magistrate had gathered folk to search the lakeshore and environs, he meant to lead your father on a tour of Aldermere."

"Search the lakeshore . . ." Grace sat up a little in the tub, felt the stroke of warm air against her skin.

"Why, of course!" Dessa laughed. Her tone lost its quizzical trait. "Two separate parties, going in either direction. How else will we learn who's been poisoning our lake? I just hope they find the culprit before he catches wind of anything and makes an escape."

Grace searched the young woman's face, the sweet contours of cheeks and brow and lips, the fawn-brown eyes. "What will happen? When they're found?"

"Well . . ." Dessa took up an iron rod, thrust it into the fire to agitate the coals. "I suppose that depends on who finds him. . . ."

Smoothing wet hair back from her face, Grace asked slowly, "What do you mean?"

"People are angry. Fishing is the livelihood of most of Aldermere. The magistrate is just and fair, and well respected, and he was clear in his expectations. But he can't be everywhere, can he?"

Grace felt a chill of a very different kind. "You don't think anyone would . . ."

"I really wouldn't know. I suppose much depends on whoever it is, how they behave when they're caught." Dessa's grip tightened on the poker. Looking at Grace askance, she shook her head. "Honestly, I don't know what to hope for." Then, with exaggerated cheer, she said, "But you don't have to worry about that. You've done your part, and can look forward to dinner with the magistrate, and returning home. Remind me again where you're from?" Her tone's uptilt returned as she set the iron poker swaying in its stand.

"Edgewoode," Grace said.

She did not know what woke her. Eyelids heavy with sleep, Grace blinked up at the broad expanse of night; at silhouette trees branched overhead, dark limbs knotted against darker sky. Peepers chorused from those stratified limbs, a multitude of voices so layered, she understood only their joy, exultation.

Beneath and around her, the wagon rocked. Boards groaned, wheels creaked with steady rotation, the teams' hooves thudded arrhythmically along the earthen track. Feasted, feted, exhausted, Grace slept in the wagon's bed, wound in her cloak, head pillowed on a burlap sack. Ahead of her, her father sat beside Sem on the bench, as Sem guided them from Aldermere, home to Edgewoode.

Except something had awakened her. A spoked wheel connecting with rock or rut; the sound of owl or nightjar, the distant howl of wolf. Thin fear hiccupped down her spine. Grace couldn't fathom her father's insistence on returning to Edgewoode at this hour, leaving the softest mattress her body had ever known.

Yawning, she felt the warmth of her own breath, the night air cool against her exposed cheek. Slow and persistent, sleep tugged, and she felt herself sliding, sliding. The threads of conversation drifted over, around her—Sem's voice, her father's. A fragment of sentence caught her ear, a shard-bright phrase.

". . . he swore he'd find her, Gaven . . ."

Grace's eyes flashed open. Sem's words, his voice—soft, uncharacteristically somber—brought her fully awake.

"Why do you think we're out at this gods'-forsaken hour?"

The low spark of her father's response, its keen edge, pierced her. She suppressed a gasp, an involuntary breath.

"And I agree with you on that point, sir." Sem paused, seemed to grope carefully for the right words. "But don't you think Grace should know?"

She felt, as she listened, an implicit threat creeping over her, tightening.

"She's *my daughter*. I won't let *anyone* harm her."

"Yes, sir, and she's my friend," Sem pressed, "and she's strong and smart. No disrespect, sir, but I think she should know."

"You'll keep your opinions to yourself. And you'll hold your tongue."

Silence. Strained silence, underscored by the horses' drumming hooves, the grind of wagon wheels against earth and stone, the cascade and lilt of peepers.

"As you wish, sir."

She heard her father's pacified grunt and Sem's dismay in his slow exhale.

Grace's heart ratcheted in her chest, jarred by the wagon's progress, by the small snippet of dialogue and the knowledge—*withheld*—this comprehension granted. She heard nothing more beyond her own thoughts racing. Sleep eluded her, swept by on distant wings.

CHAPTER THIRTEEN

To be off the road, gone from Aldermere, and in her own room again. To be *home*, restored to all the comfort and safety that engendered. Grace felt a flutter of relief, of muscles expelling tension like pollen, despite that shadow, that unspoken threat—one she was not meant to know about or overhear, one her father meant to shield her from. She held this bright insight like a forbidden fruit. Its truth seeped, red and ripe, into her heart, bruising the texture of her thoughts. She was unaccustomed to secrets.

Giving herself a small shake, Grace shifted her attention to the letter in her hands. She held it up to the oil lamp's light and reread it—once more, just to be certain. Dark ink scrawled over thick parchment, incised the smooth, creamy surface. It was a letter of gratitude, of "commendation." Touching Magistrate Bertren's seal—skin to embossed wax—she refolded the letter along two deep creases and slipped it onto her shelf, between slim book and smooth stone, alongside his initial letter of request.

Spread across her bed lay the magistrate's gift; the dress seemed to have fainted, draped over white pillow, a swoon of nubby, raw silk that spilled from bedspread to floor. She lifted it, held it before her at arms' length. Deep, sapphire blue, fitted at the bodice and from elbows to cuffs. Thumbnail-sized buttons—carved of wood, dyed midnight—ornamented the lower arms, ran down its back, from neck to base-of-spine. She held it—a fount of water, flowing. It flared gently, heavily, to the floor; seemed to glow with its own subtle light.

Carefully, she cradled the gown—a wild thing, in need of succor—against her torso and glanced about her small room. Shallow, recessed shelves and low dresser; the washstand, its hollow basin webbed in a craze of fine cracks and rimmed in clusters of wood violets. Her eyes settled on the ladderback chair in the corner—recently re-caned by her father's deft hands—and she draped the gown over. It engulfed the chair entirely, pooled and flowed to lap the floor. It had been worn only once, to dinner with her father, the magistrate, and Aldermere's prominent citizens. A dizzying affair—clamor and laughter and oblique, inquiring glances. She recalled the feel of the dress against her skin, how it had seemed to claim her form: at once holding her upright, while simultaneously restricting breath and movement. She wondered if she would experience that sensation again—if she even desired to.

A skein of goosebumps marched over her body, diverting idle thoughts. Her room's single window allowed in evening's chill breeze; the white curtain swam in its frame. She slid the sash closed, peered beyond the glass, saw only her own rippled, hazy reflection. Concealed in sprawling, undisturbed dark, the new moon hid from view.

Aldermere. The town insinuated itself in unexpected ways. Setting aside thoughts of blue silk, of lakes and magistrates, she tugged a deep green skirt from her dresser, along with a tawny blouse and dark ginger vest. Dressed in familiar clothes that skimmed her shape with neither demand nor restriction, she brushed out her hair—a changeable and inconvenient shade somewhere between gold and bronze—in long, even strokes. Putting the brush aside, she crossed her room and stepped out into the hall. The clink of utensils on glazed earthenware dishes, the aromas of bread and onions and gravy rising from below. Despite fatigue and the urge to collapse on her bed, hunger prodded. Dinner, her parents, and questions awaited. She stepped off the landing.

Murl met her midway down the staircase. "You smell different." Methodically, he snuffled the folds and hem of her skirt.

"Rude." Sylvie rubbed herself, full length, against Grace's calf.

"I changed clothes," Grace said. She sat on the steps amid a mass of green wool, held out one hand for Murl's investigation and scritched Sylvie's cheek with the other.

"You smell like *you* again." Murl licked her hand, lay his head in her lap, and looked up at her with a doleful expression. "But the new smells were *interesting* . . ."

Sylvie sneezed, unable to hide her distaste.

"Next time, I'll wait a little longer to clean up."

"Okay!" Murl wagged a broad circle with his brush tail.

Grace pressed a kiss to the dog's domed skull, stroked the cat from glossy head to base-of-tail.

"Grace?" Her mother tried, with marginal success, to contain her impatience. "Are you coming down?"

"On my way," she answered, then whispered into her companions' pricked ears, "*Come along* . . ." Gaining her feet, she followed Sylvie and Murl down the remaining steps.

"There's our girl." Her father, seated before a large bowl of soup, smiled at Grace past his own road-weariness.

"Have a seat, dear," Lettie said, ladling a second bowl full.

Grace pulled out her chair, fell into it, relieved. "Dinner smells wonderful." Leaning over her bowl, she inhaled—spring onions, tangy herbs, wild garlic.

Lettie placed a crock of sweet butter on the table alongside a tray of hot biscuits. Filling her own bowl, she sat. "I'm just glad you're both home," she said. "All the way to Aldermere . . ."

Gaven blew over his spoon. "It's not so far, love," he said gently.

"Then why weren't you home yesterday?" Grace's mother wore concern and quiet protest stamped plainly across her furrowed brow.

"I'm sorry, Lettie." Gaven reached through the warren of bowls and tableware for his wife's hand. "It couldn't be helped."

"You should have sent word," her mother said. Lettie squeezed Gaven's fingers.

"You're right." Gaven held her gaze, smiled. "I should have."

This was as close to argument as Grace had ever witnessed pass between them. "We would have arrived on the heels of the messenger, Mom," she teased.

Lettie dismissed the comment's logic and, hearing the kettle sing, released Gaven's hand, pushed herself away from the table. She poured a pot of mint tea, nesting three glazed mugs amid the crockery. "Thaniel stopped by yesterday," she said with a casual air, filling each mug.

Murl planted himself beside Grace's chair, gazed up at her with a lopsided doggie grin. "He *always* smells interesting!"

Stalking toward the hearth, Sylvie leapt easily into a chair. Chin to paws, she curled around herself, twitching her tail's tip in disapproval.

"I wish you could have come with us, Lettie."

Grace's mother peered over her teacup's brim at her daughter and let her gaze slip sideways to meet Gaven's.

"Someone had to stay behind and look after the household." Minted steam veiled her expression, softened the fine lines about her eyes.

"Fair enough," he agreed. "I can tell you, though, they won't soon forget our girl in Aldermere."

Leaning sideways, Grace scratched Murl's ruff and ears, avoided her parents' combined gazes. The dog's tongue lolled, and he thumped his tail against the rug's braided coils.

"The magistrate was so grateful, he invited us to dinner." Returned to the comfort of his own home, Gaven shed the previous two days' unease like an old cloak.

"Dinner?" Lettie set down her tea and shifted her attention between them. "*And* that dress?"

"Indeed." Gaven nodded. "I've never seen so much food on one table."

Grace straightened, leaned forward. "Mom, you wouldn't believe! There were the thinnest pancakes filled with wild mushrooms, and blue heron's eggs in footed porcelain egg cups, and white asparagus with cream sauce and dill. . . ." Detailing the menu honed her appetite. "The sweet butter was shaped into *roses*, and for dessert, there was an orange-blossom water cake with warm chocolate-tangerine glaze!"

Brows raised, Gaven shook his head. "A veritable *feast*."

Lettie moved her spoon through her bowl, caught a bright disk of carrot.

"Oh, but Mom, it wasn't *nearly* as good as *your* cooking."

"Nonsense." Lettie smiled. "It sounds marvelous. I'm sure it was wonderful."

"Well, to be honest, it was all a little overwhelming," Grace said. The scene sprouted in memory—the long table, forested with silver-branched candelabrum; white lace linens; ewers and glasses; plates and bowls of delicately painted porcelain. "There were so many *forks*. . . ."

"You work your way from the outermost fork *in*," her mother advised. "For next time."

"Next time!" her father echoed. "Once was enough! You can go next time; I'll stay and watch the cottage."

"I suppose it's only natural they'd want to express their gratitude," Lettie observed.

"She *did* save their lake." Gaven inclined his head toward Grace, winked.

"I didn't *save* it." The lake—a veritable landlocked, tideless sea—lapped at Grace's memory, frothed over and exposed the shape of accidental eavesdropping.

"You may as well have." He shrugged. "The effect is the same." He dunked his biscuit, once, twice.

"But that isn't so," Grace said. "The lake is still very, *very* sick."

"You learned the cause," Gaven said, undeterred. "You did what Bertren wanted!"

Grace opened her mouth to speak, but could not. She shook her head, swallowed against the lump in her throat. When Murl leaned his head on her thigh, she fell instinctively to stroking him.

"Lettie," Gaven continued, "she spoke to the *water*." He could not conceal his own baffled pride. "Our girl spoke to the very *lake itself*."

Lettie knotted her fingers together. "Is this true?" Her voice seemed to thrum from a distance.

Grace regarded her bowl, green onions coiled in cooling broth. Trailing fingers through Murl's coat, she met her mother's surprise and nodded.

"But . . . *how*?"

When Grace hesitated, her father answered: "She entered the lake."

"At this time of year?" Lettie was incredulous. "You could have caught your death!"

"Now, Lettie . . ."

"I didn't know what else to do," Grace explained. Her mother was right, and she shivered at the memory—the lake swallowing her feet and ankles, wrists and hands; the glassy expanse of water, accepting her; the brutal irony of the sun's brilliance overhead. She was fortunate not to have succumbed to cold, fever, or worse. Those deep waters would not approach warmth until summer sprawled into autumn.

"I don't understand." Lettie's brow creased.

"The lake," Grace said. The corners of her mouth lifted in an involuntary half-smile. "I heard its voice." Even now, that clear, blue-green eddy angled against her inner ear—patterns washing her mind's eye, arranging and rearranging slurred images; the surge and break of *understanding*.

Murl pawed Grace's skirts, prompted her hand's renewed attention.

Grace's father got up. "Apparently, there's a local—a so-called mechanist—who'd been emptying waste and oil and metal scraps into the lake. No one knew." He scraped a ladle inside the pot's curve, refilled his bowl. "The magistrate organized search parties. They found the fellow soon enough. Caught him completely unawares. Of course, he denied any wrongdoing, but they dragged him to town, regardless, where he was charged." Gaven shrugged, shook his head over the profound failings of his species. "Needless to say, he packed himself up and departed."

Grace looked up at her father. "They drove him *out*," she corrected. She felt her cheeks flush, the pattern of her heart's beat increase. She couldn't imagine being driven from her home, from Edgewoode.

"Let's say . . . they . . . encouraged his departure."

"Isn't the effect the same?" she added, arching a brow.

"He endangered his own town's welfare and knew it." Gaven sat down. "I'm sure he'd have found it uncomfortable to remain."

"Grace," her mother said, "you're not eating."

Grace turned her spoon, considered the green onions she worked around its stem. "You left out a detail, Father," she said.

"Did I?"

"The 'mechanist' made a vow," Grace said.

"Hmmm?" Gaven avoided his daughter's gaze. "I wouldn't know about that."

"No?" she asked.

"No, not to my knowledge."

"Dad, I heard you," Grace said, all in a rush, "you and Sem, talking!"

Gaven looked up, away, lips pressed. "Damn that boy's tongue."

"It's not Sem's fault."

Lettie's face paled. "Gaven, what does she mean?"

"It's nothing." Her father waved his spoon. "Hearsay."

"The mechanist swore he'd find me." The words felt flat on Grace's tongue, meaningless. She turned her spoon between her fingers, over and over.

Lettie gasped.

Gaven spoke firmly, calmly. "Idle tongues and gossip."

Lettie's gaze swerved between the two, hands clutched, knuckles white.

Gaven splayed his palms in pacifying gesture. "The judge, the magistrate, all of Aldermere came to our girl's defense."

"You *just* said it was *gossip*!" Lettie cried.

"We're home now." He reached again for his wife's hands, cradled them in his own. "It's *over*. Done."

Lettie pulled away and got up from the table. Busying herself, she spoke over her shoulder, "Please eat, Grace."

More tired now than hungry, Grace ate to remove a small worry from her mother's brow; she dipped her spoon and sipped thyme and tarragon and nettle.

Murl looked up at Grace, ears laid flat against his skull. "What's a mechanist?"

Sylvie appeared, interposed herself between canine and Grace's ankles. She regarded the dog with clear green-gold eyes. "Someone who makes . . . contraptions out of metal."

"What's a 'contraptions'?" Murl cocked his head to one side.

Sylvie licked her left forepaw, smoothed her whiskers, and said: "An unnecessary complication."

CHAPTER FOURTEEN

Each day, Edgewoode's fauna and flora reached out to Grace. Each new tongue interposed itself upon all aspects of her life.

"Hear me . . ." The great white oak's voice curled with soft burr and rustle.

"Do you hear me?" asked spreading matts of sweet white clover.

"I *know* you hear me!" yelled a jay from atop the garden arch.

"Watch your step!" The black beetle's hiss redirected her foot's fall.

Speech grew, everywhere. Twists, inflections, curling nuance. All that previously had skimmed her consciousness now caught her ear and took root. Comprehension vined, expanded. Within breaths, within days, weeks—she forgot she had not *always* heard and understood.

In sleep, her mind absorbed, adapted, translated. Her proficiency expanded with the moon's growth, diminishment, absence, and rebirth. In dreams, she practiced, refined; she conversed with earth and lichens and snails, with ravens, rain, and roses. In the star-stippled nightfall, she slept deeply, dreamlessly, her bedroom window cracked to the dark bloom of evening. Eventually, the repeated tap—like knuckles gently rapping, or the lilac reaching as-yet bloomless twiggy branches up to strike the glass' pane—woke her.

Heavy-limbed with slumber, Grace planted an elbow and rolled over beneath a layered warmth of blankets. Through slight-parted lids, she peered in the general direction of the half-heard disturbance. Dark crowded her vision. Yawning, she sipped cool air as her sight adjusted to filmy moonlight. Night swelled outside her window; yet, she detected the suggestion of movement beyond the pane's barrier. Shadow bumped against the window's warbled glass. Grace sat into full wakefulness and beheld a large owl hunched on the wooden sill. It struck its hooked beak against the pane: *tap tap tap*.

Slipping from bed, she crossed the worn wooden floorboards, and—slowly, carefully—parted the curtains, pushed the sash fully open. The owl hopped back and met her gaze, large yellow eyes wide within the disk of its face.

"Come," the owl intoned.

Grace swept tangled hair from her face, blinked. The owl remained. Its feathers—silver gray, ticked with ivory and banded brown—shivered around its beak, at its throat. A froth of pale feathers skirted heavy, sickled talons.

Pivoting on her heel, she tugged the coverlet from her bed and wound the fabric's still-warm folds about her shoulders. Grace looked back at the owl expectantly.

"I await," the owl said.

Clutching the coverlet about her shoulders, Grace watched the owl slide from her window's ledge and dip away, silent and insubstantial as the surrounding dark. Clad in shift and blankets, she hurried barefoot from her room, pulled the door quietly shut behind her, and tiptoed down the hall. Hand skimming the banister, she descended the staircase, crossed the open main floor to the cottage's door. As her fingers settled on the door latch, a familiar voice spoke.

"Are we going out?" Stiff-limbed, Murl rose from his spot on the hearthrug. He trotted to Grace's side, flop ears pricked, and scented the air. "It's night."

"Go back to sleep, Murl." She patted his head.

Murl wagged reflexively. "Can't I come?"

"Not this time," Grace whispered.

Sylvie uncurled from a chair. Stretching languidly, she half-yawned, half-mewed. "I'm coming, as well."

"Both of you, *stay*," Grace said.

Murl drooped—ears, head, and tail.

"I think we're going," Sylvie rumbled. Dropping silently from the chair, she insinuated herself between Grace's ankles. "Isn't that right, dog?"

"Yes!" Murl barked, elated.

"Shhh! Murl, please . . ." Grace inhaled sharply, glanced up the staircase toward her parents' room, just beyond the landing.

Murl dropped his voice to a low whine. "Where are we going?"

"I don't know," Grace said. She listened for the creak of floorboards, the hinge of door; she heard nothing but her father's soft snoring.

"You don't know?" Murl cocked his head to one side.

"We'll be careful." Stroking the dog's ears, she smiled reassurance.

"*You* be careful." Sylvie sniffed. The cat stretched and elongated, front paws and claws extended, back arched. "*Human*." She uttered the term with wry humor, not quite concealed in a wide yawn.

"I'll be careful!" Murl agreed.

"Good. And we're being quiet, remember?" Grace said. She angled the door open.

Sylvie darted out. "You should cover your feet." The cat's voice slunk backward through the darkness.

"She sounds like my mom," Grace whispered, easing the door shut behind them.

"Not mine," Murl huffed. Tail aloft, he trotted by Grace's side.

The night's perfume enveloped her—fern and pine and damp, softening earth. She gripped the coverlet's edges loosely about her shoulders; it draped earthward, edges trailing along the grass behind her. Darkness stretched in all directions. Turning in place, Grace searched for the owl, until movement caught the corner of her eye—on silent wings, the owl scudded by, low overhead. Moonlight silvered its wings.

"Follow," the owl instructed. Tipping one wing, he glided off.

"Owl!" Murl exclaimed.

Grace swallowed a nervous laugh, then stroked the dog's head again and hurried to follow the owl. A shadow, it skimmed the night. Without the half-moon's glimmer, she would not know their guide's location. There, it waited, an erect blot on tree limb or fence post; next, it paused on peaked roof of shed or barn or house, an elusive breadth of night that peered down, wide-eyed.

Unfazed by night's expanse, Murl trotted along easily, head slung low and snuffling. "Hole," he warned.

"Thank you." Grace sidestepped the shallow depression. Fingertips brushing Murl's coat, she navigated the broken terrain, tracked the owl's aerial path.

They made steady progress along the Bright Wood's knotted edge, though Grace wondered where Sylvie might be. When the owl exchanged forward flight for broad circles, they had reached an open field. Grace stumbled—Murl drew up short, slowed his eager trot, and angled himself bodily across her path. The dog emitted a low guttural sound, a noise caught between whine and growl. Sylvie, too, materialized, dashed suddenly between Grace's feet. Back arched, ears flattened, the tabby cat hissed.

Deep within Grace's skull, a sudden multitude of tongues whispered and shushed, like wind-rustled grasses. Gasping, she staggered, squinted through the dark, and tried to peel away light from shadow. A nervous frisson lifted the small hairs at the nape of her neck; astonishment caught in her throat.

Ahead, in a field of grasses tramped down by foot and paw and hoof, an unlikely array of creatures gathered—rabbit, raccoon, opossum; skunk and badger; deer and fox and mouse and snake. Despite the mass of creatures, an external silence prevailed, yet a static hum—personal, internal—filled Grace's head.

"Come," Owl beckoned.

Murl and Sylvie protested; Grace advanced.

The ragged perimeter of creatures that defined the field's edge drew her, pulled her forward. She felt the communal tension of the animals' ranks double, treble; saw the bright flash of dozens of moon-touched eyes. Their ranks parted. Falling aside, crowding one against another, they made room for her to pass. Something waited at the circle's heart. Something that both frightened and fascinated. Overhead, the owl switched direction, continued its spiraled flight in presumed safety.

Grace strained to see. A misshapen mound of darkness, hunched within the darkened field. Now there was no questioning Murl's low growl, no mistaking Sylvie's sideways, claw-tipped dance. They both skulked at her heels as the gathered creatures' ranks closed silently behind them.

All at once, a throbbing chant swelled within Grace's mind: a near indecipherable tide of awe, fear, respect. A single word, repeated on dozens of tongues, until word and image coalesced, resolved . . .

Wolf.

Lungs constricted, Grace's hand flew to her lips. A chill raced up her spine, and she understood the primal fear, the tension. Human and creature alike feared the wolf—its strength, ferocity, cunning. Yet she felt neither threat nor menace. In fact, of all the voices present, she detected nothing remotely lupine.

"Murl, Sylvie." Grace fought to keep her voice low and calm and even. "*Stay here.*"

Murl whined. Sylvie spat. Grace edged forward.

Wolf indeed.

Pulse accelerating, Grace swallowed, took a wary step. Another.

There. The creature lay on its side, prone, chest heaving in an irregular pattern. Blood seeped from savage gashes at its throat, crusted along its rear leg.

"Wolf?" Though she whispered, Grace's voice punctured the web of night.

A thick, wet growl rumbled low in the wolf's throat. It scented the air, and its eyes snapped open.

"You . . ." It wheezed. "You came. . . ."

Grace sucked a short breath between her teeth, licked her lips, nodded. "Yes."

"You reek of fear," the wolf rasped.

She could not argue the point—panic stung her armpits, clenched her belly.

"I will not harm you." His voice welled in his throat, compact and sticky.

Grace could not tell if the wolf choked or laughed.

"I require your assistance." Clearly a creature accustomed to commanding others, he neither pleaded nor cajoled.

"Me?" Blanket white-knuckled about her throat, Grace sat on her heels, knees to grass. A full pace away, she felt entirely too near. Her head filled with the wolf's raw, animal odor, with the rusting scent of blood. "What . . . what can I do?"

The wolf's breath heaved and rattled in his chest. "Deliver me."

"*Deliver* you?" Baffled, she repeated the words, felt the rub of them against her tongue.

"My life. Take it."

Shock slid through her, stiffened spine and shoulders. She shook her head. "No."

"You must. You will." Lifting his muzzle slightly from blood-slicked grass, he raked her with yellow, half-moon eyes. "I demand it."

Grace fell backward, struck by his authority; she caught her hand upon the earth, tangling her left foot in her night shift's hem.

"You humans." His head dropped to earth once more, too heavy. "Unprovoked, you kill. When petitioned, you cower."

"But . . ." She felt the keen edge of his disgust. "*I* haven't killed. . . . I *couldn't*. . . ."

"Paragon of your kind." He snorted, or scoffed, deep at the back of his throat.

A heavy silence pervaded the area—all the anxieties and expectations and pent breaths of all the surrounding creatures, the owl sailing overhead; the half-moon's unflinching, silvered gaze.

"I die. Slowly. With each breath." The wolf wheezed now; all thunder faded from his voice. He implored: "Please."

Trembling, Grace pushed herself back up to her knees. Hands knotted in her shift, she inched closer, to within arm's reach of the wolf. His wounds were deep. "What has happened to you?"

The wolf groaned. "Does that matter so much to you, human?"

"It does," Grace said.

"What love have you for my kind?" He exhaled a sticky snort. "You and your kinfolk . . . your traps and knives and guns . . ."

"A man has done this to you?" Grace asked. She could not see well enough to make sense of his wounds; she wished for Thaniel's presence.

"No." The wolf heaved a labored breath and closed his eyes. A mournful, low moan shuddered through his body. "I have lost my pack."

Another inch. Closer. Near enough now to reach out, to touch the bristling gray coat. Instead, she busied her fingers, pushed her hair back from her face, behind her ears. "I don't understand."

"You cannot. How could you? *Human*."

"Help me. Explain. I cannot do what you ask. Not without understanding."

"I was challenged. I lost." The great chest heaved, collapsed, expanded slowly. "Too old . . . too weak to keep my pack. My time . . . done." He spoke with grudging acceptance. "The pack's way. The wolves' way."

"I'm sorry," Grace said.

Pale eyes snapped open to regard her coolly. "I do not accept your pity." His black lip curled back against long ivory teeth. "The pack requires a strong leader. It has one once more."

The moon slipped from a veil of cloud cover and silvered the wolf, silvered all.

"It is said you are a friend to wild folk." The wolf paused. "*All* wild folk."

"I am," she said.

"Then I petition you: End me. I have no wish to feel the scavengers' teeth and claws as I die."

Grace felt the weight of dozens of watchful eyes, her mind and ears filled with the sibilance of fearful whispers. When she crept forward on her hands and knees—her blanket laying a path through the grass behind her—Murl whined and Sylvie meowed. Closer still, until her knees skimmed the hair of the wolf's skull. Close enough that she must override her own species' inborn instinct to *flee*.

Eyes sealed to his fate, the wolf spoke, softly: "I submit to this act."

Grace, with slow, deliberate movements, gathered her hair in a knot, peered at the wolf, at its inarguable immediacy. The prominent gray muzzle—not so very unlike Murl's, though sharper, more angled.

"Now." Again—eyes tight shut; tufted ears wedged back against the long, soft-bristled skull—his whispered voice: "Take up a stone."

Biting her lip, Grace extended her hand, brought her palm to rest upon the wolf's rough, matted coat. She felt the erratic motion of his ribcage, felt rather than heard his low growl.

She asked, "What if your wounds could be healed?" She winced as her head erupted with dozens of overlapping voices.

For a long moment, but for the rasping of his breath, the wolf remained silent. Then: "Death hungers . . . howls."

"Death is patient. It can wait," Grace said. "Time can heal."

Another silence. The wolf opened one moon-pale eye. "I am nothing. Without a pack."

"You can make a new life," Grace said. She held his gaze, determined not to flinch.

"I am old." The wolf shut his eyes, wheezed. "I do not know how."

"We will learn a new way," Grace said, "together."

The wolf twitched beneath Grace's hand, a ripple of muscle and sinew that belied age. She sent Murl to fetch Thaniel.

The wolf did not respond. Nor did he protest.

CHAPTER FIFTEEN

A wolf at the door.

A wolf in the fold.

A wolf . . . on the hearthrug?

Grace knelt on that hearthrug, arm's length from the wounded creature that both common sense and fable cautioned against. Arranged about her, spread in an arch within easy reach, were clean rags, linen strips, a shallow enamel basin, and a small pot of ointment.

Suspended above the hearth's low flame, the kettle began to sing. Wrapping her hand in a cloth, Grace stood and removed the kettle from its place, sending its song into a slow fade. She poured a long stream of boiled water into the basin, left it to steam and quake, then sorted the linen strips by length. Lifting the pot of ointment, she sniffed—a blend of scents, mint, rosemary, sage; hyssop, perhaps. She expressed a calm certainty of purpose, for her parents' sake; Gaven and Lettie sat at the kitchen table, stiff and ill at ease. The evening meal rang silent but for the dull, arhythmic clink of utensils. Aware of their attention, Grace kept her hands and purpose steady.

Wolf by the ears. Wolf as confessor.

Kneeling once more, beside her patient, a shiver of anxiety swept through her, from toes to scalp. Her throat tightened; fingers gripped the basin's curled lip. *Learned behavior*, she reminded herself. *We have an agreement.*

Drawing a steady breath, she spoke in a soft, neutral tone: "It's me." Recent experience had taught her any sudden movement sent all into thrashing chaos—cat and dog; parents; bowl and bandages; lupine pride. It did not do to startle him. "It's time again."

As anticipated, the wolf did not respond; she had learned to appreciate silence over protest. With her collection arranged on the floor about her, she reached out—tentative—felt the bristle of stiff fur against her fingertips. When he did not snap or snarl, she began—one by one, layer after layer—to peel back the old bandages from his torn throat. Despite her care, the action elicited a soft grumble—a habitual sound that mimicked distant thunder. Though expected, her body responded—the hairs rose at the base of her neck, along her arms. The burden of her parents' unease, the impulse to turn and see the unspoken fear she knew engraved their faces, prodded.

We agreed to this, she reminded herself, eyes fixed on her work. *We all agreed.*

Three days ago, Thaniel had clipped away thick bands of fur to expose the gash, had instructed her in cleaning and wrapping it. Gathering soiled bandages in a small pile, Grace leaned forward, her body angled sharply over the wolf. She considered the seamed, pink wound crosshatched in Thaniel's neat stitchwork of black thread. That had been a scene, she thought, and shook her head.

Speaking in a low voice, she addressed the wolf, saw his ear twitch in her direction. "I'm going to clean the wound now."

She slipped a clean cloth into the basin, water warm as flesh. Wringing it out, a thin trickle of water described her forearm, from wrist to elbow. Small droplets pattered the hearthrug, seeped into the weave of tight coils as she peered at the wound. Cloth clenched in hand, she blotted the exposed wound, the dark, even stitches. The wolf, eyes tight shut, bared curved teeth and rumbled low in his throat, a sound similar to—and yet nothing like—Sylvie's purr.

Instinct, she repeated to herself, knuckles whitening, *habit. Learned behavior.*

With great effort, she pushed aside her own visceral fear and continued to blot, to clean. Crouched as she was over him, in such proximity, the wolf's muzzle and teeth were, again, both similar to and nothing like Murl's. As she worked, she pondered the superficial resemblances, acutely aware of her beloved companions, domesticated dog and cat. She felt their presences, beyond the fire's wavering perimeter; heard the static hum of their hypervigilance, the spark of their erect postures. Their devotion so palpable, it almost distracted from her careful work. They safeguarded her, prepared to intercede; she clung firmly to the belief this was unwarranted.

"Have you finished paining me, human?" Wolf's voice, though soft, held gravelly menace.

Caught within the twist and curl of her own thoughts, Grace startled at his question. Her hand spasmed midair. Steadying her voice, she breathed. "No, not yet."

She dipped the cloth, sloshed it about in tepid water, wrung it out. Her thoughts wandered to the people of Edgewoode, whose recent display of collective and individual levels of tolerance exceeded expectation. She nursed a wolf, most feared of all wild creatures, back to health within their midst, and, with assurances and promises to all—her family and Thaniel; her neighbors, shepherds, goat- and cowherds—they accepted. Grudgingly, yes. With whispers, shaking their heads, nodding vaguely in her direction, perhaps. But, to her relief and gratitude, no one demanded the wolf's head.

She released the cloth in the basin, where it opened, a bruised bloom in cooling, clouded water. Then she dabbed the poultice over the wound, applied fresh white bandages. Shifting posture, she inspected the wolf's hind leg, trailed her fingers over his coarse gray coat, as much for her own sensation as to allow him to know her movement's progress. She repeated the procedure: peeling, cleaning, poulticing, rebandaging. This gash, too, remained miraculously free of infection.

"You *hurt* me," Wolf rumbled. Lifting his head, he revealed black gums in grin or grimace.

"I'm . . . I'm sorry," Grace said. "We must keep the wound clean."

"*We*." Wolf huffed impatience, regarding her with a pale eye.

"Yes," she said. Fingers working, she finished rebandaging the leg swiftly, deftly, her heart lodged in her throat. "We."

"There is no 'we,' human." Wolf flicked his gaze away, dropped his head against the hearthrug.

Grace watched his still form, the leap and shift of his shadow tossed against wall and floor. Nerves threatened her voice, her hands and fingers, yet she repeated firmly: "*We* have an agreement." She willed the authority of her voice to take root. Within, she trembled.

Wolf exhaled a rasping, nasal "harumph."

Heat sped through Grace's limbs, followed swiftly by chill. She gathered assorted paraphernalia—basin, poultice pot, rags, soiled bandages—and rose, arms burdened. Wolf arranged himself into an ill-managed heap before the fire's erratic flames.

"That's *my* spot," Murl lamented in a soft whine.

"You're so very good to loan it." Grace fixed an apologetic look on the dog, then addressed the wolf's curved back. "Are you hungry?"

The shaggy creature twitched, heaved a labored breath, but did not answer.

"*I* am. . . ." Murl's tail thumped without enthusiasm.

"You are ever hungry, dog." Sylvie flicked the frosted tip of her own tail in critique. She concealed her own unease, her very self beneath the table, surrounded herself in a fortification of spindled chair legs, the table's stouter legs.

"Best behavior, everyone," Grace said. She studied the wolf, marked Murl's and Sylvie's steady gazes. Crossing the wide-planked floor, she unburdened herself in the kitchen, stowed oddments in their respective places, all the while aware of her parents' watchful eyes.

Grace avoided their mutual stare, cast a glance out the kitchen's twin square windows. The sun sank and set, a surer measure of time spent in ministering aid than the fatigue of hands, limbs, spirit. Blinking surprise, she saw a soot-gray sky, heavy with the threat of storm, framed within the divided panes; heard, now, the rumble of thunder, low and insistent, that drummed against the cottage's deep walls. The south wind swelled and moaned, rattled the door within its frame and jangled its iron latch; threatened the hearth's flames and popping embers.

"What does he say?" Her father broke the silence. Leaning back in his chair, careful of Sylvie's twitching tail. He packed tobacco into his pipe, lit the bowl.

"Mostly, he complains," Grace sighed. With little comment, her parents had abandoned their evening hearthside seats to the new lupine fixture present in their household—perhaps the most striking shift in their daily ritual.

"Does he heal?" This, from her mother—concern, wrapped in steel.

"Well enough." Grace retrieved three glazed, stoneware dishes from below the kitchen basin. "No infection."

"The sooner, the better." Gaven clamped his pipe's stem between his teeth, blew erratic smoke.

"Sit, Grace, eat," Lettie said. "Your dinner is getting cold."

"Just another moment . . ."

Grace placed a bowl of scraps near the door for Murl, then tucked a second, smaller bowl between wooden legs for Sylvie—each far enough that they might take their ease and eat, yet near enough that they could observe the wolf's movements, however small. Murl swallowed his food in several sloppy gulps, ears flat against his skull, tail tucked bellyward. Though Sylvie feigned disinterest, her ears twitched and swiveled, and her narrowed gaze remained fixed on the wolf.

Walking a third bowl over to Wolf, Grace set the dish on the hearthrug, an arm's length from his muzzle. She observed the swivel of his tufted ears, the ripple of muscle beneath fur that moved from ruff to tail.

"Domestic food." Eyes sealed, nostrils flaring, Wolf spurned the bowl's contents.

Grace ignored him.

When at last she sat at the kitchen table between her parents, Sylvie huddled between her ankles, her dinner was quite cold. Questions hung—taut, unspoken—between them: How long until the interloper healed? Until his departure? What then? Grace offered no answers. She did not, and could not, know.

A thunderous clap shook the cottage. Grace jumped in her seat. Purposefully, she scooped a mouthful of cold pot pie and considered what she *did* know: They had, miraculously, established a routine. The wounds healed, and Wolf would eventually eat—the past three nights, despite daily complaint, she always collected a clean bowl.

Also, to her relief, Adelaide the lacemaker had withdrawn her son's name from a bid for marriage.

When a wolf creeps in the door, love flies out the window.

CHAPTER SIXTEEN

The twinge of guilt would not subside, stole into the periphery of Grace's thoughts unhindered. She'd left her parents, Murl, and Sylvie in the garden, with Wolf contained indoors—cranky and ill at ease with the mere thought of domesticity.

She sat within the meadow's swaying midst. For a moment, just a moment, she'd slipped away from the chaos she'd introduced, to ease a separate worry. The thought lay buried beneath the current of everyday diversion: a dull ache of memory, of anxiety, that refused to sink into the silt of forgetting. Aldermere. The mechanist. The opaque implication of threat. Through water, she had opened herself to involuntary danger. Through wind—an element that knew no barrier—she hoped for knowledge.

So, here she sat, on a small grassy rise. Eyes closed, face tilted slightly up, legs and ankles crossed. Her skirts were a woolen landscape, arranged over grass and low-creeping flowers and damp earth. Weather-worn hills of the valley's gentle upsweep defined its farther edges, while the Bright Wood formed its green flank. Above, the cloudless sky unfolded, blue as truth. All the meadow's inhabitants, like stars in the night sky, shimmered beyond her closed eyelids. She listened past these countless bright voices, gently encouraging them aside so she could concentrate on the wind.

A remarkable voice, the wind. It swept by like the suggestion of night or canyon, like the ripple and eddy of water, like song. For a moment, she might catch it . . .

"Here ◬we ◬ are."

A hushed and weaving breathless sigh that shifted, skipped, eluded grasp . . .

"No. ◬ Over ◬ here."

A breath in her ear, it laughed, knotting her hair against her cheek, her neck.

"Catch ◬ us ◬ if ◬ you ◬ can . . . can . . . can't!"

Playful, inconstant. It laced itself within the sigh and clamor of others' voices, folded itself beneath the wings of birds and insects. At once ancient and infant, wise and teasing, solo and chorus; at odds with itself, yet perfect in its dualities and infectious mirth.

"All ◬ are ◬ subject ◬ to ◬ our ◬ whim: birds ◬ and ◬ animals, trees ◬ and ◬ grasses. River's ◬ voice, we ◬

ripple ◬ and ◬ slur. Echoes ◬ of ◬ hill ◬ and ◬ mountain, ◬ we ◬ alter!"

"Yes," Grace said, mustering admiration alongside patience, "but what of the man?"

"We ◬ know ◬ no ◬ restriction, neither ◬ bar ◬ nor ◬ latch ◬ nor lock. ◬ Through ◬ keyholes ◬ we ◬ slip, ◬ down ◬ chimneys ◬ we ◬ rush, invited ◬ or ◬ not. . . ."

Grace grimaced. The wind, it seemed, was a braggart. It perceived her efforts, yet did little to support the endeavor.

"In ◬ the ◬ Wood, black ◬ walnuts ◬ ripen. Sparrow ◬ hawks ◬ fledge. Fallen ◬ log. Bees' ◬ hive. Mule ◬ pulls ◬ wagon ◬ town ◬ to ◬ village ◬ to ◬ town, ◬ follows ◬ river's ◬ course. Honeycomb. ◬ Upstream, Bear ◬ wades. On ◬ claw, ◬ fish ◬ gasps."

Grace marveled at the random specificity. She suspected that the wind enjoyed misleading, confusing, avoiding. Regardless, she repeated: "But, what of *the man*?"

"Bees ◬ in ◬ hair. Moth ◬ on ◬ shoulder. Rabbit ◬ creeps ◬ near."

Light pulsed against her closed lids. She measured time's passage in the click and whir of insects. When the wind changed its singsong monologue, when it nudged her shoulders and plucked at her blouse and skirt and hair, Grace adjusted her ear. Earnest now, no longer teasing, the wind advised in vaporous whisper:

"Rain ◬ rain ◬ rain. We ◬ are ◬ tempest. . . ."

Though she sat in a splash of sunlight, Grace understood without sight of cloud or scent of moisture, that a storm, indeed, was approaching. Opening her eyes, she shifted her gaze, considered the ranks of dark clouds forming to the west, heard the muffled drum of far-off thunder. Much as she wished to press the wind for answers, to disentangle its speech, she would not tempt the lash of lightning; she resigned herself to leaving the meadow and heading home.

As she rose, a white tumble of downward motion caught her eye. A single bloom of wild carrot—whorl of frilled white lace—fell from her skirt's folds. Bending, she plucked the flower from the grass at her toes, swept her gaze over the meadow in a broad arc. She saw no one—no one who might so neatly have plucked the wildflower and placed it in her lap without her knowing.

"Thank you." Grace twirled the sturdy bloom between her fingers. As she wove her way across the meadow, she slid the stem behind her left ear, nesting it in the wind-tossed mass of her hair.

No sooner did her feet strike the dirt track leading back to Edgewoode's heart than daylight fluttered, the storm arriving. With each step, the rain increased in strength and tempo. Pulling her shawl over her head, Grace clutched the edges beneath her chin. She wished she had worn her boots. Mud slicked the soles of her feet, oozed between her toes. Doubtless, her boots—beside her front door, thrust among papery narcissus and yellow-eyed forget-me-knots—were collecting water and would not soon dry out. Sometimes, Sylvie was right.

Quickening her pace, Grace ducked through sheeting rain, through a liquid slur of voices too numerous to parse. Yet, it seemed she heard her name—a blurred sound cast through the pelt and tumble. Midstride, wet skirts catching at her ankles, she glanced up. Thaniel leaned from his front door into the downpour, beckoning.

"Come out from the rain," he called. The torrent muted his voice.

She dashed for the cottage and stood on Thaniel's threshold. Dripping, breathless, her rain-weighted shawl slid from the crown of her head. Vines of hair clung to her cheeks and brow. Pushing rivulet strands from her face, she caught the battered bloom of wild carrot between her fingers.

"You're soaked." Thaniel shut the cottage door, shut out the rain, and caught her hands in his own. His eyes roved her face. "And your lips are blue."

"I'm fine," she laughed. "I'm not here for an examination!" His gaze, the warmth of his touch, sent a prickling across her skin.

Thaniel ignored her protest. "You need to warm up. I'll get you a towel. And a blanket." Releasing her fingers, he turned and left her on the doorsill, called from around a corner, "Take your wet layers off."

Grace hesitated, realized she was shaking with cold. The memory of Aldermere's lake swelled. Dropping the lacy blossom on a small sturdy table, she peeled the shawl from her shoulders, struggled free of her bodice. Stepping out of rain-heavy skirts, she discovered a series of small, random holes nibbled in its hem; likely, a shrew's work.

Stripped down to an ivory linen chemise, she sat on her knees, knelt before the hearth, and chafed her hands over the flames to warm them. She heard behind her the unmistakable tread, and momentary pause, of Thaniel's returning steps.

"Here." He approached and handed her a soft-worn towel, set a blanket over her bare shoulders.

Grace noted a curious quality to Thaniel's voice. Drawing the towel through her hair, blotting it dry, she was glad she heard only speech and not another human's thoughts. She dismissed the quiver in her belly, and said: "I think I brought a small river in with me."

"The floor needed washing," Thaniel said. He relocated a chair closer to the hearth.

Grace sat. "Are you always so calm?" She spread her hands and fingers before the flames.

He laughed, a soft sound, centered in his chest. "It comes with the vocation."

"Even when the unexpected arrives on your doorstep?" She watched him gather up her skirt and shawl and bodice, the ease of his hands as he draped each article carefully over assorted furniture, and position all near the fire to dry. Flames met each spattering water droplet with greedy sizzle and hiss.

"Especially then." He grinned at her. "It's good practice—you can't be excitable when working with animals."

"Ha!" She was certain, as she leaned into the warming tide, that she heard gradient laughter tucked within the fire's pop and crackle.

"Hungry?" Thaniel asked.

"Very," she said. The realization surprised her.

Thaniel nodded. "Tea, coffee, chocolate?"

She paused, fingers in her hair. "Tea."

"Let's see . . ." Humming to himself, he rummaged through the small kitchen nook, the icebox, pantry, and shelves. He measured tea into a green-glazed pot; sliced cheese and pears and brown bread; splashed cream into a squat pitcher; heaped two each of plates, cups, spoons all on a tray, with blue-checked cloth napkins. The tray chattered as he carried it back across the room.

"You could find work at an inn," Grace teased.

"Edgewoode doesn't have an inn." Depositing the tray on the side table, he picked up the sprig of wild carrot, slipped its slender stem into a small phial filled with water. He looked at her, one eyebrow raised. "Are you trying to get rid of me?"

"Why would I do that?"

Again, he grinned. "You're edging in on my territory—all my regulars ask for *you*." He sat down opposite Grace and passed her a cup of hot tea. "What were you doing out in this weather? Speaking to rain, thunder, lightning?"

Laying the towel in her lap, Grace accepted the tea, turned the cup between her hands. She heard the note of worry he tried to conceal, watched him as he spread butter and bright jam on a slice of bread—with subtlety of movement, competency of hands. Unlike so many others, Thaniel neither pushed nor pried. Always, he listened with keen interest and seemed intuitively to respect the limits and perplexities of her newfound gift and her relationship with it.

"Not the rain," she said at length. "The wind." She made no mention of why. Unrestrained, untethered, unconfined by *place*, the wind alone could tell her of the movements of that particular individual: where the mechanist might be, what he might be doing in this vast world. Unfortunately, they were details she'd been unable to coax forth.

Thaniel looked at her, expectant, and passed a chipped plate. Scarlet jam, pale butter, dark bread.

"It was a . . . lively conversation." She shook her head, amused, teacup halfway to her lips. Did the wind shush more emphatically at its mention? Her gaze slewed from Thaniel to the rain-spattered window. The glass rattled gently in its frame, a tinkling sound like laughter.

"The *wind*," Thaniel echoed.

Grace nodded and sipped—considering, remembering, committing to memory and hope of understanding. One voice, made of many, unified. Like the lake's. A school of fish, a flock of birds. Sporadic, spontaneous. Mercurial.

"What did you speak of?"

"*It* spoke . . . *they* spoke . . ." She set her cup down, gathered her hair to one side in a thick, damp rope. She recalled the broad pictures it conveyed at dizzying speed, the occasional detail that captured its attention. "A bit . . . one-sided. More of a monologue. Although, eventually, it warned me the rain was coming." She quirked a grin. "Just not quite how *soon*."

"Time is a human thing." Thaniel lifted an expressive eyebrow, winked.

"So it seems!"

"Do you need another blanket?"

"No, I'm fine." She picked up the chipped plate, bit the thick slice of slathered bread. Raspberry leapt upon her tongue.

Thaniel gauged her with a perceptive eye. Shifting subjects, he asked, "How is your rescue?"

Grace swallowed. Leaning back in her chair, amid swaddling blankets, she sighed. That twinge of guilt returned; she should be home, mediating. "He complains," she said. "With more strength and vigor with each day that passes."

Thaniel pursed his lips, considered. "In other words, he heals."

"Yes." Balancing the plate on her knees, she took up her teacup, turned it again between her hands. Contained within thin, glazed walls, the tea eddied from its center. "He heals. . . ."

"But?"

"Every day, he seems more restless, more sullen." She frowned. "He doesn't say so, but I know he questions my interference, though he chose to allow it." Her hair snaked about her shoulders as she shook her head. "Driven out," she repeated Wolf's summary, "he will not return. Insists he *cannot*." Her thoughts circled back to the mechanist, also driven out. She struggled to maintain a neutral expression.

"He'll adjust." Thaniel reached across the little table for the green glazed teapot.

"Will he?" She held out her cup to have it topped off.

"He must." Setting the teapot down, he looked at her. "That's the only path forward."

"I hope you're right." She considered the shushing wind, the pattering steps of rain falling against the peaked roof, the fire's hypnotic jig. Gradually, her hair dried and lifted from her shoulders, neck, scalp. "He considers himself alone."

"Not alone." Thaniel smiled. "He has you."

The observation unsettled her. "I'm afraid my purpose has run its course." She plucked at the blankets enveloping her, loosened their folds. "Another objective might prove helpful."

Thaniel took the empty plate teetering on her knees, prevented its fall and clatter. He said with certainty, "You are all that's needed at present."

Grace leaned sideways in her chair, crooked her knees, and pulled her feet up beneath her hip. The fire breathed warmth against her side. "He's ornery." Did she describe beast or man? "The whole house is on edge."

"It will sort itself out in time," Thaniel said. Leaning toward her, he pulled the blanket up over the half-moon of her shoulder, then sat back. "Patience."

Grace sighed, flexed her fingers toward the fire. "You sound like Thrush."

"I'm flattered."

She watched him as he set the empty cup on the table gently as a bit of down, as a speckled wren's egg. When he set his hands on his thighs to look at her, she thought she heard laughter crackle in the hearth.

"I'm glad to have caught your attention." His eyes reflected the glow of firelight.

Wind shushed and swirled about the cottage; rain tapped impatiently at the windows. Grace was now certain that yes, the flames' multiplicity of tongues—leaping and popping—snickered with anticipation.

CHAPTER SEVENTEEN

Grace resettled the satchel of oats and dried apples slung over her shoulder. Fields and farms and the surrounding landscape emerged from the storm, blinking and confused. From a cloudless blue sky—untroubled and restored to calm—the sun bloomed, cast a balm of rays over all evidence of tumult and scattered deadfall. The morning's breeze wandered through the tangle of confusion, damp and unapologetic. Birds called softly from the undergrowth—bliss at the sun's return, resolve to repair nests and replenish seed caches. In sharp contrast, squirrels skittered from various heights and barked what she could only assume were inspired profanities.

"What could that even *mean*?" Brow creased in confusion, Grace laughed, losing her footing to a mud-slicked stone. She caught herself against the split trunk of a great, silvered beech. In the storm's aftermath, while all of Edgewoode stirred with cleanup—mending roofs and barns and fences, trimming the snapped limbs of fruit trees, collecting and splitting wood—her mission lay where many townsfolk dared not venture—past the Bright Wood's threshold, through its dripping half-shadow.

"Are you okay?" Murl's concern showed throughout his posture—cocked ears, tilted head.

"She's fine, dog." Sylvie materialized from within a shiver of undergrowth.

"Thank you, Murl." Grace patted the dog's spotted head. "I'm good."

Collecting her feet beneath her, she pressed both hands to the beech, in thanks, in regret. The venerable tree had snapped at the hips. Smooth roots remained anchored, deeply coiled into spongy earth, but the tree's upper half sprawled now against its neighbors in a sidelong collapse of leaf and limbs. The air tasted of fresh-torn branches and torn leaves, acrid and tangy.

She clambered around the tree's splintered torso. Murl, snuffling, nosed his way through the maze of earthbound limbs, rejoined her on the farther side, where Wolf waited, bristling with restrained silence. His insistence on joining their expedition had surprised her. Despite wounds and a pronounced limp, it seemed a sense of ease had been restored to his limbs and movements, if not his temper. His presence leant an edge of disquiet to their small company.

"Sylvie," Grace called through veils of greenery, "I wish you'd stay closer."

The tabby melted into the distance. "If wishes were mice . . ."

Clicking her tongue, Grace pressed on. Murl, tail tucked bellyward, matched her steps; Wolf outpaced them slightly.

"Remember, she's just a filly, young and lost and frightened," Grace reminded both dog and wolf, aware that Sylvie would do as she liked.

"Horses scare me," Murl whined. "Too big!"

Wolf snorted; he stared, ears pricked and twitching, beyond the crosshatch of rain-streaked trunks.

"Well, when we find her," Grace said, "you'll all wait, and I'll approach her."

The filly they were searching for—the farrier's young draft horse and unquestionably large—had broken free of her stall and charged, storm-panicked, into night and pelting rain. After a fruitless search, the farrier turned his anxious gaze toward the Bright Wood's borders. Despite his loss, despite his own size and strength, he shrank from crossing the forest's threshold. So Grace set off where many of her neighbors—for reasons both sensible and absurd—would not. Rough canvas jacket buttoned to her chin, the boots she routinely avoided weighting her feet, she entered the Wood with cat and dog and wolf in tow. They made a curious entourage.

"Here." Wolf halted, motionless, tail outstretched. His posture expressed pointed, disinterested interest.

Murl stole forward, pressed his nose to loam several paces from Wolf. "Yes, yes, here!"

Grace ducked beneath arched hazels, bent to examine heavy crescents impressed upon the moss and mud of a narrow deer trail. The tracks threaded away between a fringe of snapped, raw twigs and bent bracken.

"Well done." She touched the prints, cool soil against her fingers, and rose. "Come along."

As she walked, she noted the contrasting effects of the Bright Wood on her companions. Wolf increased in size and spirit—ears erect, thick brush tail extended. Though he limped, his gait and posture showed a natural ease. Murl, by contrast, shrank. Tail curled, the dog padded close enough to trod her bootlaces. His ears and nose twitched nervously in all directions, though, at all times, he reserved a keen, deliberate eye for Wolf. Murl's reasons—like his tail—remained tucked within himself.

"Let's stay together," Grace reminded as Sylvie slunk ahead.

Shifting the satchel, she pushed aside a curtain of slim, rain-slicked elms. Over, under, around and through. *Deeper*. The forest settled with a damp breath. Sunlight probed, an alternating luster of wide bands and narrow shafts. Each stride took her nearer to the Wood's ever-green heart. Over muddied earth, leaf mold, and pine needles. Past curl-lipped ferns, creeping ivies, communities of toadstools. The forest wove a tapestry of conversations. Words buzzed in her head like honeybees, like falling rain and wind-blown leaves. Mentally, she culled and sorted.

"Sylvie!" Grace narrowed her eyes, peered ahead. "You're too far!"

"She hears," Murl muttered, with a small shake of ruff, "but she doesn't listen."

Grace laughed softly. In relation to the squirrels' chatter, she guessed Sylvie's general location—they barked obscenities from the canopy, betrayed the cat's noiseless prowl.

"Here," Wolf intoned, halting again.

Water laced through thick bracken; a muddy verge stamped with a flurry of prints. Wolf padded to the creek's edge, crouched to drink; Murl, with wrinkled brow and darting eye, mimicked the act.

"Drink slowly, dog; briefly." Wolf rose. "Or your gut will protest."

"I know." Murl lifted his head, jowls and whiskers streaming water.

Wolf scented the air. "This way."

Grace watched Wolf trot—a hitch in his step—along the creek's edge, through the ferns and deeper into the Wood. Glancing at Murl's expectant, upturned face, she smiled. "Off we go, then!"

Thick mud squelched beneath her boots' treads, the wet suck and release of her steps, of Murl's. A lattice of branches stretched overhead, and through them, Grace caught a fleet, flitting movement within the canopy—a rust-hued, tentative smudge of motion. Pausing, she felt her boots sink toward firmer ground, craned her neck and found Thrush, perched on a slip of limb.

"You've caused quite a stir!" Cocking his head, he aimed a bead-bright eye at her. He spoke in music.

Grace raised her hand to him, palm spread in invitation. "Me?" Pale toes curled over her fingers as Thrush alit—an insubstantial weight, light as promise.

"The company you keep . . ." Thrush inclined his head toward Murl, beside her, and the lupine figure that seemed to ignore them.

"I'm good company!" Murl wagged hopefully.

Thrush cocked his head, glanced between the two. "Perhaps it's a matter of perspective." With an avian shrug, he shook out his tail from the safety of his human perch.

"Most things are," Grace said.

"Agreed," Thrush tutted. "I'm pleased to see you're well—that was a storm to ruffle the feathers. I imagine you're here to collect your wayward charge."

"You've seen her?"

The feathers at Thrush's throat rose and quivered. "There is a refuge, of sorts, deep in the forest. A clearing. A likely spot to investigate. I'm happy to guide you."

"That would be wonderful."

Wolf rolled yellow eyes, looked away. "The domesticated creature's scent is strong enough."

"The creek bends ahead in a southerly direction." With a rustle, Sylvie emerged from shadow and underbrush. She purred silkily. "It exits the forest, and the trail divides; the eastern branch leads deep into the forest's interior." She smoothed her whiskers with one paw, eyeing the bird.

Wolf raised his head to test the wind. "The cat is correct. The scent is strongest from the east."

Murl barked eagerly and, with a sideways glance, adopted Wolf's stance and posture.

"As I was saying," Thrush said, pausing to preen speckled breast feathers, "the clearing lies east of here."

"Well, then," Grace confirmed, "east it is."

Thrush spread his wings, lifted from her palm, and piped, "Let's find your beast."

Grace followed Thrush's course, with wolf ahead and dog beside. "Sylvie," she said, "please, stay close. . . ."

With a backward glance over her striped shoulder, Sylvie slipped back beneath the screen of fern and scrub and shadow.

"I'm staying close," Murl promised.

The deer trail unfolded, swayed through fern and underbrush, dodged ever eastward. Their progress stirred the scents of pine, and decay of oak and maple and beech's leaf mold. Grace lost the leap and sparkle of the creek's chatter as the Wood's voice lifted against her ear like a tide, like dawn. Voices mingled in a kaleidoscopic pattern. The deep, deliberate intonation of trees; the whisper of wildflowers and rasp of bracken; the crickets' trill and owl's soft muttered complaint. A multitude of voices—intricate, intersecting, beautiful in their complexity.

In a latticework of limbs and underbrush that subsumed and absorbed, the Bright Wood enveloped. Each step, each voice pulled Grace deeper *in*. She walked and listened, worried about Sylvie, about locating the filly and finding their way out of the Wood before sundown. No longer able to discern the sun's progress beyond the trees' communal reach, she measured time's passage by the blisters rubbed into her toes, gnawed into her ankles.

"You make good time for the flightless."

Thrush's song curled against her ear, a melodic curl of breeze.

"We do!" Murl said.

". . . don't even realize when you've been insulted," Wolf grumbled under his breath.

"What?" Tail drooping, Murl's velvet brow wrinkled.

"Never mind," Grace whispered, tracing her fingertips between Murl's ears. "He's just grumpy."

"Ohhh!" Murl licked his own nose, resumed imitation of Wolf in posture and stride.

The track narrowed. One by one, they filed through—Murl, shadow to Wolf; Thrush, a song overhead; Sylvie, a conspicuous absence. Caught within the pluck of wild roses, the snag and snatch of blackberry, Grace lagged. The Wood hugged close with whisper, sigh, and rustle.

The track broadened, and the undergrowth's tumble and grasp fell back in stages. Loose earth dipped and rose like water. Oaks, maples, hickories, and smooth beeches parted company for slim young birches. Abruptly, like a heavy drape drawn, an expanse of meadow emerged—a broad clearing of fallow grasses speckled with wildflowers. Gold and green, pricked with pinks and violets and yellow-gold hawkweed. The field swelled and contracted in the shifting breeze.

Feeling a brush against her calf, Grace started. Sylvie, sleek and stealthy as shadow, took shape beneath her gaze.

"It's about time." Eyes half-slit, Sylvie yawned a full display of sharp white teeth.

"I wish you wouldn't do that!" Grace tutted. She bent to rub Sylvie's cheek. "You know I worry about you."

"No need. I was aware of you," Sylvie said, with a satisfied rumble. "Wolf is a predator . . . moves like a cat. But you . . . your dog . . ." One tufted ear ticked with motion. "Clumsy. You announce our position."

"Really!" Grace exhaled. She picked burrs from the tabby's flanks, and thorns from own hair and sleeves.

". . . and undermine our efforts . . ." Sylvie continued.

"We're not *hunting*." Grace huffed and held the cat's green-gold gaze. Sylvie returned her stare without comment.

"We're not *that* clumsy." Murl set haunches to earth. "Are we?"

"No. We're not."

Rising, Grace surveyed the meadow beneath the blade of her hand. Her breath caught. There in the distance—hock-deep amid flowers and grasses and pale, green-white butterflies—stood the filly, chewing contentedly.

"Your beast." Wolf's fixed stare belied his calm.

"We found her!" Murl barked. His head ratcheted with motion; his soft ears jerked.

Grace felt Thrush's wing brush her cheek, his claws fasten to her shoulder. She noted Sylvie's posture—the crook of ears, the rapid flick and whisk of tail against saw-toothed grasses.

"Wait here," Grace told them. "We don't want to frighten her."

Wolf grumbled, lowered himself stiffly, and turned his head away. Murl whined, head and tail dipping.

"Don't fret," Thrush sang. "This is a creature happy to be found."

Grace waded into the whispering sea of grass, felt Thrush lift from her shoulder. Slowly, deliberately, she followed the wide, wandering trail the filly had parted, and hoped the young horse would not bolt at her approach. Her shadow stretched over wind-ruffled grass toward the young horse, until mere strides lay between them. When the filly tossed her head, whickered, Grace slowed. Carefully, she loosed the satchel from her shoulder, unfastened the clasps.

"You must be hungry."

Eyes rounding, the creature nickered and stomped. Despite her size, she retained a young horse's awkward physique, all lanky limbs and knobbed knees.

"What do you call yourself?" Grace pulled back the satchel's flap, revealed a wealth of oats, a small bribe of dried apples. She rolled the satchel's edges down with measured turns of her wrists and fingers.

The filly pulled her head in toward her deep chest and whickered again, more softly. The name came to Grace: "Falla."

Grasses and twigs matted her mane and forelock; snapped bracken wove through her long tail.

Grace smiled. "Well, Falla," she said, extending the satchel, "this is for you."

Falla danced sideways, dipped her head and ran her soft muzzle along the length of her right foreleg. Stretching her neck toward the satchel, nostrils flared, she lifted one broad hoof, then another; one slow step forward, another and another; until she thrust her head deep into the proffered satchel.

Receiving the full force of Falla's great head, Grace rocked on her feet. Quickly, she regained her footing, lowered oats and apples to rest among the fox-tailed grasses and flowers. Gently, she touched the filly's stiff, ivory mane.

"Would you tell the others we'll rejoin them shortly?" A brief, skyward glance found Thrush circling overhead. Grace watched as, with a soft blur of feathers, he spread wings and flitted across the meadow. Then, gliding her hands over Falla's jaw and neck and shoulders, over her broad back, she attempted to assess the filly's health as Thaniel might. Thick mud crusted her coarse coat from hooves to knees, and a dried seam of blood mapped an errant path along the filly's right foreleg.

"What adventures have you had?" Grace asked. Kneeling, she inspected the wound—a jagged cut, but minor. Briefly, Falla flattened her ears and blew into Grace's hair, but she did not interrupt her meal to answer.

When the satchel was empty, Grace asked, "Are you ready to go home?"

Slipping a lead into place over the filly's neck, Grace stroked her and whispered softly, gently as Falla tossed her head. Slowly, she drew the filly along, backtracked through the meadow.

Then, unexpectedly, she saw the tree. Grace stopped, stood, stared as though struck. A tumult of noise expanded within her, stilled all the voices in her consciousness to utter silence.

There, within the Bright Wood, within this meadow, with its multitude of inhabitants, the great tree stood. It seemed, somehow, slightly beyond her ability to *see*, yet equally impossible to ignore—like a song heard at distance, windswept to particled notes. Staring directly blurred its presumed solidity, but if she let her vision stray, observed it coyly, from the tail of her eye, it became distinctly *tree* in form and structure—broad-trunked, multi-limbed, new-leafed and spreading, extending outward. It cast a stratified shimmer of shadows.

Rooted in place—in time, in *self*—Grace gripped Falla's bristled mane for support. Experimentally, she swept her vision back and forth; the tree shifted in response, in and out of focus. She laughed, her breath, her pulse rattling within her. When Falla tugged impatiently at the lead, Grace stumbled along beside her, through the swaying meadow, away from the undeniable, paradoxical vision of the tree.

CHAPTER EIGHTEEN

The kitchen glowed, stroked to radiance with the sun's setting. Board, bowl, blue water jug; her mother's profile—all burnished to warmth. The small knife in Grace's hand caught blades of westering light, scattered them throughout the room. Her eye wandered toward the window.

"Mom, I wish you could have seen it. . . ." Her words tumbled, like falling leaves, one swirled after another.

Heaped on the table between the two women, younger and elder, a pile of potatoes—dull, earth-clad and lumpy. These, Grace's mother transformed with calm eye and steady hand, removing their skins, revealing the glossy, pale-yellow bodies concealed within.

"It must be the biggest tree I've ever seen!" Grace gestured, and the little knife winked and flashed, cut patterns from dusky motes.

"Be careful with that knife, Grace dear."

"I could take you." Lowering the blade, Grace plucked up a potato with her free hand. The pile remaining shifted unsteadily. "I know the way now."

Murl, snuffling the floor, lifted his head and moaned softly. "So soon?"

"Where's your sense of adventure, dog?" Sylvie yawned, rolled over, and stretched full length in a rectangle of cast light.

"Then, you could see with your own eyes!" Setting the knife down, Grace patted Murl absently. "At least, I *think* you could."

"A tree is either there, or it isn't." A rough slip of skin fell from the knobbed potato in Lettie's hand. "I have enough to occupy me without traipsing about the Wood."

"And to think, if that storm hadn't blown through . . . if the filly hadn't become lost . . ." Grace paced a wide circle around the cat and stood before the window, looked out in the Wood's direction. "I might never have *seen* it."

"Maybe if you hadn't, you'd be more help here, *now*." Lettie rapidly halved and quartered another tuber, added it to the denuded mound.

"Oh, Mom, I'm sorry." Grace swept back to her mother's side. A faint dust of earth sifted between her fingers, curled over the forgotten potato trapped there.

"Maybe you'd rather go outside and help your father repair the woodshed?"

"Are you trying to get rid of me?" Grace teased. For a moment, she leaned into her mother, shoulder to shoulder. Then, picking up her knife with a casual grip, she shook her head. "I know. I'm a little distracted."

"Really?" Her mother raised a pale brow, continued peeling. "I hadn't noticed."

"I just can't help thinking about it, and wondering . . ."

"The Wood is large, Grace. Even you can't expect to know *every tree* in it."

"I know." Grace's gaze tiptoed toward the window again, and its curtain, fluttering moth-like. In slow increments, her hand lowered against her side. "But that's not the point."

"Humans," Sylvie rolled lengthwise along her spine within her shadow-bound square of light, from right to left. "Always inventing reasons to be dissatisfied."

"Tell me, then," Lettie said. "What *is* the point?"

Murl nosed Grace's fingers, licked the potato.

"The point is . . ." Darting a look at her mother, Grace pulled the tuber from the dog's reach and swiped it along her apron, leaving an earth-smudged trail.

"Potatoes taste like dirt." Murl ran his tongue along his muzzle.

"The point *is*," Grace repeated, "why now? Why not a year ago? Or five? Why not a year from now?"

"Is this a question you expect me to answer?" her mother asked. "Or do you have your own theory?"

Head tilted to one side, Grace called the tree up from memory—the dappled light, the breeze that slid through upswept branches. How the tree resisted solidity. "Don't you think it's curious . . ."

"*Shoo.*" Lettie flapped her hand at Murl and extracted the remaining potato from Grace's fingers.

". . . that I found the tree after I began hearing everything speak?" Grace's now empty hand fell to stroking Murl, and the dog leaned against her side, beyond Lettie's reach, his hind leg thumping rapid appreciation.

"It could as easily be a simple coincidence."

"Really?" Doubt formed a small crease in Grace's brow. "You really think so?"

"It's the simplest answer." Her mother shrugged. Rotating her wrist, another long ribbon of peel unspooled. "It certainly couldn't have sprouted overnight."

"It's too big," Murl agreed. He scratched his right ear with his rear leg. "Like horses."

Lettie gathered slick, quartered potatoes on the table into a neat mound. "Does there need to be a reason?"

"What do you mean?" Grace asked. Her eyes traveled her mother's features, examined the finely seamed brow, the curves of nose, chin, and cheekbones.

"Would a 'reason' make it any more or less true?"

Sylvie stretched, flexed paws with satisfaction. "*She* understands," she purred, "even if she *doesn't*."

"No," Grace said slowly. Her mother's hair, corded with silver, trailed in filaments about her neck and gently bowed shoulders. Many remarked on their strong resemblance.

"Did you question it when you began to comprehend all that spoke?"

Grace helped scrape undulate peels into a sloping stack.

"No," her mother confirmed. "All you speak so easily with now have, doubtless, always spoken. The tree, too, doubtless, has always been there." She applied her capable hands to a mass of sunset-orange carrots. "The only difference is, now, you're aware."

Studying her mother's profile, Grace recalled the story of that distant relative, Talbin—great-uncle or great-*great*-uncle—who had supposedly shed his own light. "But . . ."

"It's a gift, Grace." Lettie shook her head, her attention fixed on the work at hand. "You either accept it, or you don't."

She considered her mother's words; heard only reason, grounded as its source. Yet, she itched with curiosity. One phenomenon was enough, but two? Frowning, Grace dropped her gaze, found Murl grinning up at her, in anticipation of some morsel. She ruffled his fur.

"The world defies comprehension. You're not the first to notice." Lettie patted Grace's hand. "Would you get the soup pot, dear?"

Crossing the small kitchen area—Murl, ever hopeful, at her heels—Grace seized the heavy pot by its handles. Precise, measured, habitual, her movements contrasted with the whir of her thoughts. With a rustle of green leaves, woven limbs, and searching roots, the great tree rose in her mind, a rush of smooth, mottled silver bark and cascading canopy. From the hard nut of potentiality, sprouted tender seedling, slender sapling, and finally, unquestionable *tree.*

"It might make more sense . . ." She centered the pot on the worktable, and slid a slow, sideways glance at her mother. ". . . if I go back."

Her mother sliced lacy, fern-like tops off the bunch of carrots and then cleaned, stemmed, sliced a clutch of mushrooms. "*When.*" She emptied a jug of water into the pot, then scooped up quartered potatoes, bright disks of carrots, earthy mushrooms; she dropped all in by the handful. The water's surface rippled, accepted. Her mother remained tight-lipped.

"Maybe tomorrow."

"In time." Lettie cut onions, parsnip, a bouquet of soft, green herbs.

Grace dropped cubed and sliced vegetables, a cloud of herbs, into the pot, then added a thimble of salt and several grinds of black pepper. "It's just that I don't want to *forget.*"

"I doubt that's possible." With a nod, her mother inclined her head toward the hearth, where Wolf lay outstretched, a lupine obstruction. "Would you mind?"

"Wolf?" Grace called softly. "Could you clear the way, please?"

A tufted gray ear twitched, pivoted. Grumbling, Wolf rose and removed himself to the hearthrug's edge and levered down again. Bristled back facing the room's center, he set his jaw against his shins, eyes tight shut.

Lettie wiped her hands on her apron and muttered, brow furrowed. Hefting the pot in two-handed grip, she edged toward the hearth. She kept one eye on the wolf, set the pot on the hob, and stirred the flames to lick its blackened base.

Grace carefully spoke to the bend of her mother's back. "Sooner might be better."

"Oh, no. No no *no*." Straightening, turning on her heel, her mother planted one hand on her hip, brandished a poker with the other. "You are *not* going back there tonight, my girl."

Grace flinched beneath the tone and timber of her mother's voice. Stern, imperious, not-to-be-argued-with, it echoed of her youth, peeled away the fact that they were, now, if not peers, of similar stature.

"You will not be going to the Wood this night or any other. I've become accustomed to much recently . . ." Lettie's attention speared deliberately sideways toward the wolf relaxing full-length at the hearth's edge. "Very much *indeed*. But the Wood is not safe at night. Not even for *you*, despite the company you're likely to have." She did not wait for a reply but returned to the soup pot and gave it a firm stir.

Without stirring a whisker, Wolf agreed. "Your dam is right." He huffed over his folded front paws. "Heed her. You are too soft to run with the night."

"Please don't make us go." Head dipped forward, ears flattened against his skull, Murl whimpered.

Grace knelt, wrapped her arms around the dog's neck, pressed her cheek against his splotched coat. "We won't," she said, and gave him a small squeeze. "Not tonight."

"Or *any* night," her mother said, still bent over the fire.

"Or any night," Grace confirmed, exasperated. Releasing Murl, she stood.

"All this fuss," Sylvie commented idly, "over a tree." A misplaced shadow, she rose from her sunspot, approached her preferred chair near the hearth, leapt lightly up and in. Striped spine to spindles, she washed face and ears and whiskers. "And from one who has the gift of *tongues*."

"What is it now?"

"Nothing." Grace noted the wisps of steam that curled her mother's hair. Untying her apron, she hung it from an iron hook near the door. "I think Sylvie is mocking me."

Lettie tapped the spoon soundly against the kettle's rim. "I wouldn't take it to heart. Cats are funny that way."

Grace leaned against the door, watched Sylvie smooth the dark "M" between her ears with a tawny paw, the whiskers that grew there. Fire leapt and sparked in the feline's gaze, reflected keen awareness of who listened, who heard, who understood. Of all the household, the tabby seemed least concerned by Wolf; somehow, through feline resourcefulness, she had managed a pact so the two accepted and ignored one another's presence.

At her back, the door—a firm barrier, rippled glass cool against her skull. She plucked at her skirt, subdued, and her shadow stretched, obscured fading sunlight.

Closing her eyes, Grace's field of vision sparked and flashed, branched and sprouted and leafed. Impulse pricked. The tree whispered: *Now now now . . .*

"Set the table, dear."

Grace's eyes flew open. Pushing off the door, she traversed her own shadow, pulled unglazed plates and bowls, pewter spoons and butter knives from open shelves. The oak table chanted with their placement. She arranged cups and napkins, three of each beside each setting. She set the breadboard at the table's center. Unbidden—an apple falling from bent bough, or a pine releasing ripe cones—a thought slipped sideways inside her, dropped with a soft thud: of potential squandered and lost. Her heart clenched, fistlike.

"Come back."

Hands slack, Grace startled, looked down. Sylvie twined about her ankles, green-gold eyes intent and staring.

"You were lost," Sylvie meowed.

"Lost in thought," Grace agreed. The room—bare of leaves and branches, of budding possibilities—snapped into sharp relief about her. She stood at the table, a long bread knife pressed to a loaf's crusty dome.

"Thoughts are like rabbits," Sylvie rumbled. "You commit to the chase, or find yourself caught in the brambles."

"Rabbits are *fast*!" Murl jogged over, bumped his nose against the cat's.

Sneezing, Sylvie drew her head back. "Faster than some . . ."

From his spot near the fire, Wolf snorted.

"Thank you, Sylvie." Grace stroked the cat's cheek, beneath the small, pointed chin. Like water, the cat slipped beneath her hand, and she found herself instead scratching Murl's ears.

Returning to the table, gripping the knife, she drew it through the bread's rough crust. Thick slabs fell from the loaf, landing one atop the other. Murl licked up any crumbs that fell, no matter how small; Sylvie returned to her chair by the fire, both physically and symbolically above Wolf. Grace cut another slice, and the blade skipped over the bread's cleft surface.

"Here, I'll have that." Lettie took the knife from Grace's hand. "Go and call your father in to wash up."

Evening gathered beyond tea-stained eyelet curtains, beyond dimpled, watery glass. Pink and gold and violet. Grace turned toward the back of the house and the door set beneath the stairs that led to the backyard. She stood draped in shadow, her hand on the latch, and noticed, for the first time, the door's construction—the reinforced boards that stretched diagonally from top to bottom, and crossed at the center.

Even the silent door—which might once, as living tree, have spoken to her audibly—insisted she wait.

CHAPTER NINETEEN

Grace walked the wide, rutted, earth-packed track. Each barefooted step was a provocation of small stones, poking, prodding tender soles and arches. The surrounding landscape stretched outspread and unaltered, familiar as herself. Behind her, receding with each step, her family's snug home—its dooryard garden, a tumble of green growth; the clothesline, a fibrous cord of light, snapping with wash; farther back, the huddle of small outbuildings, barn and shed, chicken coop and beehive.

Underfoot, the track unspooled, captured her footfalls within itself—an impermanent, earthen record of her passage. With her or without, it would eventually wander on, through the town center, past mill and trading shop and farrier's; always dodging, always flirting with the Bright Wood's edge.

Slowly, in the middle of the deserted road, Grace paused, unable to remember where she was headed. Skirts shifting against her thigh, she felt a weight in her pocket. Reaching in, she pulled out a russet feather the length of her index finger; a budding twist of vine; a deeply lobed, serrated-edged green leaf, larger than her hand. Each, a fact within her uptilted palm.

Pivoting on her heel, she scanned left and right, forward and back. The road tramped on, curiously unpopulated. No carts or wagons; no foot traffic. The pastures fenced only emptiness, the erect pleat of grasses. Grace cocked her head, listening; her ears brimmed with a deep and prevailing silence. A voiceless breeze moved over a wordless landscape. Silent, stiff-limbed trees stippled the horizon. Concealed within dense undergrowth, creatures—squirrel, stag, starling, stoat—all held their tongues.

She wondered where Murl could be. As she looked for him, a veil of thin mist crept in. Ashen, diffuse, it scrubbed the area of light, leached it of color and clarity. She rubbed at her eyes, blinked to clear clouded vision without success. At her sight's periphery, a smudge of motion swept—the sole speck and spark of color left in the muted landscape. Cinnamon. Russet. A bird, wings spread, flew noiselessly past.

"Thrush!"

Her voice pulsed strangely in her ears; reed-thin, diminished, it did nothing to arrest the bird's flight. Oblivious to her raised and outspread palm, Thrush arrowed by, pierced the Bright Wood's obscured boundary. Grace's arms fell slack at her sides; she stared at the point of Thrush's vanishment.

"Oh, no, no, no," she said. "*Thrush* . . ." The name, the bird—a prayer unanswered—nested on her tongue.

Frowning, confused, Grace turned and headed back the way she had come. The track blurred beneath her rushing steps, dust lifted at her toes. Until she found herself at her cottage: this, too, deprived of color. She paused beneath the garden arch, the vines pricked with small blooms that exhaled a scentless perfume. At the front door, she fumbled the latch, felt the cast iron's nick and burr, chill against her skin. Pushing the door inward and open, she beheld the familiar scene—Sylvie curled, nose to toes, in the spindled chair, her tail a compact plume of striped fur; Murl, stretched in his favored spot before the hearth. The moment's relief dissolved.

"Where is Wolf?" Grace asked, uncertain whom she addressed—cat, or dog, or self.

Murl rose, wagging, tongue lolling. He padded across the room, plopped himself down before her to have his ears scratched while Sylvie opened glass-green eyes and observed intently from her chair. When the cat mewed—wordlessly, beyond her comprehension—Grace reeled, struck like a bolt.

Hands threaded through her hair, clamped over her ears, Grace commanded herself: "Wake up wake up *wake up*!"

. . . and, in a rush, awoke.

Lurching upright in bed, she inhaled sharply, overcome by the dream's lingering pall—the sense of abandonment, of utter loss. She unknotted her fingers from the coverlets, swiped away tears with the back of her hand. Slowly, her heart calmed, its rapid thudding diminished; her breath no longer rasped in and out of constricted lungs. Blinking, gulping, she drew knees to chest, wrapped her arms about them.

Thick and dark and moonless, her bedroom resolved about her. She felt along her bedside table for lamp and matchstick. The lamp's chimney clattered, trembled in her fingers' grip, but the match responded in a single stroke. Wedding flame to wick, a wreath of darkness peeled away.

For a moment, she sat in a twist of blankets and breathed, counted her heart's steady beats. Sylvie's words from earlier that evening rose unbidden in her mind. "*You were lost*," the cat had said. Now, in these thin hours of the dream's aftermath, she understood instinctively, intuitively, the statement's truth.

Grace swung her legs over the bed's edge, got up. With one hand, she held the lamp aloft; with the other, she clutched the coverlet—still reassuringly grass-stained from claiming Wolf—about her shoulders. Flamelight flickered, stroked a turmoil of long shadows as she padded from her room along the short hall, past her parents' bedroom door, down the stairs, step by step by softly creaking step. She paused a moment, a stair's tread from the landing, and beheld the scene of the main living area with relief—Murl, Sylvie, *Wolf*. The knot of tension within her loosened.

Trailing the coverlet, she negotiated the pantry with practiced ease and set various objects on the table—kettle and tea tin, cup and spoon and honey pot. She tipped the water jug into the kettle, then tapped out a drift of tea. Dried leaves, flowerheads, and petals swirled—rose and lavender and chamomile—over the water's surface. Fitting lid to kettle, she carried it to the hearth, hung it from the hob over gray ash and winking coals. With an involuntary shiver, she felt, as she knelt on the hearthrug, Wolf's scrutiny—his eyelids parted, apprehended, and then resealed.

Grace added kindling, breath, and her lamp's fat flame to ashen coals, coaxed a small fire to brightness—enough to heat a tea kettle. Sitting back on her heels, she straightened, turned. Her gaze moved over the recumbent forms of her friends and settled at last on Sylvie.

"Sylvie?" She spoke softly, aware that Wolf's ear and the damp tip of Murl's nose both twitched. The cat, however, did not stir. Neither did any of the creatures speak. The uncertainty of Grace's dream rushed over her. Creeping forward on her knees, she stroked the cat, head to tail. "Sylvie?"

Motionless, eyes closed and tail ticking, Sylvie answered: "Yes?"

Grace almost sobbed with relief. Slipping her hands under the cat's melting form, she lifted Sylvie to her chest and sat in the warmed chair. She ran her fingers over the tabby's fur, coaxed a rumble.

"Why are you up?" Sylvie yawned and rearranged herself in Grace's lap. Arching, the cat extended both front legs, flexed paws and claws. With silken motion, she settled and tucked her tail about her.

"I . . . had a bad dream." Grace shook her head to free it of the memory. But for the uninterrupted purr that filled her ears, the tremor beneath her touch, the cat might be asleep.

"So you wake me?" Sylvie groused. "I was chasing feathers. . . ."

"I'm sorry." Grace drew her hand along the cat's striped coat. She appreciated Sylvie's warmth and substance, knew better than to ask if the feathers were loose or attached to someone.

"Apologies are pigeons flown," Sylvie demurred.

Murl picked himself up from his spot by the fire and came to sit on the scalloped edge of Grace's blanket. "When I have a bad dream, I run away as fast as I can." He looked up at her. "Then, I wake up." Murl bumped his nose against Sylvie's until the cat sneezed and positioned her tail as a barrier.

"That's very clever." Grace swallowed a bubble of laughter.

"What did you dream?" Murl asked.

The sense of grief returned, of stunning loss. Her hands stilled their motion—stroking of cat's length, scritching of dog's ears. Sitting in her father's chair, coverlet tight about her shoulders, she stared at the hearth's small fire. Coruscating light skipped against the room's dark, snagged in the weave and fold of her nightgown.

"Well." She took a steadying breath. "I dreamt I couldn't hear you anymore."

Murl encroached, inch by inch, along her lap until canine muzzle brushed feline haunch. "Just me?"

"No." The word's dull heartache, its full blue depth filled her mouth, lay heavily on her tongue. "*Any* of you. *All* of you."

"Ohhh . . ." Murl's soft brown ears flopped back against his head. "That's sad. I like our talks."

"Me, too."

Sylvie shifted on Grace's lap, kneaded her thigh, and resettled so her tail flicked Murl's snout. "Wasted energy," she said.

"But—"

Sylvie interrupted: "Do you hear us?"

"Well, obviously . . ."

"Then there is nothing to mourn."

Slowly, the kettle heated; heat wisped from its spout, releasing the fragrances of last summer—chamomile, roses, mint—and of the summers to come. "It's just, it felt so *real*." Her chest tightened.

Ears cocked backward, Sylvie asked, "Do I feel real to you, now?"

"Yes, of course," Grace said, "and I so love talking with you, and understanding you."

"And me, too?" Murl nosed her hand, worked his head beneath her fingers.

"Yes, you, too." Smiling, Grace choked back a half-sob. "*All* of you."

A torrent of vapor issued from the heating kettle, and Grace lifted a limp and unwilling Sylvie from her lap, pulled her hem from beneath Murl's hindquarters. Leaving the coverlet draped over the chair, she crossed to the hearth, deprived the kettle of heat before it reached a crescendo. She poured herself a cup of pale gold tea, sipped it, hot and unhoneyed.

"The cat is correct."

Grace looked at Wolf, who lay on the hearthrug. Though his sides swelled and shrank steadily with breath, he gave no outward hint of wakefulness, or speech. Bristly gray fur regrew at his throat, his hind leg; his great shaggy head rested on snowy forepaws in a credible facsimile of canine aspect.

"Unless it informs your waking life," he grumbled, "leave dreams to the dreaming self."

Grace blew over the lip of her cup. Petals eddied in her cup, thoughts in her mind. Inhaling, she sipped again at summer, swallowed. Instead of returning to her chair, she sat on the floor, her legs tucked beneath her, and leaned against a carved leg so Sylvie remained undisturbed. She felt the cat's tail fan her shoulder, stroke her cheek; she heard an appreciative purr.

Murl shifted closer, settling himself in a furry mound against Grace's hip, his head in her lap. "Sometimes, if I have a bad dream that won't *go*," he said, rolling his eyes up beneath his soft brow to look at her, "I shake all over until it *leaves*."

"That's a good idea," she said.

Sylvie waved her tail beneath Grace's nose, and mewed. "That, I'd like to see."

Catching Wolf's snort of gruff laughter, Grace stroked the furrows from Murl's brown-and-white crown, then redirected the cat's tail tip from trailing in her tea.

Murl licked her hand and whined softly. "Do you think *he* dreams?"

"We all dream." Wolf lifted his head, held them in his full-moon gaze. "All dreams are worthy of the dreamer. But they cannot replace the here, the now." With a grunt, he returned head to paws.

Sylvie listened, one eye a green-gold slit. "What better place is there than here, now?"

"Here and now is comfy," Murl mumbled, "and together. I like together."

"So do I," Grace said. She sipped her tea, slid her palm along the dog, and listened to the cat's purr, Wolf's snores, the fire's frisk and crackle. The dream's residue faded, and a small smile reshaped her lips.

Wolf had said *we*.

CHAPTER TWENTY

With practiced ease, Grace gathered her hair in a thick mass and secured it against the nape of her neck with a length of green twill ribbon. The resulting tail switched against her spine as she walked. A garland breeze gathered about her shoulders, plucking loose tendrils free.

"It's not a challenge."

Grace—at once vexed and amused—spoke aloud to gust and breeze. With a flex of wrists, she swept the loosened strands behind her ears and turned her cheek toward the wind's oblique touch. The air smelled of wild hyacinths—crisp and sweet and clear.

Skirting the garden's willow fence, where tawny grasses yawned toward her ankles, she strode past shed and barn and chicken coop, and soon found herself swamped in a clucking, squawking froth of expectant hens.

"No scraps this time." Palms splayed in pacifying gesture, she raised her empty hands. "Later. I promise."

Cackling and fussing, the hens squabbled among themselves, cocked their heads. They eyed Grace with beady skepticism, muttered and clucked:

"Promises, promises . . ."

"Not worth scratch . . ."

"A little patience is good for the gullet . . ."

"*You've* never had to wait for *anything* . . ."

"Who said that?!"

With bone-bright beaks, the flock snatched at Grace's skirts and bootlaces; she threaded her way through a surge of feathers. Petulant, fixated, they remained unaware they were rousing the rooster's attention until, in a flourish of red and green and gold feathers, he rushed their company headlong. Crown lowered, neck extended, he blared his command: "Disperse and part!"

The hens wailed and scattered in all directions where, from a safe distance, the rooster became the subject of their collective grievances. Hunting, scratching, pecking the soft earth for seeds and insects, they muttered low in the backs of their crops and glared at him, unblinking.

"Thank you," Grace said to him.

"Not at all. It's my duty and privilege to maintain a measure of order among this assemblage." Chest puffed, the rooster looked up, head cocked; his comb sloped at a rakish angle. "There was mention of 'treats.' When can I expect delivery?"

"Oh . . ." Grace cleared her throat, matched the rooster's serious tone. "Shortly before dusk, I think."

Stretching his neck, he studied the sun's advance within the broad, uncluttered sky. "Agreed," he said. Jerking his attention back to her, he lifted his wing blades from his sides once, twice, thrice, and dismissed her. "As you were."

Grace bent and, skirts swept over one forearm, retied her boots. She listened to the wind's edge along the small, clustered outbuildings: to twitchy, dust-brown sparrows angled over the chicken coop's roof; to the rooster as he scolded and redirected his flock. She listened greedily, gratefully. After the dream of silence a few nights ago, even this disconnected and fractious discourse satisfied her.

Threaded through random ambient sounds, the scratch and scuffle of approaching feet caught her ear. Rising, turning, she found Murl pelting through the yard in her direction. He cleaved a path that raised clouds of soft earth and scattered rooster and hens.

"Where are we going?" Tail aloft, he fell into a tongue-lolling trot beside her.

Bending, she rubbed the silken tufts behind his ears. "To the beehives," she said.

"Oh." Murl bounded ahead, thrust his damp nose deep into a clump of turned earth and snuffed loudly. "Why?"

"To check the frames."

Glad of the diversion, of the dog's company, Grace resumed walking. With each step—booted, clawed—the hens' recent communal outrage faded, fell away, and the tended yard eased toward tousled overgrowth where wildflowers wove through grasses gone to seed. Countless dainty blooms, fringed in slim petals, tangled and nodded with ripe, bristled heads. Dark burrs hitched themselves to Grace's skirts, to the plume of Murl's tail. Daylight slipped through spreading tree limbs and slow-bronzing leaves in mosaic pattern. Ahead, beneath a gnarled quince tree, lay their purpose: a squat, white box gleaming softly in a splash of light.

Grace paused, knelt, and took Murl's head between her hands. "Remember," she said, holding the dog's gaze. "Don't snap at the bees."

"Bees hurt." His tone recalled a mournful note.

"That's why we don't *eat* them," she said, and kissed the top of his head.

The bees' buzz and hum increased as they drew nearer. Grace absorbed their chorus, hypnotic and soothing. Even before her new gift had stirred, stretched, and shifted awake inside her, she had possessed an apiarian intuition. Of her family, even from girlhood, she had been the one to lift the hive box's flat lid, peer inside, and check the frames for honey. Often, her father teased her, observing that the bees parted for her as they would their own queen.

With Murl pressed close to her side, Grace slipped her fingers along the edge of the hive's lid. She knew precisely what she would find within—the bees told her. Singly, collectively, they greeted her and described in dance and vibration the hive's contents.

"Be gentle with each other, friends," she said to dog and insects.

Wreathed in humming aura, Grace peered over the rim's lip—the stacked frames, filled with wax-capped cells, dripped honey. She touched her little finger to clear amber and tasted sweet, hard work; tasted a song of high, blue skies and abundant sunshine. Bees settled on her hair and wrists and shoulders; intoned of goldenrod, wild aster, and lavender, of black-eyed susans and the drowsy fading tumble of wild roses. Grace lifted her left palm to eye level in invitation. The workers took turns—moving over her heart line, fate line, lifeline—and danced the locations of lemon balm, henbit, and sweet clover. Their tiny, barbed feet scrawled and tickled.

"So intrepid!" Grace smiled.

"Me?" Anxiety blunted Murl's natural enthusiasm. He tucked his tail and pressed head and hip to the drape of Grace's skirts.

"You, too."

Trailing her fingers against Murl's ear, Grace listened to the bees. The world revealed itself to them on a grand scale; urgency determined their efforts, shaped their choral hum. They cleaned and cared for egg cells, larvae, and pupae; protected the hive against itinerant drones. They spoke of extraordinary distances traveled: over vast bodies of water; rolling swaths of field, meadow, forest; through dangerous wind and weather; beyond the reach of predators.

Reflexively, eyes closing, she lowered her hand to better hear their unified voice. The energies of each small individual strove toward a common goal—to raise the next generation, guard against the nectar-less days ahead, weather cold and darkness, keep their queen safe. Winter loomed large in their collective consciousness, regardless of the season. Their communion recalled that of the wind—active, vital, frenetic—but in well-ordered fashion.

"Do you know?" She whispered the question, surprising herself. "Where he is? *Who* he is?"

She no longer expected an answer, regardless of who she asked: wind, bees, flocks of birds. The mechanist and his implication of threat. Time's passage compressed, shrank, and smoothed those peculiar dimensions, increased her sense of safety. Yet the ghost of uncertainty remained, drifting at the back of her mind like a shadow. Wherever he may be, she told herself, he was not here, in Edgewoode.

"Where who is?" Murl asked, concerned.

Opening her eyes, she patted his head. "Oh, no one . . ." A careless answer, a careless smile.

Certain now of the bees' consent, she reached into the hive and lifted a frame from its slot. A retinue crept up her arms, over the sweep of her collarbones, the slope of her shoulders. They alit and departed at intervals too swift to predict.

Honey brimmed and trickled from the square frame, golden and translucent. Wax capped and protected countless cells—assurance of the hive's health and prosperity. Only when autumn ceded its reign to winter would the bees slow their rapid pace in response to cooling temperatures and decreased sunlight. At that time, she and her father would swaddle the hive, wrap it in batting and oiled canvas, to maintain some warmth and minimize casualties. Not yet. Earth and air and water still exhaled a balm.

Grace slid the frame back into place, replaced the hive's lid, and thanked the bees, one and all. The nimbus of bees hummed agreeably, and she stepped out of their dizzying, incessant, *insistent* communal dialogue, as she might a rushing stream.

"Can we go now?" Murl pricked his ears, head tilted in anticipation.

"Yes," Grace laughed. "Was it really so bad?"

"They're so hard to ignore," Murl whined, laid his ears back against his skull. "So many . . . *zoom zoom zoom!*"

"You did a great job," Grace said.

Leaving the hive in its veil of dappled light, they retreated along the grass- and flower-fringed path toward the cottage. One by one, the remaining bees lifted from Grace's blouse and skirts, her hair—one from her cheek; another, unnoticed, from Murl's left haunch—like shards of light. They continued their dancing flight, a complex pattern of lavender and coneflowers and airy anemones. Each tiny oblong body darted off on wings pulsing faster than vision could follow.

Earthbound, solitary, Grace trailed below in their wake. Later, she would return with a scoured, wooden pail to collect a portion of honey. She would pot up some for her family, and a bit for Thaniel, as well. Next spring, she decided, as the grass heads and wild carrots brushed against her skirts, she would plant more lavender.

CHAPTER TWENTY-ONE

Sitting on her boot heels, knees pressing matted grass, Grace angled her shoulder against the weathered fencepost, an unlikely counterbalance to the pressure her father applied. A warmth of sunlight cascaded over her back and shoulders, while the rough slat edge wriggled against her grip, gnawed the heels of her hands, and bit. She leaned more firmly against the post, body taut, muscles tensed. Somewhere among the weave of tangled grasses, a cricket chirped.

"Chisel." Grace's father extended his hand.

She plucked the tool from fresh-churned earth, thumped it into his outstretched palm, and watched as he applied it to the joint. Slips and pale tongues of splintered wood peeled off, fell away.

"Truly, I am most apologetic."

A large heifer leaned over the simple fence near Grace's shoulder and lowed softly in her ear. White and ruddy splotches stretched over the cow's sharply angled hips and spine, over the generous swell of her sides. Her tail flicked back and forth to its own internal rhythm.

"I leaned—only a moment, only slightly—to relieve an itch. I never dreamed it might break. . . ." The heifer's eyes were huge, dark, dewy; the curved plate of her nose glistened with damp.

"The post was probably already weak," Grace reassured her.

"Don't you believe it," a nearby goat nattered. Extending his bearded chin skyward, he scratched the back of his own, arched neck with the tip of a curved horn. "The clover on your side is sweeter, and she knows it. They all do."

Mortified, the heifer moaned, low and long.

"There it is," the billy said, rolling his slot-pupiled eyes, "the pretense of 'wide-eyed innocence.'"

The heifer's sleek sides heaved, and the goat cackled.

"You're neighbors," Grace said. She cast a glance at both creatures. "If you can't be kind, try at least to be civil."

Chewing silently, goat and heifer avoided each other's eyes; their lower jaws slid back and forth in syncopation.

"Besides," Grace added gently, "clover is sweet, regardless. The fence has no effect."

Head lowered, white-and-ruddy splotched neck extended, the cow grazed about her own knobbed knees in a slow, considering arc; the goat lipped up chiseled curls of wood.

"You can relax now," Gaven said. He surveyed the freshly notched post with satisfaction, turning to regard his daughter with a mild and curious eye. "I gather there's some dispute?"

"A small one." Grace rolled her shoulders, flexed her fingers. "One that will persist, no doubt."

"Some things you can fix," her father said. "Some fix themselves."

Grace sighed. "I know."

"And others can't be fixed, no matter the tools or talents at your disposal." Gaven laid aside his chisel and held his daughter with a steady gaze. "Not all arguments, not all situations, are yours to resolve."

Grace glanced sidelong at her father. Advice—solicited or otherwise—typically fell within her mother's domain; her father trusted direct experience. "Yes, but . . ."

"No." Gaven shook his head. "*No* 'buts.'"

She blinked in surprise, ear snagged by the unfamiliar firmness. Her father sat on one boot heel, the opposite knee pressed to turf; tools were arrayed about him—hammers, chisels, file, and hand axe. The pasture's grasses and wild onions grew long and abundant around the fenceposts, their seed heads wild with upward-coiling filaments.

"This is important, Grace." An earnest quality colored his voice, at odds with the goat that nudged and nibbled his shirt collar. "Tell me you understand."

"I do." Anything to pacify, to reassure, to quell the unease wriggling in her belly.

"Good." Gaven gave a short nod.

She observed the relief that softened the line of his mouth, that smoothed the divot between his brows, and she wondered when the gray hairs had stitched themselves into his neat-trimmed beard and moustache, into his temples and eyebrows.

"Now," he said, "help me guide the beam in, and we'll see what's what."

Happy for the task, for the easy comfort she expected of her father's presence, she lifted the beam's end. With its weight against her shoulder, she helped fit it into place, watched her father's calloused, steady hands make the final adjustments.

"It's the fence they're arguing about," she said. "Goat and cow."

"It's for their own good." Her father eyed his work with goat-worthy criticism. "Tell them I said so."

"Maybe they'll believe *you*," she said.

Butting her thigh, the goat bleated long and loud: "Unlikely."

Grace absently drew her fingertips over the goat's horn-knotted forehead and turned her attention toward the cottage's backyard. An animal commotion rose—the muffled fuss of hens' complaints along with Murl's welcoming bark.

"Are we expecting anyone?" Gaven levered himself to his feet, wiped his hands on his workpants, and squinted against the light.

"I don't think so." Grace swept her hair from her face, tucked it behind her left ear, saw Thaniel turn the corner of the hen house.

"Ah, Master Vet." Gaven smiled, extended his open hand.

"Please. *Thaniel*." He shook Gaven's hand, smiled past him at Grace.

The two men stood before her, conversing amiably, but Grace heard little beyond her own humming thoughts, the patter of her heart. She watched her father reach up, rest his hand on Thaniel's shoulder—the latter stood slightly taller, straighter, and unbowed. Both were quick to smile, inclined toward easy laughter; together, they gathered the tools strewn about the grass and nested them in her father's long, wooden toolbox.

"Daughter," Gaven said, hefting the laden box. "Have you time to spare?" He raised an eyebrow, allowed her to consider her own mind.

Grace nodded, quickly added, "Unless you still need me?"

"I think we've done enough today." Gaven squinted again—unnecessarily—at the sun's heightening angle. "It'll be lunch soon. I'll tell your mother you'll be home for supper." The elder man waved, turned, ambled back toward the house, gripping his toolbox.

"Come." Thaniel inclined his head toward the canvas sack slung over his shoulder where he typically wore his veterinary bag. His eyes and grin glittered. "I have a surprise for you."

Amused, curious, she walked beside him, and they laced their steps among her father's recent path—past woodshed and henhouse, past the cottage and its neat kitchen garden. Grace heard the warp and weft of her parents' conversation drift from within the cottage, Murl's enthusiastic bark.

"Do you want to invite him along?" Thaniel paused mid-path, adjusted his grip on the burlap sack.

Grace laughed. "That's his 'begging' bark. Mom's in the kitchen—we couldn't drag him away if we tried!" She slipped beneath the garden arch and through the gate that Thaniel held open.

Beyond this, Wolf sat restless among the shadows. "I will accompany you."

"Of course," Grace said. His interest surprised her. Rarely did he leave his post of self-imposed vigil.

"I will *not* beg for scraps." Rising, he shook himself vigorously, trotted slightly ahead and out of reach.

She looked up at Thaniel, unable to suppress her amusement. "It seems we have a chaperone!"

"Hmmm." Thaniel's brows rose in mock concern. "Does he know something about your intentions that I don't?"

Grace rolled her eyes. "You invited *me* on this outing, remember?"

"Ah, yes, that was me, wasn't it." He shortened his stride reflexively to match hers.

"You seem very pleased with yourself," Grace observed.

"Today is a rare day. . . ." His brown eyes stroked the broad blue sky, the lazy drift of untethered clouds. "No lame horses, infected udders, hoof-rot . . . and, Master Mills has given me a sample of his first-pressed cider."

She slid a sidelong glance in his direction.

"We," he said with a broad grin, "are going on a picnic."

Leaving the main road, they cut through a fallow pasture dotted with sheep. The flock drifted, an earthbound reflection of the clouds above.

"Wolf?" Grace's eye slewed toward Wolf, attentive to instincts.

"Food is sustenance, not pleasure." Wolf swiveled an ear in her direction. "I do not hunt when I have fed." His posture expressed disinterest, while the sheep—alert, wary—bleated distress.

"Wolf may disapprove of our picnic," Grace said to Thaniel.

Readjusting the sack on his shoulder, he replied, "I'll eat his share."

The pasture rolled on, sprawled into lush meadow—the same she had visited to engage the wind. Together, they parted a sea of red-headed grasses, goldenrod, and foamy meadowsweet to reach a small rise, where Thaniel spread a blanket, its edges snapping in protest. He and Grace sat, shoulder-to-shoulder, hip-to-hip, thigh-to-thigh.

She watched Thaniel plumb his satchel to withdraw a small round of seeded bread; a wedge of yellow cheese; two small, hard, red apples; figs and nuts and dried dates.

"You found the honey I left you!" Grace said, when he pulled out a squat, waxed-sealed pot.

"I did." Nodding, he took two shallow wooden cups from his sack. "Safely tucked beside the door." Prying the cork loose from a squat earthenware jug, he poured two splashes of cloudy cider, handed one to Grace. "You know, my door is always open to you—I only drop the bar at night."

She shifted in her seat, in her skin, followed his hands' motion as, with a small folding knife, he sliced half-moons of apple and slim triangles of cheese, tore pieces of bread and spread them with honey, how he neatly arranged all on a wooden board between them. When she sipped, cider fizzed on her tongue where speech did not.

Several yards away, Wolf sat in the meadow's late-blooming flurry. Gray ears pricked, tail twitching, he shook himself, then waded toward them through tall grasses to share the blanket's edge. Nostrils flared, he inspected the bit of honeyed bread Grace offered. Peeling black lips back from ivory sickle teeth, he extracted the piece from between her fingers and licked up any sticky crumbs.

Thaniel shook his head, impressed. "You'll have him tame as any dog."

"Never." Hand splayed against Wolf's shoulder, she felt tension rise in muscle and sinew, felt the low thrum of protest. "He's wild."

"Of course," Thaniel corrected himself. He layered a crisp apple slice with yellow cheese. "It's *you* he's devoted to."

"That's not—"

Wolf interrupted: "Your mate speaks true." His voice rumbled in his frame, through her palm. "I am in your debt. My life is yours."

Flushing, she wove her fingers into Wolf's coat and breathed against the silvered ear: "*He is not 'my mate.'*" She felt the flick and twitch of his ear against her cheek, heard the chuff of his exhaled impatience.

Thaniel leaned in an inch, as if proximity would enable comprehension. "Why do you whisper?"

Flustered, Grace uncurled her spine. "Wolf has . . . opinions." She met Thaniel's warm brown eye—the color of autumn oak and acorns.

"Don't we all!" He laughed—a sound that rippled, like shallow water gliding over smooth stones. Carving another apple, he handed her a slice, gestured toward the meadow's far edge. "What does he search for?" Leaning back again on one elbow, the apple crunched between his teeth. "Who?"

"I don't know." She studied Wolf's erect posture, the way his pale eye roved and pierced the landscape. "For someone with so many opinions, he keeps a great deal to himself."

Thaniel lowered his chin at her and arched a meaningful brow. Before she could object, he stretched full-length upon the blanket, crooking his elbow over his eyes to shield from spangled sunlight. Deftly, he switched course. "Tell me." He peered at her through the web of his fingers. "Who do you hear now, and what do they say?"

Grace considered him, this man beside her, the ease of his posture. So many asked her to listen—those in pursuit of a desired goal, some out of curiosity, a handful for entertainment. But Thaniel . . .

Relaxing, she pushed the hair back from her face, tucked filament strands behind her ears. Tilting her head, she closed her eyes and reached for that internal switch, the insubstantial lever that raised the sluicegate. A chorale of rippling voices flooded in. As always, an exhilaration. Her breath caught, like a moth, in her throat; her heart raced with birds' wings. Listening, breathing, absorbing, she gently teased and separated the shimmering verbal threads, and told him—of the grasses and wildflowers, wearied after two seasons of growth and blooming; of crickets tuning their songs in counterpoint to grasshoppers'; of the red-winged blackbird that counted the days until migration; the fieldmice's dash and scurry and fretting over fair distribution of seeds and nuts for storage; and of the earthworms' worries over rain and drought and plows, teeth and beaks and claws.

All the while, the wind whisked about her, plucked lightly at her hair and tugged on her blouse. It swelled, dipped, contracted; it breathed against her ear:

"Tell 🜁 him 🜁 we 🜁 play 🜁 in 🜁 his 🜁 hair . . . touch 🜁 his 🜁 mouth . . . stroke 🜁 his 🜁 cheek 🜁 and 🜁 you 🜁 do 🜁 not 🜁 not 🜁 not . . ."

Grace straightened on the blanket, suddenly and acutely aware of Thaniel's face and form, his well-shaped hands and tapered fingers, of the dark brown hair the wind plucked loose from the binding at the nape of his neck, strand by strand.

"We ◬ dare ◬ you. . . ."

Thaniel gazed up at her from beneath the wedge of his elbow, ever-patient.

"Tell ◬ him . . . ◬ Tell ◬ him ◬ him ◬ him!"

"The wind . . ." She shifted her gaze, eluding Thaniel's. "It taunts."

With effort, she ignored the wind's teasing. It laced through her hair, curled and goaded and whispered of Thaniel's straight nose and thoughtful brow and his lean, fine, clever fingers.

"Hush," she said. With a sideways glance, she conceded to the wind's judgment.

Thaniel cast her a puzzled look. "I didn't say anything."

"Not *you* . . ."

Before Thaniel could ask for an explanation, Wolf stiffened beside her, rose. Ears pricked, tail stretched, he expanded in height and length and stature, staring fixedly at a point along the meadow's edge where weave of grass gave way to forest.

"Thaniel." Following the line of Wolf's gaze, Grace exhaled, pointed. "Look . . ."

There, pale against the Bright Wood's shadow, stood another wolf. Though distance obscured the figure, this second wolf lacked the thick ruff and mane, the sheer mass of the animal bristling beside her.

"Wolf?" Lightly, she touched Wolf's shoulder—tension charged the air between her fingertips, his fur.

"She should not be here," Wolf growled.

Clouds scudded past, a lark's song rang clear, and Grace felt the wrench and ache of Wolf's concern, longing, despair as her own—in her bones and muscles, an itch beneath her skin.

"It is not safe," Wolf keened. "Here. In the open."

The other creature—smaller, paler—called; the lupine song rang, held, lingered.

When Wolf answered—three crisp, short yips—Grace flinched, hands-to-ears. The second wolf scented the breeze, jogged from the forest's sheltered edge. In a heart's beat, Wolf launched forward into the meadow. Tails high, the two touched noses, circled, slid along each other's lengths.

Observing the reunion at the forest's edge, Grace recalled Wolf's earlier comment, and understanding struck: "It must be his mate." She continued to watch, to listen, and her fingers walked themselves to Thaniel's. Twined among his, she felt his hand's response, and a shiver swept up her spine.

Later, they had gathered up the remains of their lunch—he, with more efficiency than she. They had wiped, wrapped, stowed; she had scattered breadcrumbs for a host of little birds, and tucked nuts and apple cores into the meadow's lush green turf for the insects, chipmunks, and field mice. Then Thaniel walked her home. Occasionally, their arms brushed as they walked; their fingertips, in passing. Always, the wind remained a coy breath in Grace's ear.

"Tomorrow, then?" Thaniel asked.

"All right," she agreed. She stood on her doorstep, awash in late day sun, while his feet were firmly anchored to matted turf; it amused her to view him at eye level. "Tomorrow."

He smoothed a skein of her hair behind her left ear, his hand grazing her cheek. Retreating along the worn, moss-seamed path, he grinned at her over his shoulder and waved.

Grace returned his wave, her hand catching sunlight. For a moment, she stood within the cottage's door, leaning deep within its frame, and allowed her gaze to linger on the space that had—for a heartbeat—held him. She inhaled autumn air, crisp and sweet. Though the atmosphere cooled—a chill breath against the exposed skin at her wrists, throat, collarbones—the house's stones recalled long spears of light and radiated warmth.

Pushing off the doorframe, she gripped the latch, and the door gave inward beneath the slight pressure of her hand. She pulled it shut behind her against evening's approach, kicked off her boots, and wriggled her toes. A cursory glance revealed an empty room. The back door beneath the staircase stood open, and from beyond its casing, Murl's bark pierced the hush, laced through with her parents' laughter. Sylvie emerged from half-light and thrust her small, compact head against Grace's calf. Stooping to stroke the cat's ears, Grace realized Wolf lay outstretched in his customary spot near the hearth.

"Wolf?"

Curiously, she approached, with Sylvie sashaying about her ankles. When she knelt on the rug beside him, the cat leapt into the fireside chair, pointedly turned her back to the room and began an extensive grooming routine. "You're *here*," Grace said.

Wolf lifted his head, intercepted her gaze; reflected flamelight winked in his eyes. "Am I no longer welcome?"

"What? Don't be silly," she scoffed. "I just thought . . . you'd stay with her. . . ." She envisioned the smaller, paler female with sharp clarity; the wolves' postures, the greetings exchanged.

"She is where she belongs." Muzzle to forepaws, he closed his eyes.

"But . . ." Grace's heart sank, her shoulders rounded.

"Together. Apart." He slid one eyelid open to look at her. "We are linked."

The back door creaked and thumped shut as Grace's parents entered and greeted her. Their arms and conversation brimmed with their day's work, and Murl trotted at their heels, wagging and grinning a broad doggie grin.

"I saved you some!" Murl dashed over, dropped a gnawed marrowbone at Wolf's front paws. Licking Grace's cheek, he romped to the kitchen worktable and sat in an erect posture as Lettie commenced dinner preparations.

Drawing the back of her hand over her cheek, Grace glanced from Murl to Wolf. "Will you see her again?"

"Indeed." He lifted his great shaggy head, snuffled the bone. "As I said, one to another, we are linked."

"All of us. Always." Sylvie smoothed her whiskers with a paw. "Connection is strength."

"Wolf?" Grace asked. She ran her hand over Wolf's coat.

Gripping the bone between his claws, he rumbled: "I have come to agree."

CHAPTER TWENTY-TWO

Throughout the following days, Grace observed a shift in Wolf's behavior—intent reshaped his form. He stood fully within his frame, no longer sulked or grumbled. She learned his cues—subtle tensing of lupine posture; twitch and swivel of gray tufted ears; the damp, dark nose alert to a trace scent scrawled over the air. She learned to anticipate when sickle claws would scrape the door's seam, when to release him, and she watched him steal toward the Bright Wood's edge to join her. His mate. Most days, this new habit delighted her; today, it worried.

"The Fair has come to Edgewoode." She set her hands on lupine shoulders, wove her fingers to either side of the great, shaggy head, through the weft and warp of his fur. "There are outsiders here, who don't understand. Be careful."

Wolf regarded her calmly, seemingly unmoved, grumbled low in his throat. "I know to be careful around your kind."

Grace preceded him across the floor, marked the click and shush of his pads as he followed beside her. Hand on the doorlatch, she hesitated, pulled the door wide on a tide of sunlight. Side by side, they stood in the doorway's frame. She felt the snag of his brushy coat against her skirt, watching him scent each wisp and curl of breeze and parse every detail conveyed. After nosing her fingertips, he loped toward the meadow—a fleet shadow, scudding.

Grace closed her fingers over that unexpected gesture, so canine in nature. Drawing her sealed hand to her heart, she squinted through mid-morning light and tracked his passage along the timber fence—a wide berth given to the cow pasture—and on toward the Bright Wood's edge. Stealthy as thought, he barely stirred the grasses.

Drawing a great breath of autumn air, she dropped her hand to her side, fingers still loosely curled over the remnant of his parting gesture. She admired his individuality, complexity, adaptability; she envied the balance he negotiated between two worlds. When she probed about his mate, he offered only gruff comment—she *should* not, it was not *safe*, loyalty to the pack was *all*. Yet there she stood vigil, again, fixated on that point where he had sprinted over the landscape and melted from view to meet her.

"I'm careful." Murl padded to Grace's side, flopped his haunches down in Wolf's spot. He looked up with big, brown eyes.

"You are just the right amount of careful." Grace smiled, and noticed, with a small clench of heart, the frost in Murl's muzzle and brows. Sinking to a squat, she ran her hands along his spotted head, behind his loose satin ears. Her original companion, always by her side. His tail swept the floor.

"It's just you and me today, Murl," she said. "What do you think of that?"

The dog barked enthusiasm.

They set out for the fairgrounds beneath an autumn-blue sky, bird-flecked and expanding overhead. Edgewoode's harvest festival mirrored the village itself—small, familiar. Visitors here, south and west of the Bright Wood, were few, and had to provide their own lodging or beg space in barn or hayloft.

Grace's boots marked rhythm with Murl's pads—two beats to four; strike and echo. Yet, she felt distinctly and uncharacteristically lopsided. In her left hand, she lugged an iron pot—its wire-wrapped handle rasped her palm, pinched her fingers' grip while a willow basket rocked on her right forearm.

"Coffee, cocoa, salt, bay . . ." She recited the items her mother asked her to fetch from the Fair.

"Bay, like Wolf?" Murl asked. He looked up at her intently, jaws parted, exposing ivory, age-blunted teeth.

"A dried leaf," Grace said, "to flavor soup and stew."

"I like stew." Murl ran his pink tongue over his muzzle.

She continued her list: "Silk and cotton threads . . ."

The dog's tongue lolled. "What kind of stew?"

"Root vegetable," Grace said, laughing. "But there won't be any stew if we don't find a decent tinker."

"A stinker?"

"*Tinker*. Someone who mends objects." She extended her left arm, held the pot up so it brimmed with light and revealed its flaw. "Our pot is cracked."

Murl drew his ears forward, sniffed the crack. "It leaks light." He licked the pot.

The dirt road widened, bending a westward curve away from the Bright Wood toward the cider mill and the fairgrounds beyond. Colorful tents and pennants bloomed and billowed as tradesfolk gathered to hawk their wares and performing troupes erected small stages and arranged their props. A fiddler's sweet air lifted and carried as he tuned his instrument. Singly, in pairs, and in small groups, folk arrived in a tide at the fairgrounds. Their passage raised a haze of dust.

"Hello, miss!"

Pausing, Grace turned as one of Edgewoode's shepherds fell into step beside her. "Mikil, how are you?"

"Look!" The usually soft-spoken Mikil beamed. "Blended, scoured, carded, spun, dyed, and ready to trade!" He peeled the edge of a canvas tarp off the hand cart he pushed, revealed a flossy heap of pale, hued fibers within.

"Oh, they're beautiful." Grace touched a cloud of violet wool. "I'm sure you'll find a great deal of interest."

"This is our best season ever," Mikil said. "After you spoke to the flock this past spring, shearing went smooth as a whisker—not a nick, cut, or scratch throughout!"

"I'm glad to have helped," she said, and angled her body to keep Murl from nosing the cart.

"Couldn't've done it without you," Mikil said. "I've put a bit aside for you . . . and I'll dye it any color you want. Green, right?"

She waved as he finessed his cart away through the crowd and became aware of a new presence at her elbow. "Ella?"

"Miss Grace!" The young woman's breath came in a rush. "I'm so glad I caught up with you. Here . . ." Her hand plumbed a deep, lidded basket that clinked and tinkled at her fingers' search. Retrieving a slim, stoppered vial of pressed glass, she held it out to Grace. "Thank you so much for your help! The groundhog dug his burrow elsewhere. The tree survived and bloomed furiously!"

Removing the waxed stopper, Grace brought the vial to her nose and inhaled. "Lilac . . ." Her eyelids drifted shut, and her head bloomed in hues of pale purple.

"Any time you feel depleted or overwhelmed . . ." Ella mimicked waving the vial under her nose.

Arching her brows, Grace glanced at the hectic array of noise and motion that spilled and sprouted about them. "Like now?"

Ella laughed. "You'll run out before you get home!"

Grace slipped the lilac oil into her basket's hollow. The Fair tugged and pulled, wrapped her in slip-and-coil scent, in music and voices, human and other-than. Wagons creaked and breezes pressed tents and pennants into erratic motion. Skimming the crowd's perimeter, she slowed her pace.

"I smell *food*." Murl held his nose aloft and scented the air. Jaws parted, he panted.

"Okay," she said. "Ready? Let's dive in."

With each stop, she added something to her basket, until it brimmed with coffee, sugar, cocoa.

"Is that a stinker?"

"*Tinker*," Grace corrected. Tracking Murl's line of sight, she shook her head, "That's a tailor."

Touching spools of thread—sleek and coarse; dyed to match every cloth, color, and mood—she selected blue silk thread and ivory cotton, adding these to her basket.

"Is that a stinker?" Murl whuffled.

She suppressed a laugh. "That's a chandler." Pale candles, joined at shared wicks, hung from a stratum of horizontal rods or squatted in pillared rows on makeshift shelving. Beeswax and tallow infused the air.

"There." She pointed past the display of candles, glass chimneys, flints, and snuffers. "That must be it." Grace threaded her way toward a nearby wagon, the cast-iron pot thudding against her leg. Her left arm complained, from shoulder to fingertips.

A once-brightly colored affair, the tinker's wagon now sloughed paint in faded yellows, pale reds, dusty blues.

The tinker himself, seated on a worn three-legged stool, seemed in a similar state—a grayed man devoid of color. He was drinking with Sem, the miller's son, whose laughter and wide grin shone in stark contrast.

"There she is—our humble hamlet's pride!" Spying Grace, Sem spread his arms wide, spilled cider in a shimmering arc. Drink and festival buoyed his characteristic good spirits. "Our very own Grace—gifted in tongues, whose speech knows no boundaries!"

A tremor wriggled through Grace's belly. Tightening her grip on the pot's coiled handle, she felt herself color, uncertain for whom she was more embarrassed—herself, or Sem.

"He didn't believe." Sem wore an incredulous expression as he tipped out more cider and swept his arm to indicate the man on the stool. Thumping his chest with his free hand, he added, "*I* convinced him."

Shaking the hair from her face, Grace addressed the tinker: "Don't mind Sem—he exaggerates."

"No need for humility *here*." The man raised his arm to wave at the barebones site. His teeth flashed.

"Our Gracie is too modest!" Sem slung a friendly arm over her shoulders.

Shifting under Sem's weight, she tried to shrug herself free—he stank of cider and stale sweat. "I only came to have our pot mended."

"I thought we liked Sem?" Murl whined softly.

She didn't answer. She fell back a step when the tinker rose, vaporous as smoke, and approached.

"He smells funny." Murl tucked his tail, sealing himself against Grace's leg.

The tinker smelled of oil and rust and blunt minerals. Hands calloused and ticked with scars, he took the pot, gave it a cursory inspection. With a glance toward the wagon, he barked over his shoulder, "Bran!"

The wagon's peeling door creaked and swung open. "Yes?" A young man, sturdily built, leaned out from the wagon's throat. Sun-blond hair wreathed his head, and he wore a neatly trimmed beard and moustache of similar hue.

"We host distinguished company, son." The tinker spat and retreated to his stool.

As gray skies part before clear, Bran sprang from the wagon. Examining the pot to assess its damage, he cocked an eyebrow. "*Distinguished*?" His gaze skipped between Sem and Grace, lingering.

"Not *him*," the tinker scoffed.

"Hardly." Shaking off Sem's arm, Grace stepped on Murl's foot. The dog yipped, circled, sidled behind Grace to lean against her calves.

"See?" Sem grinned and swayed, feeling his point proven. "Too modest."

"Oh, yes, quite." Hands spread, the tinker pursed his lips.

Grace reddened, mystified by the man's tone.

"Repairs will take about a week," Bran interrupted. Holding the pot in one large hand as if it were weightless, he fixed his attention on Grace. "I'd say sooner, but we've picked up a lot of work already."

With a nod, Grace shifted her stance, feeling Murl's shape—angle of shoulder, jut of hip—so she did not step on him again.

"You're fairly remote out here." Bran glanced about, as if consulting a mental map. "A good distance off the main road."

"Tucked away." The tinker sniffed. "Back end of nowhere."

Bran rolled his eyes and shook his golden mane. "Your smith must stay busy." He tucked the pot under his arm, wedged against his ribs.

"I suppose he does," Grace said. Navigating the shift between Bran's dazzling light and the tinker's gloom disoriented.

"Well, that makes our trip all the more worthwhile, right, Father?" Bran grinned as the other man snorted. Bran waggled a conspiratorial eyebrow at her. "Travel makes him cranky."

"So it seems." Grace wondered how this golden, jaunty man had fallen from the tinker's graying tree.

"I, on the other hand, love travel," Bran said. "I haven't been this side of the Wood in . . ." He rubbed his gold-stippled chin in thought, glanced at his father. "How long has it been?"

"Not long enough," came the grumbled response.

"This is the thanks I get, for rescuing my old man." Bran cocked his head in the tinker's direction.

Another grumble: "You talk too much."

"And, apparently, I talk too much." Bran's grin broadened.

Sem chose that moment to interject with slurred, dramatic flair: "Fair warning, friend . . . her heart belongs to another." Flinging an arm about both their shoulders, Sem lost the balance of his cider in a glittering arc and dislodged the contents of Grace's basket.

"Oh, Sem." Grace moaned, ducking away from Sem and his mumbled apologies, intent on collecting her strewn parcels.

"Allow me."

She found herself on her knees, crown-to-crown with Bran, plucking spools of bright thread, packets of herbs and tea and coffee. Flustered, she caught the tinker's flinty stare over Bran's shoulder and shivered, despite the burnished autumn sun.

When the tinker spoke, his expression revealed nothing of his thoughts, "You mean to tell me when that cur barks . . ." He gestured at Murl. ". . . it makes sense to you?"

"I don't mean to tell you anything," Grace said, and ran her hand over Murl's head.

"Never met a beast that seemed worthy of conversation." The tinker stood, then approached.

Catching her basket, Grace rose slowly, aware that Murl bristled beside her.

"But *you*," the tinker said, considering her. "You understand. You're *different*."

"I never said . . ." This man, his attitude, frayed her nerves.

"But you *are*." The tinker angled past his eclipsing son, past Sem and Murl.

"Father . . ." Bran's tone darkened, lost its glitter and warmth.

"I'll expect the pot's return within a week." Grace turned, smoothed Murl's raised hackles, tried to soothe away the rumble that grew in the back of the dog's throat.

"*Special*," the tinker said.

"Father." Bran's voice sharpened, edged sun-bright. "That's enough."

Ignoring his son, the tinker jerked his thumb at a mule tethered to the weather-worn wagon. "You mean to tell me, you could converse with *that*?"

Grace could not help a glance—an ancient creature, sway-backed, bone thin; one of a pair. Her heart wrenched.

"Oh, she can!" Sem said, immune to increased tension.

Grace grimaced, lips pressed in an unsmiling line.

"She can talk to anything—cats, dogs, sheep, birds!" Sem beamed and hiccupped. "Show him, Gracie!"

Oh, Sem, Grace thought. "I'll just be on my way." Touching fingertips to Murl's ruff again, she turned on her heel.

"You would deny a man his curiosity?" The tinker glided to block her path. "A small request; a small demonstration."

"Father . . ." Bran sharpened both syllables.

"*Show me.*"

Grace stood, rooted—Murl pressed close and whining—as the tinker strode toward one mule, gripped its braided bridle, and maneuvered the creature before her. A ridge of bones knotted its back; ribs grooved its sides. She felt another surge of pity. The mule rolled its eyes, ignored her—until it did *not*; until it swung its long-skulled head abruptly toward her.

Ears flattened, it brayed, "Leave now. *Quickly*. While you can."

Grace startled.

"Does it *speak*?" It seemed the tinker spoke from a great distance away.

"*Now.*" The mule peeled lips back over yellow teeth. "Leave. *Now.*"

Overtaken by the mule's urgency, Grace felt the tinker's scrutiny.

The second mule, hobbled beside the wagon, brayed, "*RUN.*"

"I'm sorry." She backed away, refusing Bran's outstretched hand. She regretted his look of dismay. Hearing the mule's shrilled panic, she saw the tinker wrestle the poor beast's bridle, fist raised. Still watching over her shoulder, she careened into someone with bone-jarring impact. The willow basket spun round her forearm, scattered itself earthward a second time, and she sought to free herself of the hands settled on her shoulders.

"Grace? Wait!"

Looking up through the screen of her hair, her limbs slackened. "Thaniel . . ."

"What's happened?" Thaniel frowned in the direction from which she had fled.

Grace fixed her gaze on Thaniel. She would *not* look back. "We've just left the tinker's," she said. "I tripped."

Murl's tongue grazed her cheek. "He smelled mean."

"I hope we never see him again," she breathed into his ear. "He can keep the pot."

Together, they rescued her strewn items—*again*—from boot and hoof and well-trod earth, returning each to Grace's basket after close inspection. The festival's flow of traffic coursed seamlessly around them.

"Is there anything I can do?" Thaniel dropped a final item into the basket, gained his feet, drew her up beside him.

She shook her head. "I'm just glad you're here." His mere presence anchored her.

"Well, then." He met her eye, gave her fingers a light squeeze. "I have something for you." Reaching into his vest pocket, he pulled out a small, flat parcel.

"What's this?" She glanced at him sidelong.

The corners of his mouth quirked upward as he took the basket in exchange.

Grace turned the packet over in her palm—thick green paper, bound with coarse string. It crinkled and spoke at her touch. Carefully, she opened it, found within a bloom of pale gold silk. Trimmed in green and ivory satin, its center seeded in small beads, the whole sat affixed on a small hair comb.

"It's beautiful." Grace held the comb cupped in her palms. Finely worked leaves and petals stirred with autumn's breeze.

Murl stretched his neck, snuffled the air. "Food?"

"I saw it at a vendor's stall and thought of you." Thaniel said. "Three seasons out of four, you wear a flower tucked behind your ear. I'm paying attention."

Murl's haunches flopped in the dusty road. "Not food."

"You'll have something to see you through the winter," Thaniel said.

Grace felt the absence behind her left ear. Working her fingers through her hair, she wove the flower into place, smiled up at him.

"It suits you," he said.

Keenly aware of the narrow space separating them; of Thaniel's unquestionable presence—Grace felt lighter, a sensation that persisted despite Murl's encroachment. The dog insinuated himself between, looked up at them, panting, grinning.

"Where are you headed?" Thaniel asked, "and can I join you?"

"Home," she said, "and always."

She slid her arm inside his, their elbows crooked. The basket swung from her forearm, measured the rhythm of their paired gait. With Murl trotting alongside, the fairground's noise and stir and motion gradually fell away, replaced by the warmth and timber of Thaniel's voice, the ease of his bearing. When they reached her garden gate, her earlier unease had dissolved, much as the tinker's road-worn wagon sloughed faded, yellow paint.

CHAPTER TWENTY-THREE

"Shut the door," Gaven snapped. Throwing up his hands, he scowled. "Shut it and bar it."

Before easing the door closed, Grace peeped through the narrowed gap. Two young men—strangers, fairgoers in high spirits—leaned against one another as they staggered down the cottage's garden path and beneath the blooming arch. She considered slipping out to latch the gate after them, but closed the door instead. The heavy oak bar fell into place with a thud.

"Is he selling tickets? Giving directions?" Her father rarely raised his voice. Now, hands fisted at his sides, his queries struck the air.

Grace darted a glance at her mother. The elder woman kneaded pale, billowy dough; her lips were pressed in silence.

"I might have to have a talk with Cedric about his son." Brow creased, Gaven drew a deep, shuddering breath.

Cedric. The miller. Sem's father.

"I have a mind to tie that wolf of yours out front, to deter interlopers."

Murl, tail tucked, head slung low, whimpering, "I could deter inner lopers. . . ."

Wolf's low growl hummed from the hearth, "I will *not* be tied."

Grace held her arms out, palms spread. "I don't think that would be a good idea, Father."

Her father glowered at the room. "I'll be out back." He stumped across the room and out the rear door. Soon, the dull thump of an axe, the subsequent tumble of split wood sounded.

Grace knew her father as a private man, patient; one who saw an enormous gulf of difference between curious though well-meaning neighbors and intrusive strangers. Word of her talent had spread through the fairgrounds, and she became again a figure of interest. Though it sat on the periphery of Edgewoode, her home seemed to have been annexed to the fairgrounds themselves. At all hours, the curious, the desperate, the disbelieving tramped down the packed, earthen track along the Bright Wood's fringe to her family's cottage, overrunning her father's sense of privacy and eroding his patience.

"Don't worry, dear." Wreathed in a halo of flour-dusted light, Lettie looked up from her breadboard. "He'll come 'round."

"I hope so." Arms folded at her back, Grace leaned against the door's questionable barrier.

"We've all had enough for one day." Her mother scraped the elastic dough into a ball on the kneading board, punched it down, and applied the heels of her hands in practiced motion.

Grace nodded. Yes. Enough. Too many asked too much. Today alone, she had spoken to countless individuals, in numerous tongues—people and pigs; horses, heifers, and hens; ducks and dogs and donkeys; even, unbelievably, a parrot from so far beyond Edgewoode, an ocean had been crossed. She could barely think straight; she had declined—politely—to judge both the sheepdog and falconry trials; she had translated for a small girl and her kitten; she had directed a young family and their ailing goat to Thaniel; and she had failed thoroughly to impress an old woman with an equally uncooperative goose.

"You *take that back*. She never would say such a thing! Why would she? She wouldn't, that's why," the old woman had argued.

"Believe what you will," Grace had finally snapped, as if she could make up such nonsense. Then: "The two of you deserve each other." Which had surprised all involved.

Now, she thought of her father, angry—angry with *her*. Wilting against the door frame, she watched her mother knead and shape and slash pliant dough. Motes of flour dust lifted through the air.

"Your father loves you. Never doubt that." Lettie paused and pushed a sleeve back up past her elbow. She regarded her daughter. "Go on out back."

Grace blinked, considered her mother. She may not glow bodily, or float a hand's breadth above the earth, nor speak to animals and elements, but her perceptions remained nonetheless uncanny. Crossing the room, she wrapped her arms about her mother's waist in a grateful hug, then pivoted toward the rear of the house. Murl met her at the rear door.

"You stay here, all right?" she said.

Murl drooped. "To watch for inner lopers?"

She smiled. "Just *watch* for them." Heading out the door, she swept her gaze around the room to include Wolf and Sylvie. Once outside, she stood a moment and soaked in the westering light.

"Who is it this time?" Gaven looked up at her, axe handle caught in his knuckled grip. "Someone with a gloomy goat? A cock, won't crow come sunup? A sheepdog, thinks herding beneath him?"

Despite herself, Grace laughed, a small, constricted sound.

"It's not right, and I won't have it," he said. He fixed his daughter with a stern eye. "No daughter of mine is a sideshow attraction."

Barefoot, she descended three short steps, conscious of the wood's grain beneath the balls of her feet, rasping at her heels. She studied the arc and sweep of her father's axe. The blade flashed and struck the chopping block; split wood fell cleanly away to either side.

"I'm sorry," she said.

"You!" Gaven exclaimed. Planting one foot, he pried the axe blade free of the block. "It isn't you who vexes me, my girl—it's the opportunists and the busybodies and the . . . the . . . the bacchanalians!"

She massaged her brow, rubbed her temple with a wince. "They don't realize—"

"You'd feel differently if the shoe were on the other foot." Her father swung the axe again. "If it were *your* daughter, *your* flesh and blood being harassed and pestered."

"Probably," she admitted. Axe met block, lodged, and she approached her father, lightly touched his arm, the rough weave of cotton beneath her fingertips.

"Ah, my girl." Gaven released the axe's haft, covered Grace's hand with his own, clasped it. "You are so like your mother. I can't stay angry in your presence." Leaning forward, he kissed the crown of her head, then stepped aside to resume swinging and chopping.

Grace collected wood, stacked it in the woodshed. With each armload, she thought of how her talent had affected her parents, altered the pattern of their lives. The "hearing" had engulfed her in burgeoning, riotous spring. Now, seasons changed, days shortened. Nights expanded with winter's approach. In the comparative quiet, she observed with increased clarity and a pang of regret as the natural world grew hushed. Not silent—as she had known it prior to those earliest conversations—but distant, introspective. The voices folded in on themselves, leaving an echo where they once resided. Migrations began—blackbirds, buntings, swifts, and sleek swallows stippled the sky with restless, inky motion. When a flock passed overhead, she wondered if Thrush was among their numbers. She had not spoken with him since the Fair arrived.

At the woodshed, Grace stacked rough logs crosswise in neat rows, one atop another, and saw the spider—large enough to disrupt thought. To her dismay, her breath caught, and she took an instinctive, backward step, clutched wood between forearms and sternum. She felt the prick of splinters.

"Too close for comfort, eh?" As the spider spoke, its hollow jaws clicked.

"Forgive me," she said, recovering herself. The creature was large and brown and half the size of Grace's palm.

"No need." The spider waved an appendage, finely haired. "Used to it."

"I really am sorry." She took a deliberate step forward, laid the last length of wood to the pile's far side.

"Never mind." It spoke conversationally, in a voice like spun shadow, and scaled the stack with ease. "You've never taken a swing at me. Appreciate it."

Grace cleared her throat. "Oh, I wouldn't do that. . . ."

"Afraid of the mess?"

"What? No!"

The spider crouched and laughed, a faint, raspy sound like dried leaves.

Grace looked at the creature, its juddering head, its clicking jaw. "Are you . . . teasing me?"

"What, too many legs for a sense of humor? Or is it the eyes?" The spider blinked a series of tiny, glistening black orbs in a convulsive pattern. "It's the eyes, isn't it?"

"No, I just never thought—"

"It's okay, it's okay. No need to explain. Let's let bygones be bygones. Shake?" Lifting several legs, it moved them hypnotically. "Is this working?"

Grace frowned. "Is what working?"

"Never mind. It was worth a shot." The spider cocked its head at a disconcerting angle. "You would've fed my family for generations. . . ."

"What?"

"Joking! Humor, remember? Seriously. I'm a good neighbor. Artistically inclined, catch pesky insects—you *know* I'm not an *insect*, right? I don't eat your food stores, like *some* I could mention. . . ."

A series of small, indignant squeaks protested from the woodshed's various dusky corners: "It's all just *there*, neatly packed and organized . . ."

The spider shrugged five of its jointed limbs. "See what I mean?"

Grace laughed.

"Hey, let the other uprights know I'm here, eh? So they don't yell—makes all my hairs stand on end, all over. Deafening. You folk are big. Loud. Scary."

"I'll tell them."

"Nice to make your acquaintance." The spider waved a forelimb and scuttled away. From between dark cords of wood, a single word rasped: "*Fin*ally."

As she backed out of the woodshed, into welcome autumn light, Grace heard the spider's scrape of laughter and caught her father's curious glance. Before she could explain, a figure strode around the corner of the house. Afternoon sun flared, bound the figure in shadow. Though clearly a man, this was neither Thaniel, nor anyone else she recognized. Grace squinted beneath her hand's spread palm, and the man, taking this for greeting, waved and advanced toward them with even strides.

"Hullo," he called. "I knocked at front, but no one answered."

From the corner of her eye, Grace saw her father bring his axe to rest in both hands. She tensed, hearing the measured breath of his recent exertion. Then recognition dawned, sharp and abrupt. This young man wore the sun, carried it draped about him, burnished and golden.

"Bran." Grace dropped her hand, exhaled relief.

"You know him?" A low drone of irritation bit neatly through Gaven's voice.

Grace nodded. "Sem introduced us. At the fairgrounds."

Her father uttered a noncommittal grunt. "*Sem*."

Bran reached them and extended his hand. "Am I intruding?"

"Bran, is it?" The elder man sized up the younger. Shifting the axe to his left hand, he met Bran's grip, firmly.

"Is our pot fixed so soon?" Grace noted the cast-iron kettle snugged—seeming near weightless—between Bran's bicep and ribs.

Bran's smile slipped. "Given our initial meeting, I felt we owed you some speed." He lifted one shoulder, his expression sheepish. "As a matter of good faith."

"What's this about, now?" Gaven's brow creased.

"I hope you'll accept my apologies?" Bran rubbed the back of his neck with his free hand. "My father is a . . . difficult man."

"That's all right." Memories of the encounter sent a stiffening chill up Grace's spine. Shifting in her boots, she knotted her fingers at her back.

Gaven, observing the exchange, rested the head of his axe on the chopping block and leaned on its haft. He fixed Bran with a serious look. "A man should apologize for his own actions, son."

Bran laughed, but there was little humor in the sound. He shifted the kettle against his ribs and considered his worn, dusty boots. "That's not likely to happen, sir." Tilting his golden head, he looked at Gaven with a lopsided smile.

"I see." Gaven charged the words with gravity far beyond their two syllables.

Grace felt her father's searching glance, understood his restraint as an unspoken appeal for guidance. "I'll finish stacking the wood, Father."

Gaven paused, then inclined his head toward Grace, "I'll be inside." Abandoning his axe, he took the mended kettle from Bran and tramped across packed earth and up the cottage's back steps. The door thumped shut behind him.

"Let me help," Bran said. Immediately, he bent, collected splintered wood, and tucked the pieces where he had recently held the kettle.

Silently, Grace picked up a piece of fresh-split wood, then a second. She felt Bran's eyes, gliding blue over her, searching.

"Honestly," he said, "I'm sorry. For the other day."

She saw, in a quick glance, her own unease reflected in Bran's expression, in his eyes—the high, clear color of summer.

Bran continued, with a twist of expression: "I'm sorry for my father. . . ."

Again, the man rose before her mind's eye—his pallor and flat, gray voice, his stare. She blinked away the memory. "This way," she said. She led Bran toward the weathered shed.

"He doesn't mean it." Bran fell into step beside her.

"Doesn't he?" She glanced up at him.

Bran flinched, but for a breath, said nothing. Then, softly, he amended, "I guess I'd like to think he doesn't."

Grace unloaded her wood—opposite the spider's corner—and directed Bran to follow suit. She studied his profile as he stacked each cord. She noted the small hump that crooked the bridge of his otherwise straight nose, the small scars and divots—at his hairline, riding his left cheek. Too clearly, she recalled his father's balled fist raised against the mule, and speculated.

"We've been separated for a long time," he said. "I hadn't seen him in years, until recently. It surprised me. A fresh start, I thought. Maybe . . ." His voice trailed off, caught in possibility, disappointment.

Grace considered him, not so much older than herself. A kind face, even features; the fair brow, creased lightly with thoughts unspoken; broad shoulders, stiffly held. He was a ray of light compared to his father's clouded aspect. To have such a man for a father . . . Her heart tightened. Exhaling a faint smile, she nodded, said, "Come on inside."

Bran laid the last of the firewood on the stack. "Thank you." His expression cleared; relief lightened his voice. He shortened his strides to match hers.

Her thoughts roiled—over Bran and his father, over that tiny particle of doubt lodged in her heart. She entered the house, swept the room's interior in a single, swift glance—her father, pipe clenched between his teeth, paused in his chore of mending a chair to glance in their direction; Sylvie swiping at his tools; Wolf, hearthside; her mother in the kitchen area, turning two loaves from their pans onto a wide board. The scents of fresh bread and sweet tobacco coiled and mingled in the air.

"Bran, is it? Thank you for mending our pot." Her mother covered the loaves with a linen cloth. "Will you join us for dinner?"

"No, thank you," Bran replied. "I've already stayed longer than I intended."

Murl dashed forward, fixated on Bran, pressed his nose to Bran's pant legs. Standing stiff and still, with tail extended, he whuffled the young man from toe to calf to knee.

"Inner loper! Inner loper!" Murl barked sharply.

Grace turned, beheld her beloved dog with astonishment: "Murl! That's enough!" Then, she saw creeping from the room's edges Wolf and Sylvie—Wolf, with head and tail slung low; Sylvie dancing forward, sideways. The animals circled, and Bran braced in response.

"Dog," Wolf growled softly, "is this the man you witnessed?"

"He was there," Murl yapped. "This is the man's pup."

"Murl, Sylvie . . ." Grace stepped closer to Bran. "Wolf. *Stop it.*"

"The dog told us," Sylvie spat, "about the man at the Fair." The tabby slipped between Grace's booted feet, wound herself through Grace's ankles.

"*He* is not here." Grace spoke with forced calm, laying her hand on Bran's arm. She closed the gap between them as she minced around and over Sylvie's clever paws.

Wolf raised moon-yellow eyes. "And if he were?" His voice rumbled at the back of this throat.

"He *isn't*," Grace said firmly. She felt the muscles of Bran's forearm tense beneath her palm as wolf and dog and cat continued their slow, circling survey. A creeping, preternatural tension trembled, a sibilance beneath her skin and within her head, behind her ears. She felt her parents' sudden, sharp attention—her mother drew her hands carefully along her apron, her father removed the pipe from his teeth and rose slowly to his feet.

"If *he* comes," Sylvie hissed, "we claw . . ."

"We bite . . ." Murl barked.

And Wolf finished, "We rend."

"Stop it, all of you!" Grace cried. She heard her words, her own voice, through a leaden ear—muffled, and thick with strain. She circumvented Sylvie. "*Now*."

"Grace?" Gaven spoke his daughter's name carefully. It hung suspended in the air like smoke or scent.

She did not answer. Instead, she met and held each creature's eye in turn—lambent yellow; warm brown; clear, quick, gold-flecked green. Wordlessly, she appealed to each of them. They grudgingly heeded, not because she demanded or compelled or threatened, but because she desired it. The cat, the dog, and Wolf completed one final circuit around Bran, then dispersed to the corners of the room. Settling in their preferred spots, they continued an unblinking survey.

Grace heard Bran's expelled breath, felt his rigidity diminish.

"I really should go." He cast an uneasy glance about the room, flinching at the scrutiny of each creature.

"That's . . . probably best," Grace said. Noting that Bran's gaze lingered on Wolf in particular, as if he seeking the creature's permission to move, she slid her hand inside Bran's arm and escorted him through the room, to the front door. His bicep jumped and seized beneath her fingers' touch. At the threshold, she saw Bran's pale eyes dart backward over his shoulder.

Lettie followed, cradling a loaf of bread, wrapped neatly in linen cloth. "Thank you for returning my pot." Wearing a thin smile, she extended the loaf. "Will you take this home with you?"

"You're very kind." Bran shook his head. His smile did not reach his eyes. "Maybe next time."

Gaven spoke around the pipe clenched between his teeth and quirked an eyebrow, "*Next* time?"

At Bran's flushed expression, Grace cast her father a pointed glance and pushed the front door open, led Bran out into cooling twilight. Releasing him, she closed the door behind them.

"Now it's my turn to apologize," she said, arms folded beneath her ribs. "I don't know what could have gotten into them." Gazing at him, she could not help but draw comparisons against Thaniel. Though both men were tall, Thaniel was lean, Bran, sturdy; Thaniel's features finely carved, Bran's open with laughter. Thaniel, a moonlit night to Bran's midday sun. Her breath caught, and she appreciated Bran's interruption more than perhaps she should.

"The animals . . ." He stood among the fragrant herbs of the dooryard garden—thyme, marjoram, sage, and rosemary. Fading sunlight sparked in the nimbus of his bright hair. "They really speak to you."

"We understand each other." Thoughts racing like hares, she gathered her hair in her hands, coiling the ends around her fingers. His blue eyes penetrated, disconcerted.

"I just thought . . . I mean . . ." Rubbing the back of his neck with a broad hand, he offered a lopsided grin. "I guess I don't know what I thought."

"So you came to see for yourself." Feeling strangely deflated, she recalled her father's earlier wrath.

"No!" He waved her words away, shook his head. "It's not like that."

"You were curious." With a half-shrug, she folded forearms to ribs. "I understand."

"Wow, I've really made a mess of things."

"It's fine," she said, a little too sharply. "There's no 'thing' to make a mess of." The sun continued its westward slide, cast a foxy glow; birds sang a prelude to evening.

Bran sighed, then ventured once more: "Will you come again to the Fair?"

Grace hesitated. "I don't know."

"I'd like another chance," he said, "to win your regard." He nodded in the direction of the house. "And theirs."

"We'll see." She dropped her arms, laced her fingers before her, thumbs touching.

"We leave the end of next week." He retreated backward down the brick path, away.

Grace nodded.

"I'll look for you," he said.

She remained on the doorsill, watching the herbs and wildflowers sway with his passage.

"Until then." At the end of the path, he drew the whitewashed gate closed and paused beneath the arbor. His teeth flashed, a crescent moon framed within his neatly trimmed beard and moustache.

Grace stood, hands knotted against her skirt's front, tracking his slow departure. She answered his wave with her own raised hand. Pushing her hair behind her ear, she felt Thaniel's bloom there, and watched Bran's departure. Slowly, her fingers traced the shape of each silk petal until, like a snuffed candle, Bran was swallowed by shadow, gone.

CHAPTER TWENTY-FOUR

Autumn yawned, stretched, settled; and Grace's world grew strangely quiet.

Seated on her doorsill, huddled in woven shawl, woolen skirts, and knit stockings, she shivered. Each breath lit her throat, nose, lungs—crisp and glitteringly cold. Morning light shimmered, thin and tenuous, over the garden arch's tangle of vines, over dried seed heads of herbs and flowers bunched about the little dooryard. Extending her hand, she caught a single, spiraling snowflake and watched it melt against the lines in her palm.

Voices that days and weeks ago had been vibrant and active were now softened, hushed, slipping toward slow dormancy. Grace perceived the encroaching silence throughout her bones and being. It surrounded and deepened. *Such* a silence, unlike any she had ever known before. Folded within it, she heard the hollow knock of encroaching winter.

Summer's end, autumn's festival and hectic harvest, the preparations of collecting and drying and preserving in advance of winter left little time to breathe, much less ramble aimlessly through the Bright Wood, for human and other-than-human alike. She had missed Thrush's departure. Trying, now, to recall his song—so dear to her, once as familiar and recognizable to her ear as self—she wavered. Memory alone could not reconstruct the complexity of lift and tone and pattern.

A slim, small talon of regret pricked, and the stone sill's cold crept up and in. Closing her eyes, she stilled and searched for some anchor within the prevailing, unbound quiet. She searched for the collective voice—the chlorophylled dream of half-slumbering trees; the slurred, stumbling speech of water; the earth's deep dreaming. She found instead the wind's perennial voice. It sidled up and stroked her cheek, curled against her ear, while lesser drafts stole between the seams and folds of shawl and blouse and skirts. For a moment, it teased and whispered of lands where now, at this very moment, spring unfolded gently, where summer's step had yet to sound. It invited her to follow to warmer climes and skip altogether the bare, exposed bone of winter.

Despite its teasing, its capricious nature, the wind remained a valuable ally, carrying and relaying intelligence from beyond Edgewoode's borders. Eyes closed, Grace framed her question with care, drew an image in her mind, let it sit a moment on her tongue and melt. Amusing itself, the wind tugged at her clothes, tangled in her hair.

Finally, she asked, "Is Thrush safe?"

She wondered at the foolishness of her question, that one small being might be distinguished from myriad flocks by an element so erratic. But she waited all the same, and the wind wandered, gusted, sang. She inhaled its frost-sharpened voice, felt it define her shape with its very self, and, eventually, a passing breeze, a gust, a whisper brushed against her ear replied: Thrush, safely arrived in his summerland destination, whole and well.

Grace spread her hands, palms upturned, fingers wide in gratitude. The push and pull of air currents wove between, receded, dispelled. She dropped her hands into her lap with a sigh.

"Oh!" Murl trotted over, sank his haunches on the stone steps. "It's snowing!" His nostrils flared as he scented the chill air.

She slipped her arm about the dog's shoulders. The flakes increased, multiplied, spun lazily down. Not a blizzard, not a storm, but a promise of things to come. The snowflakes gathered—white lace embroidered upon the brick path's mossy seams, atop the margins of fallow grasses.

"I like snow!" Murl snapped at drifting flakes. His front paws lifted from the sill and his teeth clacked air.

"I do, too," Grace said. "A little. In small amounts."

She held no love for lean, rawboned winter, when narrowed light and the well-stocked pantry's finite stores measured prospective health and well-being. Winter was a season to be endured, a grinding test of body, mind, and spirit.

Grace sighed long and deep. Knowing that Thrush was well—that she might hope to see him again in a season's time and hear his song—conferred a spark of hope upon the coming winter's certain uncertainty.

CHAPTER TWENTY-FIVE

With Wolf beside her, Grace sat on a folded blanket on a small hillock within the meadow—the same meadow where she had picnicked with Thaniel, and where she had first listened for the wind's voice. She strained ears, mind, and self to hear past winter's muffling quiet, to ascertain the difference between the world that slept and that which moved with near-silent efficiency and purpose. The pale midday sun floated overhead, stretching and pulling her shadow nearer its isolated roost.

"There." Wolf's voice caught between rumble and growl. "Do you hear?"

Cocooned in heavy wool, she suppressed a shiver and blew into the fibers of her mittens. The blanket was a poor barrier. Straightening, she pushed her hair back from her right ear and heard a small snatch of sound, brief and sharp—a ribbon of consequence within her mind. A single, distant, rose-gold note pierced the atmosphere.

"Is it . . . fox?" She glanced at Wolf for confirmation.

Wolf huffed approval. "Vixen," he specified. "She calls her kits."

Grace grinned, delighted, and scanned the bowed interlace of faded winter grasses. Snow fell—gently, insistently; it gathered on her cap's brim and collected in the folds of wool snugged about her. The foxes remained beyond her field of vision.

"Do you speak fox?" She wondered, as the question left her lips, if he would find it rude.

"I do *not*," Wolf growled.

"But, if your paths crossed?" She peered at him. Disdain curled his black lips; white flakes stippled his thick coat.

"They *would not* cross," he snorted, staring fixedly over the snow-glossed field. "We respect territorial boundaries."

"But, what if . . ." She held her tongue as Wolf turned yellow eyes on her.

"We would understand each other," he growled at last. "With scent. Posture. Eye contact. Words are unnecessary." He paused, stared, then pointedly shifted his gaze. "A human need."

Grace ignored the prick of judgment, leaned against him, into him, past the sheath of cold air trapped in his fur to the warmth beneath—the whole of his being radiated trapped heat. He neither moved nor complained.

"Now," Wolf prompted, "do you hear?"

With furrowed brow, Grace tracked the sound, focused on a distant, rapid pattern of pure, clear notes.

"It's chickadee," she said. "He tucks seeds into the bark of a spruce tree."

Wolf regarded her. His ear twitched, though he remained otherwise still.

"What?" She peered at him through a skein of snow-laced hair. "Did I mishear?"

"No. You are correct." He lifted his shaggy head, scented the air, added: "I heard only the bird."

Grace hitched her shoulder, let it fall. "I've seen them do this. It made sense. And he's concentrating very hard on his work."

"Do not apologize for accuracy," he interrupted, then abruptly changed the subject. "You are cold."

"I'm all right." She snugged wool more tightly about her.

"Your lack of fur cannot be ignored," he grumbled.

"You have enough for both of us." Grace huddled into his sinewed warmth. She followed his gaze as it roved the Bright Wood's edge and the tree-thickened darkness beyond. "Can you really never return to your pack?" His thick coat nearly muted her question.

"No."

Blunt, gruff—his denial struck the air, rang through Grace's bones. She persisted: "Not even to her?"

"She belongs with the pack," Wolf huffed.

"Maybe—"

"No more talk," Wolf snapped. "Listen."

Grace held her tongue, adjusted herself on the rough blanket, each indrawn breath a frosted shard that pierced nose, throat, and lungs. Closing her eyes again, she sealed out distraction, allowed the hush to unfold in her mind.

Winter crowded close. Its voice embodied restraint, its dialect an exercise in brevity. No longer must she screen for a chorus of voices; now, she pursued the vapor trails of breath and slumber and stealthy movement. Beneath the snow's soft, tinkling silence, she turned her intention toward hearing the dormant earth's shared dreaming.

She became increasingly aware of Wolf's breath streaming from his flared nostrils in deep, even respiration. Although her eyes were closed, she faced the distant crease of field and tree, and her ear found and measured the steady pulse and immediacy of his heart beating within his deep chest. Once she identified and recognized his, she found others—countless others—as if a door in her mind yawned open and swung wide on a constant thumping, thudding rhythm that underpinned the quiet—an asynchronous vibration of interwoven beats. Amid this throb, this pulse of sound, she distinguished individual patterns. A rasping cry confirmed the ink-dark pulse of a crow passing overhead. The silvery twitch-and-brush patter of a squirrel darted among the nearby oak's knotted gray-brown branches. A collective thunder of buff-and-dun heartbeats—the percussive thud of so many hooves—as a small herd of deer streamed beyond the distant Bright Wood's pine-green edge.

Curious, she turned her attention inward, and her own heart's beat and rhythm scrolled and struck, a distinct song cast within the great multitude. Grace's eyes flashed open.

Wolf regarded her. "You have heard something worthy."

Her breath caught hard in her throat; she met Wolf's lupine gaze. "I hear hearts . . . beating. The hearts of the living things surrounding us . . ." Her words echoed, a faraway sound to her own ears; she could not tell if she whispered or shouted.

"That is . . ." Wolf's tail tip twitched; one ear swiveled toward her. ". . . unexpected."

"Is it?" Grace laughed. Wide-eyed, breathless, she did not wait to hear his answer, if he had any to offer. Her attention scrambled elsewhere, past Wolf. She heard no audible sound of approach—neither footfall, nor rasp of dried grasses, nor crunch and scrape of crusted snow. Yet she *perceived*—a felted, stripy heartbeat: achingly familiar, though previously unknown in this way.

From the snow-burdened meadow's braid and tangle, a shadow moved, separated, peeled away. Sylvie emerged—silent as dream, but for the velvet purr of her heart. Lightly, her jaws held trapped a small, limp form. The cat took her place before woman and Wolf, placed a field mouse on filmy snow where it lay, quite still.

Wolf spared a brief glance for the late rodent, then lifted his head to address Grace. "There is nothing more I can show you. You must be patient. You must practice. You must be dutiful of habit." He turned his moon-yellow eyes to

Sylvie: "Cat." A simple greeting, plain acknowledgment—a measure of respect for a fellow predator.

Grace watched him rise, shake himself free of clinging snow, and depart—a blue-gray shadow cleaving the frost-tipped meadow in the cottage's direction.

"Well," the tabby said, "that's one less mouse to feed."

"Was that . . . a joke?" Grace's brow furrowed.

Sylvie yawned. "More a play on words."

"It isn't funny," Grace said. The fact of the dead mouse, of Sylvie's nature, of the reality of relationship, predator to prey, raised a fragment of grief within her.

"They can't all land," Sylvie said, curling striped tail about her sandy paws. "But you're right. Death is always a solemn affair."

Grace dipped her head, acknowledged the apology.

"We are family," the cat said. "You provide for me. And I, you. Balance is all."

Grace's gaze slid from Sylvie, settled on the white-breasted, hazel-gray curl of the mouse, a sooty crescent on the snow's crust. Gently, she lay her mittened hand over the creature, committing its design, its shape and form to memory—slack whiskers and stroke of tail, limp paws curled pinkly inward. No manic, quicksilver tattoo of a heartbeat issued from the mouse's small breast. She heard only silence.

"I understand," Grace said. "Thank you." She removed her hand from the mouse's still form. "Are you coming home?"

"Soon," the cat said.

"Soon," Grace repeated.

The mouse lay on the snow between them. A gesture. An offering.

Grace rubbed the tabby's cheek and buff chin, stroked her from peaked shoulders to tail, and felt a twofold rumble within the feline's angled chest—heartbeat wrapped in purr.

CHAPTER TWENTY-SIX

Grace felt the bag's contents shift, slide, slosh against her ribs and stomach—a burlap pendulum. Snow lay white and shimmering, and she kicked through wayward drifts to arrive at her destination, a compact dwelling of buff plaster and rough, time-blackened timber. Snow swirled along the roof's worn blue slates, collected in its eaves, added further contrast.

For a moment, Grace paused on the doorstep and smoothed her forest-green woolen skirts. She shook snow from her hair and, almost in afterthought, adjusted the pale gold and green and ivory bloom secured behind her left ear. Thaniel's door was an arched slab of paneled chestnut, time- and weatherworn to a subtle sheen. Shifting her burden, she raised her mittened hand, coaxing a muffled sound from the hardwood. She did not wait for a reply, but gripped the patinaed doorlatch and let herself in.

"Ah." Thaniel halted mid-stride at the room's center and smiled. "It's you!"

"It's me."

Grace returned his grin, setting the overfull sack carefully against the wall. Hands free, she pulled off her cloak and mittens, stomped slush and mud and grit from her boots. In her stocking feet, she hefted the bag again and met Thaniel at the small kitchen, then set the burlap to slump sidelong on the square, squat maple table.

"What's all this?" Thaniel laughed.

"The fruits—and vegetables—of our labors." She noted the curl of his dark brown hair, pulled into a short tail at the base of his neck; he smelled of pine and cedar and sandalwood. "Mother worries after you." His proximity sent a flutter through her abdomen. "Here . . ." She plucked wax-sealed glass jars from the bag, setting each on the table's worn surface with a light plunk. "Stewed tomatoes, corn relish, cucumber, and onion. Pickled eggs, spiced peaches, and . . ." With both hands, she wrestled a large, rough-skinned oblong from the bag's bottom. ". . . a pumpkin. For your root cellar."

Thaniel accepted the bright orange squash from her and held it in his hands as if determining its weight. "I don't think I've ever heard you utter so many words at once." He placed the pumpkin on the table, where it hulked, a great orange giant among glittering, rainbow-hued jars.

Folding the bag over on itself, she made a face at him.

"All right, I exaggerate." He laughed again, then added, "You're always *listening*." He took her hand. "Thank your mother for me."

Under the warmth of his gaze—deep and brown, certain as oak or earth—the flutter in her belly grew, moving through her limbs. "I'll . . . put these away," she said, though she remained fixed in place, immobilized.

"No need. I'll do it. Later." He squeezed her fingers gently, then released her hand. "Actually, I was on my way to find you. Master Herris's old draft horse needs tending." Crossing the small room, he lifted her cloak from a peg and held it open to receive her. "Can you come?"

"Oh. Of course."

Grace scooped up Thaniel's veterinary satchel from one of the round-backed kitchen chairs, traded it for folded burlap. Shrugging into her cloak, boots, and mittens, she could not name the feeling that swept through her—a disconcerting mix of chagrin, release, relief.

Thaniel pulled the door open and followed her into the pearl-gray world beyond. Their boots thudded and crunched in soft rhythm, collecting a rime of slush. Their cloaks, her skirts, whispered and shushed. With great effort, she ignored the wind's persistent and unsolicited remarks.

"What?" She felt Thaniel's gaze drift toward her, slew away, wander back again; she felt the quick gleam of his smile.

With a casual lift of his shoulders, he tilted his head back and observed the leaden sky. Thick, soot-bellied clouds massed on the horizon, hinting at more snow. "You're wearing my gift."

Lightly, Grace touched the silk and satin flower to ensure its fixed spot behind her ear. "Has it worked loose?"

"No, no, it's fine." Thaniel met her eye. "It reminds me . . . of milder days."

"Yes."

Maples, hickories, ashes, and thick oaks spread bare branches within a paling world, limbs sifting snow. A single, unfallen leaf flared red in exclamation, and Grace let go the idle hope that, just this once, winter might pass easily. Shivering within her cloak's folds, she appreciated her woolen layers.

"Tell me," she drew a frosted breath, "what's wrong with Master Herris's horse?"

Thaniel shook his head, brow furrowed. "The boy left moments before you arrived and was sketchy on details. We'll know soon enough."

The road's rough course—churned by wagon wheels, boots, and hooves—bent left, swayed right. Thin panes of ice, fragile as spun sugar, spanned muddied ruts and splintered beneath their steps. Soon, the track deposited them at the Herris farmstead, a compact arrangement of quilted fields and modest structures bound by the polite suggestion of a split timber fence. The farm itself jutted sharply into the Bright Wood's hip, with snow humped around it in broad swaths.

Herris met them at the fence and, swinging the gate wide, carved pale blue arcs into the accumulated snow.

"It's old Birt," he said by way of greeting, leading them to a well-kept, squat barn behind the house. "He's off his feed these past few days. I didn't think overmuch about it—he's a big one, Birt—but this morning, I found him down in his stall, and he won't get up for anything."

His words tumbled out one atop the other, and he alternately crushed his hat in overlarge hands and rubbed fiercely at his whiskered chin as they walked. Herris heaved open the barn's large door and preceded them into straw-dusted half-light. He paused to light a compact lantern.

As her eyes adjusted to the interchange of light and shadow, Grace inhaled the scents of sweet hay and old timber, of earth and damp and animal musk. Rough-hewn wooden ribs rose to either side of a broad-planked, straw-strewn aisle that bisected the structure's packed earthen floor. This terminated at the farther end in a great, hay-filled loft reached by a bowed ladder. Following the two men down this informal corridor, their footfalls thudding softly, Grace passed between roomy stalls arranged to either side and overheard the murmurs of the barn's other inhabitants—three spotted cows, two mares, a shaggy donkey.

"He won't eat." A dew-eyed cow spoke ruminatively around a mouthful. Her lower jaw slid back and forth as she chewed.

"Won't?" asked her neighbor, tail switching. "Or can't?"

The third cow extended her black-and-white neck, swung her head to peer beyond her stall's impediment: "He's prone . . . can't get up . . ."

"He can *hear you*, you know," a sorrel mare whinnied. She stamped a hoof, tossed her head up, and set her dark forelock in disarray.

"Hush." A gray-and-white dappled mare nickered softly. "They're concerned."

Grace, momentum hindered, felt a soft tug on her sleeve.

"Excuse me . . ."

Pausing outside the donkey's stall, she met the creature's clear dark eyes.

"Will he be all right?" The donkey released his mouthful of green linen. His voice hinged softly.

Shaking her head, she placed her hands to either side of the donkey's. "I don't know." With her fingertips, she traced the twin arcs of his gray-furred jaw.

"He's my *friend*." The donkey's long ears drooped back against his neck.

"We'll do what we can." She smoothed her hand over the tight, snowy whorl at the center of his broad forehead.

Herris, observing the exchange in silence, opened a stall door wide and bid Grace and Thaniel enter; he touched Grace's shoulder as she passed.

"I'm glad you're here, miss." He spoke thickly, words constricted in his throat.

Covering the man's rough, worn hand with her own, Grace smiled up into his cragged face and stepped into the stall. It surprised her, the horse's great size—a vast, equine landscape deposited lengthwise. The huge, heavily ribbed barrel chest stirred in listless intervals with shallow breath. Four great iron-shod hooves winked from a bristling veil of straw. Birt seemed somehow larger for his inert posture.

She removed her cloak, draping it over the stall's door; she left her mittens atop the spill of evergreen. With careful steps, she wove through the recumbent weave of Birt's heavily thewed rear legs and thick tail, slipping around the broad curves of his rump and back. Kneeling in sweet-scented hay at the gelding's massive head, opposite Thaniel, her attention flickered between horse and man as Thaniel began his deliberate examination. Birt huffed and heaved but accepted these ministrations without complaint. All the while, Grace moved her hands along the draft horse's bunched withers and beneath his tousled forelock; her fingers learned the dimensions of his broad jaw and elongated, muscled neck. The great horse nickered softly, lifted his head, dropped it heavily into her lap.

"Please." Herris, half-choked on his words, could hold his silence no longer. "Please, can't you tell me what ails him?"

Thaniel rocked back on his heels and stood, his expression carefully neutral. After a moment's consideration, during which he silently gauged Master Herris, he arrived at a tacit decision. "Birt's breathing is labored; his heartbeat slow and weak." Gently, he asked, "How long has he lived with you?"

"Oh," Herris murmured. He avoided the vet's eye, looked up instead at the stall's peaked roof, at its thickly cobwebbed corners. "He's been with us for ages. . . . I remember the day he foaled." A grin altered Herris's features. "During that storm . . . Was it twenty-five autumns ago? Thirty? The one that took down the old hickory." His gaze sobered, dropped to meet Thaniel's.

"Birt has had a good long life." Thaniel left the thought unfinished.

"But . . ." Herris glanced down at the great horse, at Grace, back to Thaniel. "He's a good, solid soul. Is there nothing . . . anything?"

Thaniel, lips compressed, clasped his hands before him, shook his head. Catching Grace's eye, he took a backward step.

"Master Herris." Grace drew the old farmer's attention, held it; she chose her words with care. "Birt is tired. *Very* tired." She glanced down when Birt once more lifted his great head, chuffed and snorted, then dropped his head back into her wool-clad lap. She returned her attention to Herris. "He grieves to leave you."

Choking back a sob, Master Herris dropped his hat and levered himself on creaking knees to the hay-strewn floor. Half-kneeling beside Grace, beside Birt's head, he placed his large, callused hand on the draft horse's grayed and stubbled muzzle.

"Ah, Birt," he rasped, and the great horse blinked dark, beclouded eyes.

"Would you like me to leave?" Grace felt the fog of Birt's breath through her woolen skirts, against her knees and thighs.

"No, please, Miss Grace." Herris's voice was constricted, roughened. "Please. Stay."

With Herris beside her and Birt's head in her lap, Grace remained.

"There's not another like you, Birt." Herris bowed over the horse's head, speaking softly into the large, tufted ears. "Nor ever will be." He bent awkwardlyand pressed bewhiskered lips to Birt's bristled jowl. Straightening his spine in small increments, he looked at Grace, and said, "Nor like you, miss. Would you tell him—would you tell him . . . tell him I love him?"

Birt flicked an ear, whuffled softly. He blew a damp breath against Grace's palm.

"Oh, Master Herris," Grace said. She swiped at her cheek, and smiled a small, bittersweet smile. "You don't need me to tell him that. He knows. He's always known."

Vaguely, distantly, she heard Thaniel's quiet exit.

Beneath the slow leak of westering light and the lantern's dance and flicker, with Birt's great bay head a weight in her lap, Grace kept vigil side by side with Herris. The old barn creaked and sagged about them while the cows lowed muffled devotions, the mares blew soft lament, and the donkey brayed his quiet, lonely grief. Outside, the wind buffeted and moaned. Late, late into the night, they watched and waited, until Birt closed his great dark eyes and heaved his final breath. Then, Grace and Master Herris sat together until they both, quietly, wept themselves dry.

When Grace at last departed for home, the night sky stretched overhead, swept clear of clouds—vast and dark, star-stippled, imprinted with the waxing moon's bright crescent. Heart heavy, wearied beyond reckoning, she leaned back against the barn's coarse exterior and gulped the cold air's tonic. She did not flinch when shadow peeled from shadow, resolved into Thaniel's shape.

"You waited?" Shoulders quaking, she heaved a ragged breath, but she did not question the conviction of his presence.

"Of course." Despite the thrall and dark of night, his tone suggested a weary smile. "I'll always wait for you."

Grace, folded in the snug circle of his arms, head tucked beneath his chin, realized she had still more tears left to weep.

CHAPTER TWENTY-SEVEN

A small breath of surprise escaped Grace's lips. Her needle's fine point had pierced the tip of her index finger, drawing blood. Quickly, she put her finger to her mouth, tasted scarlet, and glanced to the right, through the curtain of her own hair. Though her mother's head remained bent over her own work, she knew Lettie had noticed—a single, silver eyebrow arched to crease her mother's forehead.

Seated in a hard, round-backed wooden chair, several paces from the fieldstone hearth, Grace was helping with the mending. A large basket spilled over the floorboards between them, and she bent her meager energies to the task as much to occupy her mind as her hands. A veritable cascade of cloth—fawns and ivories, greens and grays and ochres; wool socks and lisle stockings; shirts and skirts and aprons.

Gazing left, she observed her father. Somehow, he placated Sylvie, his hand smoothing the cat's fur in even strokes while he read a faded, clothbound book—an indulgence rarely afforded him.

Next, her eyes fell upon Wolf and Murl, stretched across the hearthrug, distorted mirror images. With spines to the fire, their tail tips scraped the edges of her mending.

Winter shaped their current domesticity, pressed them close to the hearth's refuge, to cackling, crackling fire and the stones that trapped and held its heat. Outside, a fierce, cunning wind—unfamiliar in voice and character—bore sleet and snow along its quickened edge. With each gust and squall, it shook and rattled the barred door, keened at shuttered windows in search of entry. Grace shifted in her seat. For all the wind's insistent howls, she understood neither thrum nor swell nor downdraft.

Frowning at her finger's tip, at the small, precise hole inserted among spiraling parallel lines, Grace turned a critical eye on her work. Uneven stitches staggered along the apron spread across her lap; the cloth puckered with gaps; there were far too many broken threads. Clutching needle and thread and fabric, she dropped her hands into her lap. Of all her skills, mundane or unusual, her mending begged improvement.

"When does Thaniel return, dear?" Her mother continued to slide her own silver needle effortlessly in and out of combed homespun the color of faded beech leaves. Eyes fixed on her work, she patched Gaven's shirt with near-imperceptible stitches.

"He hasn't returned yet?" Her father looked up from his book, his hand stilled mid-stroke along Sylvie's length. Pushing wire-rimmed glasses to the end of his nose, he peered over their rims.

Grace sighed, leaned back against the hoop of her chair. "He meant to return by week's end. Middton is two full days' ride, but with this weather . . ." Trailing off, she glanced over her shoulder, where a shuttered window leaked flat gray light. Beyond cribbed, wooden slats, the glass panes stuttered and knocked in their frames. Another frown stole over her features.

"What business does he have in Middton?" Her mother looked up from her needlework.

"Trading and replenishing supplies, assisting as needed." Grace's hands remained idle and upturned against her thighs. Thaniel had asked if she might join him. But the shadows of Aldermere crept in, swelled. Though it meant separation, she had chosen the safety of her home. As the days stumbled over one another, and Thaniel's absence stretched, she had too much time to ponder her choice.

Now, she watched absently as Sylvie leapt from her father's lap to curl among the mending pooled at Grace's feet. With each shifting drift and accumulation of snow, Grace felt a keener sense of isolation. Time and again, her thoughts returned to that moment outside Master Herris's barn—the night of the crescent moon, when Thaniel had held her as she wept. The shared warmth and comfort of his embrace. Arm in arm, their breath had found unison; their hearts, mutual pattern.

He had been gone, now, a full week—one that stretched beyond itself.

"I'm not good at this." Grace spoke with dull finality. Cotton spilled from her lap, joined pale linens and earthen wool heaped at her feet. Sylvie, disturbed, meowed complaint.

"Stitching?" Needle poised, her mother probed gently. "Or waiting?"

"Either," Grace said. Knotting her fingers together, she grimaced. "Both."

"Few of us are." Lettie nodded. "Patience is a trait hard learned."

"Patience is the dominion of cats," Sylvie observed.

Stowing her needle in her apron's hem, Grace stared at the hearth's teasing flames until her eyes ached, tried to ignore the wind's keening. She considered the tabby's wry comment, suspecting it contained some truth.

"Why don't you make us some tea?" Lettie suggested.

Grace rose, grateful for a task she could manage, and drew Sylvie in her wake. The cat stretched, yawned, wound about her ankles, followed her to the kitchen. The tabby's steady grass-green gaze tracked her movements as she drew mugs from the open shelves and set sugar bowl and tea tin on the counter alongside a little jug of cream.

"Sylvie," Grace declared at last. "What is it?"

The storm's sudden onset had prevented a trip to the well. She tipped a blue-glazed jug, heavy with snowmelt, into the kettle. In her haste, small clots of ice water splashed her knuckles, spattered the counter's top.

Unblinking, Sylvie sat on the coiled rag rug, surveying Grace's every movement with white-tipped tail curled neatly over her front paws. "It has occurred to me . . ." The cat spoke with rare candor. ". . . your behavior is quite like Wolf's."

Grace cast a glance at Wolf, stretched and bristling in gray-stroked fur before the hearth.

"How so?" She felt the tick of impatience.

Sylvie offered a long, slow, deliberate blink; she yawned wide, so her whiskers curled back against her jaw. "You each pine for your mates," she said.

Grace halted mid-stride. Intent on reaching the hearth and setting the kettle on the hob to boil, she stood arrested, looking at Wolf's prone form. Though he sprawled appreciatively before the fire's warmth, she heard the quiet ache of his self-imposed separation.

"There's no shame in it," Sylvie said. Arching her back, she padded lightly across the rug, brushed her tail against Grace's skirts. "It's good to love, to be loved."

Grace gripped the kettle, listened to the faint chop of water caught within its copper-wrought margins. She found it a peculiar sensation, to be the subject of another's keen observation, to have herself laid bare, her heart so plainly defined in such a manner. She felt more impressed than she should be by Sylvie's perceptiveness, and the fact humbled her. "How can you . . ."

"I am Cat," Sylvie purred. "I know things." Lifting, stretching, she swished past and reclaimed her seat by the fire in Gaven's lap. With fluid motion, she leapt atop his book and lifted her head to have her chin scratched.

"Is something wrong, dear?" Lettie looked up from her mending.

Navigating the tangle of lupine and canine limbs, Grace stopped to hang the kettle over a bright, chittering curtain of flames. She shook her head. "Sylvie has just reminded me of something."

"What's that?" Her father shifted his book clear of tabby cat.

"That old saying," Grace said slowly. "Of absence and hearts . . ."

"Ahh." Her mother exchanged a knowing glance with her father. "'Absence makes the heart grow fonder.'"

"That's the one."

Deeply, tenderly, she felt into the sting of Thaniel's absence. Arms folded about her ribs, she stared at the hearth's flames. Each spark snapped and chanted of hope and desire, love and passion, hunger and yearning—an intense creative force that, poorly handled, consumed all; or, deprived of fuel, expired.

CHAPTER TWENTY-EIGHT

Knees pressed to the floorboards of the henhouse, Grace appreciated her father's handiwork. From without, it resembled in all ways an elevated shed, built with remainders from the local sawyer, with limbs and branches foraged from the Bright Wood's edges. Vented, roofed in deep-grooved cedar shingles, insulated with straw, it leaned slightly on its squat, sturdy footings. Years of use and constant repair leant the structure a certain rustic charm.

Inside, the humble structure was a small sanctuary—snowless and replete with the heady, hay-sweetened, slight tang of avian warmth. A lacework of straw gathered along the front and hems of Grace's skirts and apron. Her breath hatched in small white clouds. Light seeped past vertical plank walls in dusted segments, stumbled along the rear wall's shelves. Here, beneath the sloped roof's eaves, nest boxes snugged one against another, arranged in rows and columns at deliberate intervals.

"Good morning." She pitched her voice soft and low, reached beneath a nest box occupant's flounce of creamy feathers. Despite her measured approach, she received a firm peck on the wrist before her fingers curled over a single, smooth-shelled egg.

"Oh, dear, how thoughtless of me. I'm so sorry!" In a fit of agitation, the hen apologized. "It's habit, you know. I simply can't help myself."

"I understand." Grace extracted a pale brown egg, settling it against the others in her basket. She cupped her right wrist with her left hand, rubbed the thin skin there with a slight wince. A small hole gaped in her mitten where the yarn had been repeatedly pecked; it revealed a raw, red blotch of flesh. She wondered vaguely if she might develop a callus.

"So hard to break, so easy to start," the hen clucked and muttered without interruption. "Or is it the other way 'round? Habits, of course."

"I suppose both could be true." Grace sat back on the heels of her boots, smoothed the feathers along the hen's compact body.

"I'm certain I don't know anymore," the hen complained. "Especially after recent events . . ."

"There, now." Grace attempted to soothe and encourage, as she had minutes earlier with two red hens, a buff, and a black-and-white. "Maybe *you* can tell me what happened?"

"Oh. It was awful." The hen—following her flock mates' pattern—fell into near incoherence, tutting and muttering. "Awful! Terrible! Dreadful! The shock! The fear! Simply horrible!"

"Hush now, hush," Grace said. Unable to quell the hen's distress, she stroked creamy feathers, from base of juddering neck to upthrust tail feathers. Thus far, Grace had amassed nine eggs, seven sound jabs, but not an inkling of the reason for the flock's collective anxiety. Their anguish, a frantic buzzing within her skull, pecked as achingly as their beaks. Stymied, she stood, fingers gripping the basket's handle.

"You won't get a straightforward account from any one of them."

Turning, Grace saw the flock's lone rooster framed within the henhouse door.

"Such a shame." He spoke dismissively, with an indulgence born of presumed superiority. "Busy as they are with their various maternal endeavors. Easily overwhelmed by hysteria."

Arching a brow, Grace bristled at Rooster's comment, chided herself for taking offense. "But *you* can tell me what happened?"

"Of course, of course," Rooster crowed. He strutted over on spurred legs, all arrogance and glossy, russet-gold plumage. With his scarlet comb flopped over one orange eye, he cocked his head to one side and peered up at her. "Intruders!" With a jerking motion, he cocked his head again, still farther, until Grace realized he meant for her to follow him down the central aisle.

"There," he pronounced. The feathers at his neck separated as he stretched to indicate a darkened corner beneath the lowest shelf at the back of the henhouse. "Shoddy upkeep. Disgraceful."

Again, ignoring the rooster's critique, Grace set her basket aside and returned to hands and knees to investigate. Pulling away drifts of fallen straw, she scraped the corner clear. And there she found it: a small hole, freshly gnawed about the corners. Cold air funneled inward. Grace leaned on the heels of her hands.

"Mice?" she wondered aloud.

"I assure you, Female," Rooster said, lifting one foot, talons curled. He huffed with indignance. "A *mouse*, I would efficiently dispatch."

Grace held her tongue and stood up. "I'd best take a look from outside." Though she loomed over him, her height did little to dwarf the fowl's ego.

"I should think so." Rooster goggled up at her.

Shaking off skeins of straw and cobwebs, she took up the egg-laden basket, and strode toward the henhouse's small door, ducking out. She pulled her shawl over her head. Unabated, the snowfall continued lightly, gently, added a fresh dusting to the previous night's accumulation.

"Remember," Rooster said.

Grace paused on the single stone step to look at him. He jerked his head about in an unnerving manner.

"*We never spoke*," he croaked beneath his breath and peered from beneath his comb with suspicion.

Grace held a finger to her lips, nodded, and shut the door behind her. Kicking through hummocks of snow, she made her way to the rear corner of the henhouse. White drifts climbed the structure's exterior. Pushing through them, she slid her fingers below the henhouse's edge, up and through the small hole in the floor; its rough-gnawed edge snagged her mittens, pulling at loosened yarn. Scanning the area beyond layers of freshly cleared snow, she spied—leading back and forth from the hole—a peculiar trail. A well-worn and repeating track of small, ice-slicked, shadow-filled impressions to either side of an equally strange, unbroken, and undulating channel.

Having discovered this set of small, clawed paw prints, Grace followed. So light were the tracks, they barely creased the snow's surface. Her own heavy boots were coarse bass notes to their treble. She pursued the trail away from the coop, hiked up her skirts, and clambered over a wooden stile. In a flounce of fabric layers, she followed across dormant, snow-flattened fields that, a season ago, had sung with crickets, grasshoppers, meadowlarks.

Curiously, the small steps continued their back-and-forth shift, ever to either side of the wobbling trail they accompanied. Both sets of tracks dodged beneath brush and bramble, skirted the Bright Wood's edge.

"Stop!"

Grace, intent, did not immediately hear the command.

"At *once*!"

The basket swung on Grace's forearm, rattled eggs.

"Halt! Now!" A small shrill voice, authority-filled. "On pain of injury!"

Straightening, Grace stopped, pushed loose strands of hair back from her face. Heart knocking, she searched the brambles' twist of dark canes for the voice's source, saw the brush tremble faintly. A small head thrust out. Flint-dark eyes shone. Weasel's sharp nose twitched.

"Not another step," Weasel commanded. Her ferocity contracted, relative to Grace's static posture. "A trap. Beneath the snow." She studied Grace intently, nose wrinkling. "Can't you smell it?"

Grace tensed, shook her head. "No."

"Rust and iron," Weasel said, tsking and chittering. "Hopeless. Helpless. As a kit."

Grace squinted through snow-dusted shadow. Weasel's sleek body had shed summer's coat for winter's, a piebald mix of thick white and chestnut brown. It seemed to Grace as though something was supporting Weasel, as if the creature leaned forward with its small hand-like front paws folded over a smooth ovoid shape.

"Remain, remain." Weasel folded, ducked, and thrust the ovoid out of sight, back into the underbrush. Leaving the protection of twig and briar, she slunk out and marked a broad, paw print circle through the snow, passing within inches of Grace's boots.

"Right here," Weasel said. "Limb biter. Body breaker. Orphan maker." She quickly returned to the relative safety of the bramble's edge.

Grace stepped back, away; found a stout, knotted tree limb, a dark slash stabbing up through white snow. Returning to the area Weasel had marked, she thrust the limb through the snow's crust, pierced the circle's heart. Wood struck metal; concealed jaws snapped. Broad, rusted teeth splintered wood. Despite the warning, despite actively searching, Grace recoiled. She released the branch's remains and sought Weasel's clear, knowing eye. One hand pressed to the base of her throat, her heart thumped steadily through woolen gloves.

Weasel tsked and blinked at her. "There are others," she said. "Near the brambles. In the meadow. Bad business."

Grace expelled a wreathed breath. She studied the weasel, who now sat up on her back legs, exposing a smooth-furred white underbelly. Soon, she would be a specter within the snow's expanse, entirely white but for eyes, nose, and tail tip.

Weasel blinked at Grace and said, "You've come about the egg."

Grace considered the basket she still carried crooked over one elbow, its contents full of eggs. Before she could speak, Weasel folded back upon herself, almost in two, and disappeared again into the underbrush. As quickly, the creature returned, clever paws rolling a brown egg end over end in a wobbly, undulating trail. Paws folded, Weasel leaned on the egg.

"Ahh . . ." Grace breathed a realization.

"You know how it is," Weasel said, her voice high, rapid. "Family of kits. Mouths to feed. Long, hollow winters." She paused briefly, nose twitching. "I have a proposition. An arrangement. Of mutual benefit."

"Yes?" Grace asked, intrigued.

"I show you . . ." Weasel's eyes glittered. ". . . where the other traps lay hidden."

Grace studied the creature, its bright eyes and sleek curve of form. "And in return?"

"I keep the egg," Weasel said. She flicked a backward glance, past the screen of thorny brush behind her. "Feed my kits. An exchange. An agreement."

Grace turned, stretched, curled her mittened fingers around another fallen tree limb and tugged it free. "Show me where the traps are," she said, "and I'll see that you get an egg for each."

CHAPTER TWENTY-NINE

Body biter. Limb breaker. Orphan maker.

Over the ensuing week, Grace and Weasel scoured the surrounding orchards and pastures for traps. They tripped and collected dozens of various size and animal purpose; the single shared feature of each device, its wickedly strong metal jaws and cruel intent.

Neck snapper, foot cracker, ankle crusher.

Grace trudged homeward—toes cold despite her boots and stockings, fingertips numb inside her mittens; she hadn't yet mended the hole in the right hand. She winced into the wind, bone-chilling and raw. Snow hushed across her path, over fallow field and meadow, coated each upswept tree limb. A pale smudge within the sky, the sun cast a distant, bleary light. She imagined Weasel, returned to her leaf-lined burrow, snugly curled.

The day's collection swayed against Grace's back, clanking and chanting curses against their chains. Broad jaws caught at her hood, pulled her cloak tightly against her throat, like a choking hand. She didn't realize she was frowning until her head began to hurt—a dull throb of light behind her skull, between her brows.

Distraction shadowed her in thought and form—the traps, Thaniel's absence, winter's all-consuming hollow. Her head became so crowded, she narrowly avoided stumbling over Sylvie when the sleek feline form melted suddenly into view.

"Have a care!" the cat hissed.

"Oh, Sylvie!" Grace caught her step as the tabby dodged and flicked her tail in crisp accusation.

"Lost in thought . . . *again*." Sylvie sniffed.

"Did I step on you?" Crouching in the middle of the path, Grace ran her mittened hand over Sylvie's spine.

"If you *had*, you wouldn't *ask*."

The cat lifted at her touch and slid along Grace's snow-flecked woolen skirts to inspect the grisly relics that rocked against her back.

"A grim business," Sylvie spat.

Grace shrugged her weight of jawed metal. "I only hope I've found them all."

"As do we all." Sylvie sniffed and stared wide-eyed, slit-pupiled, unblinking. "Though it's unlikely."

Giving the tabby at final pat on her head, Grace rose, swept her gaze over the white-robed landscape. "It'd be easier if it weren't winter."

"The same goes for most things," Sylvie agreed dryly.

Following a channel carved through snow, Grace retraced her path back toward the cottage with the cat dodging her steps. The traps clattered dissonance, rearranged themselves with her gait. Blue and violet tree shadow stretched across the snow, dipped and pooled within the path's margins. To the west, the Bright Wood's crown snatched up pale sunlight.

"A man called at the house." Sylvie said.

Grace nearly tripped midstride. "Thaniel?"

"Did I *say* Thaniel?" Sylvie gazed up at her. "He did not enter the house. I was napping," she added. "But it did not sound like Thaniel. Also, you humans sound much alike—speaking when you should be silent, silent when you should speak."

A man, but not Thaniel. Grace exhaled disappointment, her breath a garland of white, hovering. She watched Sylvie—whiskers extended and tail a banded verticality—dash ahead.

The tabby paused, looked backward over her shoulder. "Are you coming?"

Thoughts churning, boots chuffing, Grace nodded, pushed forward through a lattice of light and shadow stroked over snow. Her strides were heavy, deliberate compared to Sylvie's brisk staccato—the cat moved nimbly over fresh snowpack, darted off the path every so often, and just as swiftly returned.

Ahead, the garden gate's arbor bore spring and summer's withered vines. Brittle, brown, the over-twining knots clutched clots of white. Sylvie brushed past her legs and slipped up the cleared walk to the door. But Grace, pausing beneath, considered those other steps pressed into the snow along the cottage's brickwork path. Forward, retreating. Each deep hollow collected small drifts. Her brow furrowed slightly, and her burden of traps bit into her neck and shoulder as she lingered within the gate's mouth, thoughtful.

"I'm *waiting*," Sylvie yowled.

Hinges rasping, the gate knocked shut behind Grace as she mixed her footsteps amid those unknown prints. At the cottage's front door, she scuffed her boots' thick treads along the iron scrape. Ice and snow fell in muddied chunks. Sylvie, impatient, mewed, arched her back, and set sickle claws against weathered wood. When Grace pushed the door open, the cat whisked between her ankles into the house.

"Ahhh, you're home." Her mother, wooden spoon in hand, looked up from the mended cast-iron pot that rocked above the hearth's bright flames. A mobile dilation of shadows swung about the room.

Closing the door, shutting winter firmly out, Grace watched her mother straighten, press the heel of her free hand against her low back. She felt a twinge of guilt for being gone so long.

"What luck have you had?" her mother asked.

Grace held up her collection of traps, shook them so they chattered. "That depends on your definition."

"I hope they were . . . well . . ." Her mother's grim query hung on the air.

Murl trotted over, sniffed at the assortment of teeth and jaws, and whined. "They smell like hurting."

Seeing Murl crouched into himself, anger licked up Grace's spine. She lowered the clamped, clenched teeth, and they jangled dully against one another from their lengths of chain. "They were all unsprung," Grace confirmed.

"Good," her mother said. "Take the awful things straight out back. I don't want them in the house. Your father can sort them out when he returns."

"He's still out?" Grace crossed the floor's wide planks, avoided the braided rag rugs to open the back door; the traps dripped a trail of rusty snowmelt behind her.

"You know your father—if someone needs help, he won't quit until the task is done. *Correctly*."

Grace leaned out into the afternoon's fading lavender light. She dropped the traps in a heap beside the back steps, where they winked with leaden portent. Suppressing a shudder, she ducked back indoors, pulling the door firmly shut.

Her mother asked, "Does anyone know who set them?"

Kicking off her boots, Grace shook her head, tongue stilled. Each door she had knocked on, each neighbor she queried uncovered only surprise, alarm, anger. The traps remained a rust-toothed mystery, clamped tight over their origins. With a huff, she shook herself free of snow, hung her cloak and scarf and mittens on their customary pegs.

"I doubt you'll get any confessions," her mother said. "Anyone who would set them without notice is unlikely to admit it."

"That's just it, isn't it?" Grace joined her mother at the fireside, released her fists into fingers splayed before the fire's warmth. "It's not like Edgewoode is *big*—it's a small enough thing to let everyone *know* you've put traps in their pastures."

"That's always been the case before."

Grace threw her arms wide. "It's common courtesy!"

"Can't they tell you?" Lettie's gaze moved between cat and dog.

Dropping her arms to hug herself, Grace shook her head. "They catch the scents of pain and brokenness and fear; nothing else." Thought of the traps—of tarnished metal teeth stroked with old blood, with wisps of fur—made her grimace. It took no special talent to imagine agony, exhaustion, vain struggle. A small sob escaped her. "I *hate* them." She suddenly found herself wrapped in her mother's arms, held tight as tears slid down her cheeks.

"I know, dear," her mother whispered, stroking Grace's hair.

"Why would anyone do this, here?" Cheek pressed to her mother's shoulder, she breathed in her scent—lavender, Sweet William.

"I don't know, Grace." She felt her mother's fingers move through the tangle of her snow-damp hair, straightening, taming.

Grace pushed back from her mother's arms. "Have you seen Wolf?" Cold fear swept over her.

Lettie hesitated, then said, "Not since earlier."

"What if?" Her question remained half-born.

"I'm sure he's fine." Her mother spoke with firm intention. "He's a smart one."

"Oh, no." Grace put her fingers to her temples, shaking her head. "No, no, *no* . . ."

"Grace . . ."

"I'm going back out." She whirled away, grabbed her cloak, her scarf and gloves, tripped over her boots.

"*Grace!*"

"Mom," she said, turning to face her mother, "I *have* to go." The protests died as her mother helped her into her cloak and set one hand on Grace's shoulder.

"I understand." She stroked Grace's cheek with the back of her hand. "I didn't before, but I do now. As much as I'm able."

Standing there, arms full of outerwear and the room tilting around her, Grace fastened her gaze on the anchoring presence of her mother.

"But you must be sensible," Lettie continued. She wound the scarf around Grace's neck, settled the cloak about her shoulders, slid mittens over her hands as she would a small child. "You have an hour until sunset. I want you back by that time."

Grace nodded, unwilling to speak for fear that her voice would break, that *she* might.

"Go to the well." Lettie fetched the blue water jug, handed it to Grace. "Bran sent a message that he wished to meet you there. You can search for Wolf along the way, and come straight back. I want you home for dinner. Do *you* understand?"

"Yes." Another nod, swiftly followed by a small frown of confusion. She held the jug in both hands, pressed to her abdomen. "I just . . . I thought the Fair and all the tradesfolk left weeks ago."

"I imagine a tinker might pick up work enough to linger." Lettie returned to the hearthside. With the hem of her apron wadded about her left hand, she opened an iron door to the compact bread oven set deep in the hearth's wall. "Bran . . . he seemed like a nice young man."

"I suppose," Grace agreed slowly.

"Is there any chance he harbors . . . intentions?" She slid a wooden bread peel inside the hearth wall's cavity, withdrawing a loaf of dark bread.

"I don't see how he could," Grace said warily. She had no room for Bran's intentions; she felt only a pressing and immediate concern for Wolf's safety.

Her mother sniffed. "Men have a staggering capacity for self-delusion." She rapped knuckles on the loaf's smooth, coarse crust and, satisfied, shut the little iron door firmly. Crossing the room, she set peel and bread on the table.

Grace bit her lower lip in thought, and trailed in her mother's wake, drawn by the bread's aroma.

"It's best to clear up any confusion as quickly as possible," her mother said. She put the loaf on a cutting board, covered it with a clean towel. "If there is any."

Grace said nothing, her thoughts tumbling one into another. Setting the jug down, she slipped her feet into her boots without bothering with the laces.

Lettie kissed Grace's brow, brushed a lock of hair from her face. "Don't forget to come home."

Grace nodded, hugged her mother, and grabbed the earthen jug. "I won't."

"Remind me when you get back, and I'll tell you about Rahbert."

Grace paused, hand on the doorlatch, and gave her mother a curious look. "Who?"

"Let's just say," Lettie said, winking, "that Rahbert was my Bran. . . ."

"There is no *Bran*," Grace said. Then, surveying her mother: "Does father know about this 'Rahbert' person?"

"Of course he knows." Lettie lifted her chin. "Your father and I have no secrets."

Grace's cheek ticked with a small half-smile. "Oh, I'm sure!"

Lettie cut the heel end off the still-warm loaf with a long, serrated knife; it bit through the crust, scattering crumbs. "Take Murl with you."

Hearing his name, Murl bounded for the door, yipping and sneezing.

"Come along," Grace said. She patted his head, then opened the door.

"Sylvie's coming, too!" Murl wagged his tail with enthusiasm.

"Always the dog," Sylvie observed dryly. "No one ever thinks to invite the cat. . . ." She did not wait for Grace to make a counterargument, but whisked ahead, leading the way through declining light.

Bracing herself, with Murl and Sylvie beside, Grace ventured out into winter's thin heart in search of Wolf.

CHAPTER THIRTY

"Wolf!" Grace called, the name a white plume on her lips.

"Wolf! Wolf! Wolf!" Murl's front feet lifted off the ground with each barked repetition.

Through slopes and swells and tumbled snow, Grace searched a landscape devoid of tracks or signs of Wolf. A panorama transformed and folded upon itself; all concealed in gleaming white, smooth and flawless, gliding past, indifferent to her objective. She leaned forward, called again. The wind overrode her. No longer the mischievous voice of spring and summer, nor even of autumn, its collective now tolled in mournful notes of isolation, despair, exposure.

Grace shuddered, pulling her cloak tight against her throat with one hand. Murl bounded ahead and back, snapping at random snowflakes, while Sylvie melted into the frosty distance. On her initial forays with Weasel, Grace had cleared these paths of traps—all the small tracks that wound to the well. This allowed her mind to wander, to consider her mother's parting comments. The remarks nettled, and Bran's visage emerged from her memory—golden sunshine, broadly smiling. He was no "Rahbert"—she did not *know* him; there could be no "confusion." Brow furrowed, she went, yes; but Wolf drew her forward, and only Wolf.

Squaring her shoulders, she shifted the water jug within her mittened grip. "Wolf!" she called again. His name shivered the air, and the wind mourned: *Lone* ◬ *lone* ◬ *alone* ◬

Immediately, her thoughts turned to Thaniel. She missed him: the timbre of his voice; his forested, sandalwood scent; the warmth and ease and certainty of his presence. She adjusted the silk flower in her hair, Thaniel's gift; it was a reminder to herself, a signal to others. Its edges caught the wind's breath, a rosette of delicate, beating wings.

Far above, a wedge of geese punctured the leaden sky, their cries too distant for her ears to decipher, while the sparrows' rapid chatter filled the prick and snarl of snow-clotted undergrowth. Flurries spiraled, drifted, and softened a landscape otherwise drained of color; scarlet berries of holly, bittersweet, and barberry shone in stark relief. Winter wielded its own unadorned beauty. The world slept, dreamed; would reawaken come spring. She drew this conviction into her lungs in long, even breaths, drinking it through her pores.

"Snow tastes like stinging!" Murl barked excitement, then whuffled a particular patch of snow with great interest.

Despite herself, Grace laughed, distracted by his antics. While the dog wagged furiously and thrust his nose along the ground and raised a shallow furrow, a rustle in the underbrush drew her attention. Sylvie emerged from a bristled scrub, whiskers tipped in snow.

"A man waits at the well," the cat said.

"Bran?" Grace asked.

With a flick of tail, Sylvie stared bright-eyed at Grace. "I feel as though we've already had this conversation," she said archly. "There are far too many of you to keep track of. . . ." The cat's voice thinned to vapor.

Loss △ *loss* △ *lost* △

The wind soughed in Grace's ear. She frowned, considering, and watched Sylvie slink back into the scrub as Murl circled round to stand beside her. The dog peered into the distance with nostrils flared and tail extended out behind him. It seemed to Grace that he stood taller, somehow, on his own four feet, alert to something beyond her abilities to discern. Her sweet dog's resemblance to Wolf clutched her heart.

She ran her mittened hand over his raised hackles. "What is it?"

Muzzle angled slightly skyward, Murl whuffled the air. "Stranger."

The wind curled about her: *Storm* △ *storm* △ *storming* △

Her brow furrowed. Murl's posture, the wind's laments, unsettled her. The path slipped on toward the well, a stream of snowpack and blue ice. Soughing and whining, the wind rose, coiled against her: *Back* △ *back* △ *away* △

A sudden squall buffeted with such strength that she stumbled backward and trod on Murl's foot. With a yip, the dog lost all semblance of height and stature, reduced to his familiar, un-Wolflike posture. Another gust struck Grace squarely in the chest, *pushed*, so she caught her boot in the twist of her skirts' ice-freighted hems. Throwing her arms wide, the world gyrated, spun, and the water jug arched from her grip. It wheeled, struck some exposed crown of stone as she went to ground. Her left knee and the heels of both hands met frozen earth. She avoided landing atop Murl only because the dog dodged nimbly aside.

"Ohhhh . . ." Head slung low, Murl said, returning to Grace's side. "That *hurt*." He licked her face.

"Wolf needs me," Grace muttered, with a glance skyward. "Stop it, please."

Tucking his tail, Murl asked, "Me?"

"No, oh no, not you," she reassured the dog. Then, dazedly, she brushed her hands briskly together. Clumps of snow fell from her mittens, one now hatched and scored—the former, unmended ragged hole of torn knitting gaped wider, framing the base of her thumb. Scored tracks pearled with scarlet beads. With a wince, she swept grit from exposed flesh and, blankly, stared at the shattered water jug. A mosaic of blue-glazed earthenware ornamented soft hummocks of snow, arranged in a chaotic semicircle around the jug's curved belly. Murl nosed the detached half-moon handle as she plucked it from the snow.

"I'll replace it." Picking herself up, she stowed the handle deep in her skirt pocket, thought of her mother's chagrin when she returned with neither water nor jug.

Home △ *home* △ *go* △

She dismissed the wind's howls, bent her head against its voice, and pushed on. Each stride measured a song of blunt pain from her knee, the tender base of her thumb. Advancing with Murl padding at her side, the path soon widened, opening out into the well's clearing.

Here, she paused, shielded her eyes, and squinted past swift veils of snow, past flakes that stung her cheeks, her nose and chin. A figure, diminished to shadow by swirling white and distance, stood beyond the stone well's far side near the unmistakable form of a mule. Stout and shaggy, the creature hunched with its head lowered against wind and cold.

Pulling her cloak tight, Grace lifted her hand in half-hearted salute. She blinked, the wind in her eyes, a knot in her stomach. Scraping her hair from her face, the wind tossed and twisted, pressed like a great hand upon her chest as she moved forward with dragging steps. It sighed, a dirge in her ear.

Mere paces from the well—that small, familiar wood-and-stone structure, its shingle-roof shedding snow—she slowed. The wind's multiplicity of tongueless voices hissed in her ears, in her head. At her side, Murl whined; a brief lateral glance revealed Sylvie's absence. Despite the sting and bite of blowing snow, Grace lifted her gaze. With each grudging step, the figure before her resolved until, slowly, she froze, an ember of alarm stirring within her.

Not Bran. Neither as tall nor as broad. This man lacked the mass of bright hair. He wore a short tail at the base of his neck, enough to catch gray hair in an annotated pigtail. No, not Bran at all. Unsmiling in face and posture, there stood Bran's father. Waiting for her.

"You came." A broad grin spread over the man's features, of surprise or satisfaction. His teeth, though straight, seemed gray as he.

"Where is Bran?" Glancing about, she exhaled a pent breath, a cloud of doubt, slow to dissipate. Dimly, she felt Murl's shape against her left leg, the ache that throbbed bruise-bright in her knee, felt the very air tug at every bit of her.

"Not here." The man's pale gaze remained fixed as he shook his head.

Brow furrowed, Grace shook her head. "But . . ." The wind slashed and dragged.

"He's off at the wheelwright's, getting materials for the caravan's repair." His grin slipped. "We hit a rough patch of road a bit west of here—split wheel, broken axle, mule pulled up lame. Found our way to a wayfarer's shack on the outskirts of Edgewoode."

"That's not . . . not what I meant. . . ." She noticed the lean, vertical slash that projected at an angle from behind his left shoulder—the dull wooden stock of a musket. "He sent me a message to meet him."

"No. That was me." He shrugged, his eyes never breaking from Grace's face.

"I don't understand." Dropping her hand, aware of the wind's curl and moan, Grace sought reassurance in Murl.

"I've wanted to meet you for a long time." His eyes narrowed against cutting snow.

"We already met." Grace sketched a backward step, into the wind's lament. "At the Fair."

"Hardly." He laughed—a humorless sound, a contained noise cut short. His hand tightened on the mule's slack reins as he shook his head. "We're overdue for a *real* conversation, don't you think? But not here. Come with me. To the caravan." He extended his arm, his hand dark-gloved and wrapped in frayed, worn cloth.

Grace gaped, then laughed. The sound escaped her throat like a green fern uncurling from compact fiddlehead, a sound utterly at odds with the moment or season. "No," she said with a shake of her head. "I don't think so."

"I'm asking." His voice grated and he thrust his spread hand wide. "*Politely*."

Grace wished neither to speak with this man, nor share his presence. Pivoting, she turned away. The wind cried, the mule brayed, and Murl whined deep in his chest.

Too ⟁ *late* ⟁ *late* ⟁ *late* ⟁

With unexpected speed, Bran's father closed the distance between them. Seizing her by the upper arm, he wound his fingers about her bicep, tugged. "Do you even *know* me?"

"You're Bran's father." Half-turning, she shook his bruising fingers free, faced him. "A tinker." Murl's whine evolved to low growl.

"Oh no, girl," he corrected. "That's what *you made me*."

"What is that supposed to mean?" In the back of her mind, she thought he was making as little sense as a squirrel.

"You speak to *beasts*," he scoffed, "but you understand *so little*."

"Before the Fair, I'd never set eyes on you," she cried, exasperated. Flexing her fingers inside her mittens, damp with blood or melted snow, she balled her hands into fists.

"And therein lies your true talent!" He thrust a finger at her in accusation. "The ruin of a man's life from a lake's farthest shore, having never laid eyes on him!"

"*What?*" But as the question left her lips, comprehension dawned with a dark thorn's swift, sharp clarity. A small gasp escaped her.

"*There!*" With a single, sinuous step, he uncoiled toward her, finger arrowing forward. "There it is. Your eyes betray you. How I've anticipated that look. . . ."

"You're the . . . mechanist?" Grace stumbled over the word as she appraised the man with new eyes, with wary curiosity. "From Aldermere?"

He snorted. "Is that remorse?" Breath huffed from his nose, from the grim line of his mouth.

"*What?*" Grace laughed—a bright note against the surrounding monochrome. Alert to the plaintive wind, to Murl's whines and the mule's snorts, she beheld the man before her: his pallor and sharp features, the creases about his flint-gray eyes. The corners of his mouth were drawn down in a perpetual grimace beneath ashen stubble. "*You* contaminated Aldermere's lake, not me!"

"A man has a right to fashion a living for himself!"

The wind ratcheted and squalled, a diffusion of crisp, particulate flakes that sawed through the clearing, then swept off through the surrounding trees' naked, upswept boughs.

"Not," she challenged, "at the expense of those around him." Heart hammering against her ribs, she turned and struck out for the path, for home; she felt her momentum instantly checked.

"We're not done here." The man's tone bit through waning composure.

"*Let me go*." Straining against his grip, she felt his hold tighten.

"Not yet," he hissed. "I want to *talk*."

She gaped at him. "And this is how you go about that? False messages? Lies?" She heard the well's thick rope agitate against its pulleys; she heard, laced through their rasp and rattle, Murl's low growls.

"It was necessary. To get you here. So you *know*. So you *see* . . ."

"See what?" She wrenched at his grip.

"*What you have reduced me to!*"

The thunder of his voice rocked her, and she staggered, held fast in his grip. The world shrank, spiraled down to the precise foci of their connection—the intermingling curls of their breath, the slow grating of their eyes' fixed attention.

"You took *everything* from me!"

In a slow-moving instant, sound and motion erupted in a hectic blur.

The wind howled.

His grip tightened, fingers digging, bruising.

Grace cried out.

And Murl—all teeth and sudden fury—launched from his crouched posture and clamped jaws—*down*, *in*—on her assailant's arm.

The mechanist snarled in shock and pain, wrestling against Murl.

Grace found herself flung to hands and knees, suddenly and unexpectedly freed. Untangling her limbs from her skirts and cloak, she gained her feet and saw, through snarled hair, the human-canine struggle; saw the arc and sweep and curve of the musket's butt, the nauseating thud that followed its connection. Her gentle dog's uncommonly savage growls were cut short. She saw the man stand grim-faced over Murl's sprawled form, watched him swing again—up, around, *down* . . .

She hurled herself between the blow and its target.

Curled over Murl, head tucked, she awaited the shock of impact. When it failed to land, she hazarded an upward glance, saw the mechanist's flushed features as he loomed, panting, over her. His torn sleeve wicked blood, crimson as the small puddle staining the snow beneath Murl's jaw.

"*Please* . . ." She held up a staying palm. A peculiar, remote calm colored her words. "Don't. We'll talk."

Teeth clenched, face contorted, he spat: "Good." He hauled her to her feet, away from Murl.

Grace nodded agreement, a series of stiff, repeated jerks. Reflexive. Involuntary. Anything to diffuse the situation.

"Let's talk. We'll take Murl back home. We'll clean your wounds. And his."

Numbing cold crept past the woolen barrier of her clothes, filled her bones, spilled down her raw throat. "We'll talk as long as you want."

He snorted. "Do you think I'm stupid?" His chest heaved with effort; breath streamed from his mouth and nostrils. Expression grim, his eyes were shadowed, flinty. "The *caravan*," he said.

Motionless, choking back her tears, head roaring, Grace nodded again. She glanced at Murl, saw his chest stir with breath, bit her lip in relief. She wanted only to creep to his side, let her fingers define the mysteries of his injury, but she would risk no further harm to him. Scrubbing her sleeve over her face, she watched through the tangle of her hair as the tinker—*mechanist*, some distant part of her mind amended—stalked to the mule. With one hand, he rummaged through worn saddlebags; the musket, re-slung across his back, was a dark slash of implied threat.

Motion at the thicket's edge caught her eye, a shadow within the briars, a pattern of dark and light that mimicked the weave of thorny twigs and stems, of snow-hummocked sallow grasses. A steady, green-gold gaze met her eye. Sylvie. A gasp caught in Grace's throat and hope flared behind her ribs. Stealing a quick glance over her shoulder, she assured herself of the mechanist's distraction, then called to the cat in a voice too soft for human ears: "Sylvie, help Murl. *Get help.*"

Sylvie, shrunk within the dark lace of underbrush, blinked silent understanding.

At the approaching crunch of heavy boots, of hooves, Grace flinched. The mechanist tugged the mule forward through the snow, then waited opposite her. To her vague surprise, she realized they were of a similar height; she need only lift her chin—just so—to meet his gaze. She noted the scar above his lip line, the hollows beneath his eyes; she caught her breath when he scowled. He clamped his hands over her waist, thumbs and fingers digging into her hips.

"I can do it myself." Her voice sounded calm, foreign to her ear; she felt immediate relief when his hands fell away. Ignoring her knee's complaint, she put her left foot to the saddle's stirrup, throwing her right leg over the mule's broad back. Her skirts plumed heavily, her cloak spilled over the creature's rump. She slipped one hand deep into her pocket, felt the jug's broken curve of handle snag against her mitten, wondered at its sharp-edged potential.

The mechanist seized the bridle and jerked the beast's head as it bawled grievance. They lurched forward, and she spared a sideways glance. She spied Sylvie slinking, belly low, to lie beside Murl.

Loss ◬ *loss* ◬ *lost* ◬

Bran's father, the mechanist, led her away—from the well, from Murl and Sylvie. From home and Thaniel's return. Toward the Bright Wood's fringe. Onward, into uncertainty.

"I warned you. . . ." The mule muttered a somber declaration. "You should have run."

CHAPTER THIRTY-ONE

Grim-faced, the mechanist pulled on the mule's reins, drawing the mule and its burden through palls of snow at plodding gait. Grace swayed astride the laboring mule, alert, back arrow straight. Beyond her left shoulder, the sun sputtered and sank, sending their shadows sprawling, blue-black between inky trees. The Bright Wood's periphery inched forward, even as snow climbed the mule's forelegs, the mechanist's calves.

"They expect me home for dinner." Her tone, carefully neutral, lacked the heat of argument.

"Quiet."

"They'll come looking for me."

The sun's light snuffed out against the horizon, and she thought, dismayed, of her father searching for her through the night, in this weather; of Murl, prone, slowly folded under layers of snow.

"Be *quiet*."

Grace persisted, couldn't help needling: "I thought you wanted to talk?"

She glanced to her right, past humps of barberry and wild rose canes as he grumbled imprecations beneath his breath. The wind prodded, suggested, and she considered leaping from the saddle, hurling herself away. Thoughts of Sylvie prowled; she envied the cat's instinctive ability to act, wondered at the strength and trajectory required to send herself clear. Leaning forward and sideways, she curled over the mule's shoulder as if to adjust her boot in the stirrup.

"Go ahead." Unflinching, the mechanist met her stare, eyes agleam. "*Try it. . . .*"

Grace jerked at the pulse of anger his voice contained. Adjusting her posture, she gazed down on him—this ashen man, this cipher, wraithlike amid whirling shrouds. The image chilled her, beyond mere physical sensation.

"Trust your fate to night and storm," he scoffed. "To the *wilds*. To the beasts you speak with."

She contracted, surprised by his perception, by her intent's transparency. Her stuttering lack of resolve humbled her. The tangled Wood shuffled nearer, distorted by blunted angles and circumstance into a creature unknown. Vast and fathomless, lit by an earthbound light that seeped up from the snow's reflection. The Wood, transformed to unfamiliarity.

Her thoughts crowded with the mule's discontent and the mechanist's rancor, the wind's frost-sharp lament. To still her hands' trembling, she pushed her hair from her face, smoothing her fingers over it. With a twist of heart, she felt the absence of Thaniel's flower. Serrated and tooth-branched, the Bright Wood closed around them, swallowed.

When, neck extended, the mule stumbled, Grace pitched forward. She clutched the saddle's pommel and exhaled a clouded, breathy gasp. Pulling herself upright, she stroked the mule's withers, smoothed her hand along its neck. Ears flattened, it snorted plumes of distress and lashed its ice-threaded tail—it had not spoken since issuing its somber judgment. Grace peered through its stiff-brush mane as the mechanist swatted at random, piercing limbs. His curses grated the night air.

"Have you . . ." She hesitated, then reframed her question. "Are we . . . lost?"

The mechanist was leading such a convoluted path, she wondered if he were truly disoriented, or if he intended misdirection.

"How can *you* be *lost*?" A sharp tug of leather reins drew the mule's bawling protest.

Feeling his temper's lash, its switch and flicker, she stilled her tongue. Turning her attention to the darkened Wood, she sought the known within the unknown—curve of trunk or twist of bough, slope or rut of earth, fur or feather or distant voice. The forest breathed and slept and dreamed, not in utter silence, but in slumbering shape and language, a frisson within her mind, against her ear, slinking, rustling, softly agitating. Her eyes, having adjusted to the sun's absence, peered beyond darkness, found subtle color layered within fretwork shadow. Navy, midnight, indigo folded and uncurled over slumped snow.

Chaffing her hands, she squinted past the vapor of her breath. It seemed a small, pale light hung among the twist of dark branches ahead. Not the moon, which had not yet birthed beyond the trees' crown. She fixed her gaze upon the wobbly glow. Gradually, the light bloomed, grew, a mote of warmth and conviction. The mechanist noted the light as well—she heard his grunt of satisfaction as he course-corrected toward the beacon. The mule lifted its ears, offered no complaint now when hauled forward through hock-deep drifts.

Hair twining through the mule's mane, Grace ducked a low limb. She felt the heat of the mule's body against her cheek, heard the saddle creak in counterpoint to the creature's leaden step. Hoisting herself upright, she seized again upon the light—it dodged between a thicket of branches. A fallen star; a peel of moonlight, sloughed. It defied the limits of its dimensions, steadied, grew, and soon defined a rough structure tucked within the understory.

The mechanist pushed aside a pine bough's curtain, pulled the mule through into a small clearing, then drew up short. There, beyond the long green fringe of needles, huddled a simple wooden structure—the wayfarer's shack. A second mule stood hobbled beneath a generous, overhanging roof, and beside these, another impermanent structure. Though recently painted, the caravan's bulk was recognizable to Grace. The vehicle listed to one side, its front axle buttressed by a stout log, and a new wheel leaned against its yellow length, awaiting placement. Near the caravan's azure door, a single window shone brightly. Smoke rolled from a cylindrical, metal stack that sprouted from its bowed roof. Under his breath, she heard the mechanist mutter scathing profanity.

"What is it?" Grace's stomach knotted. "What's wrong?"

One hand slicing air, he silenced her. After a moment's calculation, he gripped the mule's bridle and, giving the yellow caravan's tiny window and bright blue door a wide berth, led them around its back toward the shack. He tied the mule to the overhang's post beside its fellow.

"Down," he hissed. His eyes flashed bright as flints in the dark. "Not a word."

Grace swung her leg, dismounted, and thumped lightly to earth. She searched out the caravan's light, oriented herself toward its bright stroke within the dark. Slipping her hand into her pocket, she fit the jug's broken handle—sharp-edged in blue—against the curve of her palm; slid her gaze toward the mechanist. She tried to see him as formless shadow, a void of humanity, and gripped the earthenware's jagged curve more tightly. She willed herself to strike and slice, to wound; to free herself.

"Wait." The mule whickered, a low creak and shudder of sound. "This is not the Now. You will know the When."

Startled, Grace choked back a flurry of questions. She flinched when the mechanist cuffed the mule, then gripped her bicep and maneuvered her, stumbling, through deep snow to the shack's entry. He lifted a battered plank fitted against the door and thrust her inside.

"Not a word," he hissed. Consumed in shadow, light etched his form. "I'll be back."

Before the door closed and the bar knocked into place from outside, she threw herself at its obstruction. It rattled, groaned, would not yield to her battering. Arms slackening, she turned and pressed her spine to the door. Hearing her own ragged breath, feeling her heart's rapid beat, she stilled and tried to make sense of her surroundings, to recall the interior's dimensions based on a moment's glance.

The shack's dark contours pressed close—thick with the scents of damp wood, animal musk, and neglect; faintly cushioned in sawdust underfoot; hemmed by the weight of objects shared, discarded, forgotten. When she inhaled, the very air coated her nostrils, lay heavily on her tongue: damp wood, rust, and grime. She inched forward and instantly caught her left foot on some obstacle. She stumbled. Hands thrown out, she discovered an intersection of confused angles—a small, gouged plank table; an old chair with broken spindles; wooden crates, stacked carelessly, pried open. Something dislodged from above, fell, and struck her sharply on the crown of her head—a tarnished, scattering sound further described the room's scope as minute pieces flew, jangled, bounced. Gingerly, she touched her head, wincing; the rising contours of a small lump swelled beneath her hairline.

Time crept—imprecise, unfocused, immeasurable. Beyond Grace's confinement, the world prowled, and each passing moment drew the mechanist's imminent return. A jolt of panic lanced through her limbs, hiccupped through her heart's hectic beating. Outside, tree limbs lashed the structure; wind knifed between the boards' seams, flecked her cheeks with snow. Vaguely, she recalled the mule's cryptic words: "*You will know the When. . . .*" She frowned, thoughts rabbiting, and pushed the riddle aside; she focused her energies on her solitary and immediate need—*escape.*

Again, snow-pricked air met her cheek. She started, sucked breath. This breeze—slim, elusive—hinted at exit. With renewed urgency, she moved toward it. The windblown shack creaked and shuddered as she groped her way around the table, edged through the room's dark center past the scratch and scrape of crates until she reached the shack's far side. Here, knot-holed planks snagged her mittens as she felt along the wall for any gap, hole, window; she found none.

Disheartened, she choked back a sob. Then a rush of movement drew her attention—a stir of shadow so swift, so quiet, she almost failed to notice it at all. Faint noise found her ears—a skitter and patter, the softest of treads; a comingled shrill of bright intention. Grace gasped when the prick and tickle and whisper of numerous small, warm bodies climbed her boots, spiraled up her heavy skirts, her cloak and bodice and sleeves.

Field mice. Scores of them.

They did not speak, but Grace heard their purpose within her mind in a quiver of singular voices, joined. Standing motionless, she felt a multitude of tiny claws, the trace of whiskers as, in coordinated motion, the creatures leapt and swam—one after another, singly and in pairs—from her arms, torso, shoulders, to the rough-hewn wall, skittered, drew her attention up up *up*.

Tracking the flow of mousy motion, Grace noticed an odd patch of wall, a piece out of place. The mice slipped over, under, *through*, and hope rekindled. She retraced her steps—back, around the crates, to the gouged, sorely used table. Finding the chair, she fastened hands on it, dragged it behind her, and set it against the wall below the biting, chewing, gnawing, squeaking. Carefully, hands reaching, fastening, she climbed, stood, stretched. Carefully, she felt through the soft-furred, quivering bodies, found the crude outlines of a window, boarded over. She pried at its edges, strained to pull the boards free, could not secure a grip. Then, in a flash, she remembered the jug's handle, stuffed her hand deep into her pocket.

Fingers curled over the broken piece, she wedged it beneath a board, levered and pried. Bits of handle shivered, splintered; rusted nails whined complaint; the board broke free, lifted away, and cold air licked her face. Elated, she applied the fragment of handle to the next board, and the next, wedging, prying, freeing. Dried boards, weather-bitten nails, chips of blue pottery dropped at the chair's feet until the window shed a square of light, and the shack's obscurity peeled away.

For a moment, Grace saw a sickle moon—silver bright—caught in a net of tree limbs beyond the window's cavity. Then, as suddenly, a tremor of noise rose from beyond the shack—the mechanist's voice, recognizable though warped and distorted by weather, scope, reach. Blunt words, clipped, staccato phrases met a second voice, as argument swelled and rose in pitch and volume.

Grace poured her attention on the small opening in the wall—a crooked square of hope, just above her head. Several mice clung to the cobwebbed sill—small tufts and tails in the cold air's wash. Abruptly, the shimmering, falcate moon was swept utterly from view. A hurry of mice swam from the sill, down the wall, over Grace's body. She teetered on the chair. The handle's worn curve flew from her hand, striking the floor in a plume of powder.

"Steady thyself." Wide eyes illumined, a small spectral owl was perched within the rough opening. Its voice slid like a moonbeam on falling snow. "The mules ready distraction."

Grace blinked, understood—the Now, the When was approaching. Hopping down, she navigated the room. She seized a whole, sturdy crate and set it atop the chair. Casting a swift glance over her shoulder at the barred door, she lifted her heavy skirts and scaled the tottering stack. Once her boots were set, she lifted onto her toes and found the owl hunched within the window frame. She met its wide, yellow eyes, tracking its gaze as it swiveled its head toward the Bright Wood's dark, entangled trees, then back to her. Clicking its beak with impatience, it glided on spread wings to a nearby branch where it waited, ghost-like.

From Grace's vantage point, balanced on the crate and facing possible exit, the window seemed impossibly small. Cold air struck her face, and she gulped it down. Covering the sill with her cloak, she hoisted herself up, elbows bent, knees scrabbling. A push, a wriggle, and she filled the space entirely. She heard the crate topple, the chair overturn. The frame narrowed about her hips and shoulders; snarled mittens and skirts and stockings; bit ribs, shins, forearms. Straining, extending, her heart was a wild creature trapped. One final kick, and she fell from the window, expelled outward into cold and dark and snow.

Bruised, battered, Grace untangled her limbs from cloak and skirts, then took several headlong paces. She anchored herself against a young, silver-skinned beech. It still held summer leaves that shivered, skeletally—sere and bleached of color. With a slantwise glance, she beheld the wayfarer's shack through snow-limned lashes—a crooked structure of spare boards and humble intent; the blind, vacant-eyed gap of her escape. She saw, arranged in chaotic pattern on the shack's exterior, the dull gleam of wide, rust-toothed metal jaws. She saw, with a constriction of breath, animal skins—dried, stretched, nailed. Fox. Weasel. Badger. Anger flared, rooted in her belly and uncoiling. Mentally, physically, she shook herself, forcing her gaze elsewhere—her left hand, fisted against the beech's smooth trunk; the crescent moon's deliberate grin; the countless intersections of light and dark, snow and earth and slumbering flora. Every moment she tarried winnowed her choices. She must move forward, onward. Away.

An eruption of noise, a tumult of sound broke the night's stillness—the mules' sudden, desperate brays, long and loud and urgent. A man's voice, angry, hostile; another's, desperate, beseeching. The sharp crack and bang of a door slamming—wood meeting wood with aggressive force. While the clamor of mule and human discord rang, she pushed off the slim tree's support.

Away.

Grace fled. Her only thought was to increase the distance between herself and the shack and mechanist, as quickly as possible. Masses of snow dragged her steps, freighted her skirts. Each breath burned her throat and lungs; her heart throbbed in her skull. Heedless, she ran straight for the Bright Wood's heart.

Branch and bramble snatched at her hair and clothes, snagging at exposed skin. She wondered, fingers numbing, what had become of her right-hand mitten. Pushing forward, deeper, the Wood's subtle design became intelligible, a secret revealed. Trees arranged themselves in a sinuous pattern. She moved between them, along a narrow aisle of snow.

Pulse matched her footsteps' tempo, inhalation matched exhalation of breath. From the corner of her eye, she realized the little owl was gliding silently to her left. Occasionally, its wing tips brushed fallen snow from her shoulder. The wind pushed from behind, an urgent pressure against her back; it tugged her forward by hair and cloak. She skimmed hummocks of white, buried stones, snagging roots. Tiny flakes multiplied—a steady, shielding drift. A thought bloomed in her mind, both comforting and unnerving: *No one will ever find me.*

Trees, slim with youth and ragged with age, pressed close on all sides, weaving a lattice of branches overhead and around her. Dried leaves quaked on bent-fingered branches, scraping and sighing. All about her, formless and malleable, stooped the moon-filtered dark. All sense of which way she had come, how long, how far she had run, slipped away. The realization shook her, and she slowed her step to gain her bearings.

"Don't 🜃 stop." The trees wove their slow, ligneous voices together.

"Swiftly 🜁!" The wind's voice, a sibilant hiss in her ear.

"This way." Overhead, the little owl circled, a patch of pale, fluid shadow.

"Runrunrun!" This last, a piping assertion, came from the depth of her skirt pocket.

Thick with cold and fatigue, the fuel of panic spent, Grace's headlong flight stumbled, slowed. She slipped her hand into her pocket; soft fur grazed her skin, whiskers and small, sharp teeth: a fieldmouse. She laughed—a desperate sound scratched from the night air—while her interior continued a whirring flood of motion. She passed her sleeve over her streaming face, caught a scorched breath, and pressed again into movement.

The owl skimmed on, wove through sheeting snow and steepled branches to lead the way, while the wind continued to push and tug and urge. Grace faltered, unable to recover that shared, synchronous pulse; steps and heart and breath were now in conflict. She picked her way, each step's placement laden by her cloak and skirts, weighted and laced with ice. Damp, graying cold seeped past leather boots, through thick stockings. Fingers, toes, ears numbed. Worry hatched within her. For Murl—his motionless form dull in her mind's eye. For her parents—surely by now, they knew of her absence. For Wolf and Sylvie and all those she cared for. For Thaniel. For herself.

The Bright Wood reared, all-pervading, and Grace stood static amid swirls of snow, amid her own darkening thoughts, unaware, deaf to wind and owl and mouse's entreaties, to the crescent moon's witness high on the night sky's tempered brow. Bone-biting cold and deep weariness settled, and she slipped, knees and toes and hands impressing snow. Lungs heaving, her chin dipped toward her breastbone. Her hair sprawled, loose over broken snow. Absurdly, her thoughts drifted to spring, to Thrush, to sleep and dream . . .

A sudden bright crown of pain dazzled her. Jerking into the present, she reemerged to an urgency of wings. The owl beat about her head, prepared to deliver a second blow. Shielding her face behind her hands, she weathered the well-intentioned assault of beak and talons and wings.

"Steel thyself," Owl said. "Soon, there."

Grace picked herself up and lurched forward, surrendering herself to the owl's flight, the wind's urging, to the retinue of shadows that detached from surrounding dark to flank her. Deer. Long-limbed, slender necked. Powerful. Near silent. Her head filled with their manifold urgings until they distilled into unified tongue and voice:

"Don't stop."

"This way."

"Soon."

"Swiftly."

The steady thud of hooves in her ears sketched a new pattern for her own heavy feet to mimic. The herd moved together, a nimble river banking, edging, swerving. They swept her along in their cervine current, and when they stopped, supported her amid the muscled warmth of their bodies.

Grace swayed, breath sawing, lungs rasping. Her escort scented the wind, slashed their tails, snorted and stamped snow to slick ice. They had reached a thinning of the Bright Wood's depth, where trees and bracken gave way to a broad clearing. Tenuous moonlight spun the snowy plain with silver, delineating the owl's slow ellipse. The wind curled gently over and around her, while at her side, a doe thrust her head beneath Grace's arm, pressing against her, neck and shoulder and body. Grace cherished the doe's sturdy warmth.

After her mad dash from threat and through blizzard and nightfall, owl and wind and deer and trees had led her here, to this place, to presumed safety. Mystified, Grace knew they waited upon her as she scanned the area, straining to comprehend. Slowly, the snow's intensity slackened, thick clouds dispersed, and the clearing took on a vague, identifiable aspect. Blinking snow from her lashes, she swept her face clear, peered through the opaque stream of her own breath, and suddenly saw. Understood.

Grace inhaled the night's ache in a long breath. There, in the middle distance, limbs webbed and silvered with moonlight: The unmistakable form of a great tree grew from the darkness. Not merely any tree; the very same marvelous tree she had discovered all those months ago, the one she had gushed about to her mother, had intended to return to. Eyes shut tight, she shook her head, opened them—the tree remained. Extremities gnawing with cold, she stood exhausted, gazing at the very same tree under which she had found the filly.

A nudge prodded the small of her back. The shape and contour of a deer's skull pressed against her spine and—gently, insistently—urged her forward. Still, she hesitated. With one mittened hand and one bare, she clutched at the deer beside her, conscious of the tight, bristle weave of coarse fur. A flight of deer advanced, grunting, blowing, tails upright, while the herd's body remained at the tree line. Her doe paused, turned, and looked back at her with huge, ink-dark eyes. Bone-weary, Grace followed on heavy legs beyond the protective coverage of trees, over and through an impossible distance of billowing snow toward an improbable goal.

With each step Grace took forward, the tree consumed the night sky's expanse—more than it rationally should. Its massive trunk ascended from snowy earth, a smooth column that supported a graceful and complex fretwork of gradually tapering limbs and branches. She continued until she stood at the tree's base. Neck arched backward, her gaze swept up the tree's undulating patchwork bark. Ivory, dove-gray, creamy brown. Beneath her touch, the trunk radiated . . . warmth. Surprised, Grace pressed her cold cheek against toothless bark, felt a slight, welcome, and undeniable heat.

A small choking sound escaped her as she slid down the tree's length. Collapsing among its roots, she folded her body against the generous trunk, absorbing unlikely warmth through sodden wool. Like twilight, awareness of her surroundings flickered, hovered—the small owl above her on bent branch; a deer, its head in her lap, and another pressed to her side; the fieldmouse curled asleep in her pocket. Deftly, the wind rose, blew a semicircular drift just beyond her bent knees. Consciousness dwindled. Her eyelids slid shut, and Grace sank, succumbing to exhaustion.

CHAPTER THIRTY-TWO

She dreamt. The strength of her roots wound deep within the earth, through leaf mold and loam and soil, until she curled tendriled toes around stone and anchored herself securely into rocky fissures. Stretching, she lifted strong, graceful limbs upward, smooth in grain and gesture and of pale shifting color, in both light and shadow. She shook her crown of leaf-green filaments until it spilled to the very tips of her fingers. She drank deeply of sweet rain and deeper, earthbound water, of sunlight. Her veins coursed with amber sap.

A gown of velvety green moss flocked her torso and limbs. All of life sheltered within her arms, within the crooks of her elbows and behind her knees, in the deep hollow of her throat and belly, and at the very base of her spine. She was filled, entirely, with sibilant whirs and shushes, rustles and whispers, and she fed and nourished each and all on small-petaled flowers and spheres of seeded fruit, on leaves and bark and cambium.

Heir of earth and water, sibling to the wind, descendant of sun and moon—she was all of these. Whole. Eternal. Beyond time.

CHAPTER THIRTY-THREE

When—like fading song, drift of leaves, arc of seasons—the rime of sleep fell slowly away, Grace resurfaced, remerged in creeping increments. Gradually, she lifted from within the tide of verdant, whispered dream, and comprehension slewed. How diminished her frame, how rootless, fragile, solitary.

Time—suspended in lengths both measurable and *not*—roused, yawned, and repossessed her in a faint clamor and cascade of voices: interwoven, overlapped, confounding. She labored to join in, respond; with lips and mouth and teeth, to speak . . . *to speak?* Again, confusion. Words would not come. Bark dry, her lips and throat; brittle as autumn leaves, her tongue. Dormant, chlorophylled, a hush of breath escaped her . . . inarticulate. A rustle and stir of sound, distinct from those persistent voices that pressed, *impressed*, from all sides, from without.

Amid intermittent darkness, disorientation shifted, surged. Consciousness grew—a soft glow about the edges, small pricks and sparks of light and color, trailing, vining. Memory skimmed slowly as Grace struggled briefly to *see*, to open her eyes. She winced at the field of white that consumed her vision, dazzling compared to the patterned darkness of her closed lids. Two smooth white plains, bound in dark ribs, sloped upward, met and flanked a central shaft's stroke. It hurt to look at them, straightened and shaped, driven through with iron, separated from their source. She heard, now, a moan—soft, low—joining the susurrant voices.

Squinting, blinking, she understood at length, that she beheld a ceiling, that she was *inside*. Stiffly, she stirred her limbs, turning her heavy crown toward the light's source. Bright luster, trapped within a square transparency—a window, four watery panes of glass, bound and trimmed and set in a white-plastered wall. Eyelet curtains, cotton white and sprigged with white embroidery, stirred gently with the breeze. She considered the shifting curtain, the window. The four-square panes of glass opened on a truncated segment of clear blue sky. Deep within her core, beyond confusion, recognition flickered.

Assembled on the window's ledge, chattering to themselves, huddled a quarrel of sparrows. The creatures bustled in and out of focus—small, robust, chaotic;

composed of earth and dust. They reacted to observation, bobbed and flitted, chittered noisily: "*Awakeawakeawake!*" The air thrummed with wing-stirred excitement.

Grace shifted and drew one limb—her *arm*; how pliant, how frail, exposed, and unprotected—from beneath a layered weight of fabric. Vaguely, she understood that she lay in a bed not of moss and earth, but of wool blankets, cotton sheets, and coverlets. Lengthening her arm toward the window, toward the commotion of sparrows, she gestured, opening her palm. The motion sapped all her strength, and she let her arm fall back against rumpled blankets. The sparrows' squabbling increased.

Her fingers—crooked, spare—extended over the bed's edge, and she felt something graze their tips, damp and cool, insistent. Here vision sparked as she worked her way up on stiff elbows, levering trunk and limbs partly upright. Again, the breath and breeze channeled through her as she peered, blinking, past the cascade of blankets, the spill of crisp sheets. Her heart understood before her thinking mind, connected and attached to deep-rooted memory. Flop ears, brown-and-white coat, neck ruff; lopsided doggie grin.

"You're awake!" Murl yapped.

Grace struggled to form the name, her tongue to speak it: "Murl . . ." An image flickered—the dog's limp body sprawled over white snow. She blinked the vision away.

"You slept and slept and slept!" Murl interrupted. Sweeping his tail in a wide arc, setting his front paws on the blankets. "I missed you. You walk *with* me." He licked any exposed skin with enthusiasm, sloppily smudged her chin and cheeks and jawline, the tip of her nose.

Swiftly, the otherwise static room spun into motion. A surge of other voices lapped one against another. Hands upon her, arms about her—Grace felt herself lifted upright from pillows and bedclothes, wrapped in a fierce, warm embrace. Cries of disbelief and delight, released like small flights of birds against her ears. Hot tears—was she weeping?—traced the contours of her face. Scents of orange blossom, of lily of the valley . . .

A word, both name and title, chafed in her throat: "Mother?"

"Oh, yes, my girl," Lettie cried. Between sobs and laughter, she kissed Grace's cheeks. "*Yes, yes, yes.* Oh, I'm *here.*"

Grace felt clothed in the embrace—a garment of sunlight, wreathing ivy, a frill of lichen flung over her neck and shoulders. When her mother released her, eased her gently back against heaped pillows, re-tucked sheets and smoothed blankets, Grace studied her face, reading an unfamiliar story there. Fine lines traced her mother's eyes and mouth. Emotion flickered across it—grief and pain and joy rekindled—like trees' spring-born leaves, meadow grasses, light shivering over water.

"Gaven!" her mother called out, voice thin, high, trembling. She tethered herself to Grace with one hand, pressing her other hand—fingers splayed—over her own heart. "Gaven, come! Quick! She's awake!"

"All this fuss!"

A near-imperceptible thump—more felt than heard—depressed the mattress near Grace's shoulder. Swiveling her head, the room swam and slurred; fur obscured Grace's view as whiskers pricked and tickled her skin.

"*I* knew you would return." Sylvie slinked past Murl, dragging her tail along the dog's snout. Purring, she struck her small, hard skull against Grace's chin, scrubbed up along the bare, smooth length of human jaw.

"You got help for Murl. . . ." Grace felt the cat's deep rumbling through her periphery, vibrating inward.

"Of course." Pragmatic and unoffended, Sylvie kneaded the blankets.

Steps sounded beyond the bedroom door, rapid as pulse or rain or woodpecker's drumming. Hurried, thudding. With tilt and turn of head, Grace's vision smeared anew. She saw her father enter the crowding room, Wolf padding at his side.

"Ah Grace, Gracie . . ." Her father knelt awkwardly at the bedside, clutched at her mother's free hand. Blinking back tears, his gaze skated between wife and daughter. "Our girl is back." He dropped his gray head between the curve of Grace's neck and shoulder, choking back a sob.

Wolf sat a pace away, moon-yellow eyes steady, unblinking. He wore a mild lupine expression. "Your blood is fierce," he growled with soft approval.

From all sides, Grace emerged from slumber, surrounded. Voices—human, animal, elemental—filled her head, ears, bones, and flesh. A wave of elation lifted her—her parents', her friends'. The small room clamored, swelled, expanded with sensation near to bursting; near to engulfing, swallowing her whole, so much so that she did not, immediately, see Thaniel behind her mother and father, to the left of Wolf. Standing in the doorway, still as thought. As wish. As truth.

Her vision settled on him. Despite the whirl of emotion, of senses oversaturated, she felt swiftly anchored in place and time. In this moment. Here and now. Her ears sang with her parents' weeping and laughter, and her flesh absorbed the warmth of their embraces. Soon, her mother and father paused to trace the line of their daughter's vision; through the cleft of their shoulders, their joy, they settled on its source. Stiffly, Gaven pressed himself up from his knees, and, smiling, Lettie placed a kiss on Grace's forehead.

"Thaniel, oh, please, please come in." Her mother rose, patted the bedclothes, and beckoned him to take her place. Turning to Grace, she said, "He has been to see you every day."

With her mother's words drifting softly against her ear, like the sparrows strutting on the windowsill, Grace watched Thaniel enter, saw how he clasped her father's hand and bent to receive her mother's hug. She wondered if her parents were somehow smaller, diminished, or merely seemed so when measured against Thaniel.

"We should have tea." Lettie dried her eyes on her apron. "Tea and bread. And a pot of jam."

Gaven put his arm about his wife, drew her gently to himself and guided her from the room. Looking back, he smiled at Grace. "Daughter," he said. Simple affirmation. Unadorned delight.

Listening to their steps, Grace knew they had paused in the hall; she heard her mother's muffled sobs. She pictured her parents holding each other close, her mother weeping against her father's chest while he stroked her loose-bound hair. The image both warmed and wounded her.

As Thaniel approached and sat on the bed's edge, Grace fixed her full attention on him. He did not speak; he was content, it seemed, simply to look at her. She felt the brush of his enfolding gaze—calm, grounded, full of banked heat. Idly, he scratched Wolf's ruff until Murl whined and trotted around the foot of the bed, expectant. Sylvie arched and stretched, curling against Grace's ribs so the cat's purring underscored the increased beating of her own heart.

It seemed, as Grace returned Thaniel's gaze, that the reality of him remained obscured by the haze of sleep, or memory, or dream. She blinked, tilted her head, unable to assemble the whole of him in a single glance. Slowly, carefully, she considered him: the smooth planes of his cheeks and jaw, the angle of his chin, the eloquence of his mouth. It was as if she needed to commit him to memory, to inscribe his image indelibly in her mind's eye. With a sharp constriction of heart, she saw concern in his eyes, and adoration, and . . . something other. She recalled—so recent, so long ago—the wind's teasing.

"I have *missed* you." The words shifted and rustled in her mouth, tasted raw and green and whispery. Her voice remained as strange to her ear as it did to her tongue.

"And me," Murl woofed, "and *me*!"

Wolf swung a silencing gaze in Murl's direction.

"Hush, dog," Sylvie rumbled, eyes closed.

Thaniel, unaware, laughed softly. "*I* have missed *you*." He took her hand, netted his fingers with hers, and shook his head. Sun-stroked brown hair chased about his bent shoulders. "You have been away far longer than I." The assertion sounded raw on his lips.

In a vague, detached way, deep in her cells, she understood his statement as true. Nuance crouched in his voice; shadows flickered across his face, caught in his eyes. She relished the warmth of his hand, his skin against hers; she shifted her gaze sideways, slantwise, tried to remember . . . something, something important and vast, otherwise and elsewhere. Brow furrowed, she brushed her fingers' tips to one temple. A weight of exhaustion flooded her limbs, throbbed within her crown, against the front of her skull. The memory remained shrouded, blurred in a tangle of green.

"Don't . . ." Thaniel said.

She felt his hand on her brow as his voice, like a breath on glass, pulled her from green entanglement, back toward him. Calm, smooth, forcibly unruffled—his tone evoked rushing, dormant recall. Visits to homes and farms and barnyards, in all seasons and all weather. Thaniel—placating, healing, easing distressed creatures and their human fellows. He spoke so to her now, amused, confused, troubled. Inhaling deeply, she intended to tease him, struggled instead to lift her lids. When had she closed her eyes?

"Gently . . ."

Hearing the churn of emotion in his tone, in his choice of words, roused curiosity within her. Ignoring him, she struggled against overgrowing torpor to inch herself up a bit higher.

"Why?" A small, dried, leaflet word on her tongue. She sank her elbows in the mattress, clutched blankets, levered herself *up*.

"You'd do well to heed him." Sylvie stretched, flexed paws. Yawning, she rearranged herself against Grace's side, settled in with tail tip curled over her front paws.

Yielding to her own weakened limbs, Grace sank back within a filter of green-tinged peripheral vision. She half-frowned, puzzled by her heart's rapid skip and scamper, amplified by Thaniel's measured quiet. Yet when he ran his fingers over her hair, smoothed back the mass of wayward filaments, her tension bled away. Carefully, she studied his expression, the subtle shifts in his countenance as he leaned over her—slight compression of lips, narrowing of eyes, the unnatural calm. The scent of him, pine and cedar and sandalwood, rippled through her as, with deft fingers, he separated a tress of her hair.

"Look," he said, and lifted the lock for her inspection.

Grace stared at him, reluctant to let go the upswell of associations taking root in her fixed attention. At length, she allowed her gaze to slip from his face and beheld, twirled loosely in his fingers among strands of her hair, the unexpected. A curiosity. A pale green vining tendril coiled through the hairs' length, entwined through the filaments. Sprouting from the vine at even intervals were smooth, oblong glossy leaves, marginally toothed.

Chin tucked to shoulder, she touched her hair, lifted another length, found it similarly adorned. The vine itself was warm to her fingers' touch. Gently, she tugged, feeling the report of her scalp. As she let the loose curl fall from her fingers, her vision stumbled, veered toward her forearm. Slowly, she rotated wrist and elbow, studied the thin veins traced beneath the skin—pale blue, violet, and palest green.

"I . . . what . . ." Even now, her voice shushed in her ears like wind-stirred leaves. She wondered when, *if*, surprise or alarm might register. She sought clarity in Thaniel's face.

"Not all things are for our understanding." Half-smiling, he met her gaze and shook his head again.

She knew he chose his words carefully, heard the calming tenor he utilized to soothe, to pacify. His smile, though—the curve of his mouth, one corner lifted slightly—she knew the expression, its authenticity.

"Some things," he added, "are for *accepting*."

His fingers, warm against her skin as he lifted her hand, traced the fine faint green veins branching from her wrist to her elbow's crook. Where they slipped from view beneath the sleeve of her nightdress, he reversed his finger's defining path, back down to her wrist. She watched as he turned her hand over, lifting it toward his bent head. The loose brown waves of his hair screened his features, but Grace caught his breath, his want, his kiss within the hollow of her palm.

"I lost your gift," she whispered with vague memory. "The comb."

Thaniel lifted his head, eyes bright. "*You* are here."

The calm of his voice slipped sideways inside her, his words caught in the web of her being.

"Nothing else matters."

CHAPTER THIRTY-FOUR

Each day announced itself in segments: small flourishes followed by extraordinary change. Grace learned to accept that she had spent the winter in dormancy, buried first in snow, then in a deep sleep filled with arboreal dreaming, green and alive. She had slumbered through the winter solstice and awakened to the seamless buzz of tender, early spring. Memory bloomed in ordinary moments—an owl's nocturnal query, a too-firm embrace, the patch of furless skin that silvered Murl's jaw. She integrated, slowly—the old and new, the before and after, the *all*—with her small, singular, solitary self. To her vague surprise, she wore these truths—large and small—easily, like a veil of light, of mist.

"Here, Grace, dear." Her mother set a cup on the small table, alongside a vase filled with butter-yellow primrose. "Drink some tea."

Grace glanced up, not precisely startled, but reminded, slantwise, of where and when and how she presently existed.

"Mom," she said, smiling up at her mother, reading clearly the concern Lettie hoped to conceal. "I can make my own tea. I'm fine."

"And disturb Sylvie?" Her mother scoffed and shook her head, folding her hands over her apron. "Don't be silly." She appeared, to Grace's eye, leaner, narrower; worry etched the thin flesh about her eyes, threaded her hair with spun silver.

Sylvie yawned and stretched. "You haven't yet been awake nearly as long as you slept." Resettling herself in Grace's lap, the tabby cat angled her chin over her front paws. "Allow your dam her comforts."

Picking up the teacup, Grace laced her fingertips around its glazed curves and sipped.

"Rosehip," she said, and leaned back in her chair, face upturned to meet her mother's eye. "It tastes like summer. Thank you." Blinking her eyes closed, she accepted the kiss her mother placed on her forehead.

She sat before the licking hearth, aware of winter's lingering chill. The room swam with particled light—bright, brash, and fresh-rinsed in improbable spring. Shutters were pressed flush against white-washed walls and offered a glimpse of the world beyond that shivered with nascent warmth and life and small, green budding things. All the household's members hovered near at hand—her parents in the kitchen; Murl stretched on the hearthrug to her right, with Wolf to her left; and Sylvie rumbling contentment in her lap. All within a pace's reach, vigilant, attentive.

Fingers still curled around her cup, she sipped rosehip and honey, and noticed anew the veins on the backs of her hands. No longer a tracery of slim blue rivulets, but rather the pale, lively green of fiddleheads and Solomon's seal, of luna moths' dusty wings. Tea in hand, steam warming her face, she extended her legs, bare feet—similarly veined and hued. She flexed her toes at the hearth's low-banked flames.

With uncommon grace, she *accepted*—although frequently, her head swam.

Her attention was lingering over the rim of her cup when a knock sounded at the door. The cottage constricted slightly, protectively. The sound of the knocking perforated the room. Shining with the subtle light of a five-pointed star, an ivy leaf, tendriled through her hair, slipped forward over her shoulder.

"I'll get it," Gaven said. Swiping the spectacles from his eyes into his shirt pocket, his heels thumped a sharp tattoo against the floor. Pipe in hand, he pulled the door open.

There, on the doorstep, awash in light, stood Bran. His shadow—blue-black contrast to his own burnished gold—fell across the threshold, over her father. Daily, Bran called, with the consistency of cock's crow, moonrise, or a herd's instinctive return from pasture. She had observed the pattern from the staircase; from the backyard; from the small window of her room, scattered with doves and sparrows, that peered down over the kitchen garden. The newly established interaction held the formality of dance. Often, the door itself remained beyond reach—her mother or father or both intercepted him at the front path, gate, or garden arch. Time and again, her parents denied him entry, shook their heads, turned their backs, firmly shut gate or door. Always, Bran left without argument, head bowed like a sunset.

With each of his visits, the green-clad portal of her memory yawned, widened, spilled a froth of soft-edged images. Grace set down the cup, drew in her outstretched legs, and noted—as Sylvie protested, as both Murl and Wolf, in unison, lifted to all fours—the stiffening of her father's posture, the erosion of Bran's.

"Bran?" she called—in recognition, in welcome, her words a verdant rustle on her tongue. She felt the weight of her father's deliberation, observed him searching out her mother's eye as the two lingered in wordless communication. Frowning, her father nodded, spoke to Bran in a voice pitched too low for Grace to hear, words punctuated with small, sharp thrusts of his pipe's stem. She watched Bran extend his hand, saw her father stare at it, unmoved.

"Let's not be hasty." Gaven surveyed the younger man, speaking around his pipe through a wreath of smoke. "It's a partial welcome. And a conditional one." Hands thrust in pockets, he stepped aside.

Bran—clearly astonished to gain entry, and fearful it might be revoked—crossed the threshold. Approaching Lettie, he handed her a clutch of violets, purple with yellow throats. "It's not enough, I know," he said. "I'll make it up to you, all of you."

Lettie took the bouquet. Her smile, though worn at the edges, held warmth. "In time." Her gaze wandered over Bran's shoulder to her husband, and she repeated: "In time." She patted Bran's hand lightly. "Can I pour you a cup of tea?"

Bran shook his head, scattering rays of light.

Grace felt his hesitancy, the race and skip of his heart's beat, his restricted breath. She felt her father's protectiveness and her mother's wary, faded cheer. Murl and Wolf moved to flank her chair, the staccato click of their claws scoring wood, jaws clamped on full-throated growls.

"He smells of the other one," Wolf said, snarling, head swung low.

Where once Murl greeted visitors happily, now the fur lifted from the base of his ruff, a whine issuing from his throat.

"Hush." Grace's tone defined all the small, recent heartbreaks in an attempt to soothe both dog and wolf, mother and father; to reassure and pacify. Then, although Sylvie remained near-motionless in her lap—ears and tail tip merely twitching—she smoothed sparking fur and repeated, "Hush."

Grace tracked Bran's measured progress through the cottage until he stood—head bent, shoulders bowed—at her chair. Chin lifted, she observed him—this near stranger, this almost-friend. A bright young man, so near her own age. His hands flexed and closed, one over the other, on emptiness. Though he neither gasped nor recoiled, his lips parted on silence. Unprepared for the change he was witnessing, his eyes registered a jolt, reshaping his features.

"You found me, didn't you?"

Did her hair merely shift against her shoulders, or did the threading vines react to his presence? She extended a hand—traced with green veins—to him.

"At the tree?"

She saw him falter, his light waver and dim as the great tree's image grew between them: a vast network of pale branches that screened and separated, of spreading, underground roots.

Bran stared at her hand, her fingers, and shook his head. "*We* did." He tipped his head toward Wolf, avoided connecting with that feral gaze.

"I'm indebted to you both." She set her hand in her lap, curled it loosely with its mate, like two leaves sprouting from her skirt's folds.

A small, restricted sound escaped Bran's throat—a rabbit, snared; a mink, trapped. He passed a hand over his eyes, broad and strong, and moaned, stumbled, knees to floorboards. Sylvie leapt aside as Bran lay his head in Grace's lap.

"I didn't know. . . ." His frame heaved and shook as he sobbed. "I swear it. I didn't know . . . but I should have . . . should have suspected . . . something . . ."

"It's all in the past now," she said.

His grip bruised her shins, her calves. Lightly, she touched the mass of sun-bright filaments, moved her green-veined hands to cup his jaw's contours. She heard threat thicken the throats of her self-appointed guard, and insisted, "Over. Done."

"How can you say that?" With an upward jerk of his head, he stared at her, blue eyes clouded. "After what he did . . . what he might have done?"

Collecting the shards of his words in her lap's hollow, she quirked a small smile. "This past year has been . . . an education. In the unexpected. In change." She grazed the stubbled line of his jaw with her fingertips, then turned over her hands and held them, fingers spread, for his inspection.

Hesitantly, he brushed a leaf-green vein at her wrist, then withdrew his touch, hand rounded into a fist. He heaved a great sigh and, lifting a hunted gaze, whispered, "I'm sorry."

"I know." She inclined her head toward him.

Choking back a gasp, he bowed forward again; he professed all, everything, to her lap and knees, to her green-veined hands and exposed forearms. Without interruption, she listened with the whole of her being to his vows, his pleas, his plans of recompense: his anger toward his father—the tinker, the mechanist.

"After so many years apart," he said, bitterness eclipsing his words, "I thought he wanted to begin again. I thought he wanted a son . . . *me*." Reflexively, he gripped her skirt. "Please. Forgive me."

"It wasn't you," she said, though her own recollections crept and roiled. She regarded these memories—distant, vague—as peculiar offspring, wounded creatures to be soothed and tended.

"I should have known." Voice scraping, he repeated his earlier refrain. He looked at her askance—eyes blue as grief—and shook his head. "I've been a fool."

"He's your father." Grace wondered at the term—for herself, one of trust and endearment; for Bran, something emphatically . . . other. "You love him." She heard, behind her, Gaven snort and mutter something about apples, trees, and falls of brief distance.

Color flared in Bran's cheeks. "As I said, a fool."

"Is it really so foolish? To hope for the good in others?" she asked.

Expression darkening, he grimaced, nodded. "Yes. Sometimes. More often than I'd like."

Grace heard the lopsided click of Murl's claws as the dog—ruff and tail lowered—sidled closer.

"He's sad," Murl said. Inserting a damp snout beneath Grace's elbow, he slid it under her forearm, fitting his head beneath her ribs.

"Very," Grace agreed. She stroked his white-splotched fur, rubbed the small silvery scar on his jaw. Though Wolf and Sylvie remained aloof, apart, she felt the friction of their doubts and suspicions, as well as those of her parents, who made a veiled pretense of attending to mundane tasks.

Her mother called a gentle yet firm conclusion to the visit: "Dr. Endrue will be here soon, Grace."

Bran dragged himself to standing, and Grace followed him—her green-shaded steps rustling and whispering—to the cottage's door. Feeling the trace of his stare, she held the door wide. Sunlight flared off him, while her own skin drank it in, internally transformed it.

"Oh." Bran blinked, swallowed, then reached into his pocket. "I found this. In the snow. Not long after . . ." His voice trailed off, words mislaid, and he pressed something into her palm.

She knew before she saw it: silk and satin cupped in her hand—Thaniel's bloom. Bruised, muddied, feather-weight petals limp.

"Ah . . ." She exhaled and caught it to her sternum, beaming at Bran.

"Grace?" Her father's voice, studiously neutral.

"It's all right, I'm going." Bran stepped outside, a blaze among the dooryard garden's cool moss and fiddleheads. He paused, turned; his glance swiveled between the cottage's interior and Grace. With a sidelong look, he asked her, "Will *they* forgive me?"

Still cupping silk and satin, she shrugged and looked at him. "*I* do."

CHAPTER THIRTY-FIVE

As when her gift first claimed her, word spread through Edgewoode from tongue to ear—her encounter with the mechanist-turned-tinker, her flight to the great tree, her transformation and return. After an appropriate span of time had elapsed, the town's populace arrived—singly; in pairs; in small, curious knots. Knuckles rapped upon the family's cottage door, separated at times by days, more often by mere hours. They arrived bearing gifts of food and household goods, hoping to look, marvel, and set eyes upon the extraordinary and remarkable, their very own "Other."

Wolf raised his head from his paws, ears pricking. His moon-yellow eyes were fixed upon the wooden door. A low rumble filled his throat: "Another approaches."

"At this hour?" Sylvie yawned, displaying neat rows of sharp white teeth. She lay stretched upon wide oak floorboards in a drift of midmorning sunlight, one ear swiveled backward.

Grace lay her book down in her lap and listened beyond the cottage's fieldstone walls. She heard patterns of dappled light and the slow growth of vines clambering over the garden arch.

"Is it Dr. Endrue again?" Resignation colored her tone.

Murl trotted to the door and pressed his nose against its seam. "I smell muffins." His tail swept a wide arc.

Alert to her daughter's sudden shift in attention, Lettie looked up from her mending. "Should I put on the kettle?" She searched Grace's face. "Or open the back door?"

In a moment—a breath, a heartbeat—Grace would succumb to questions, idle chatter, side-eyed scrutiny. Slipping from her chair, she said, "Back door."

Having regained herself, she more typically welcomed the visitors—their curiosity and trepidation, their wonder. The men turned their hats in their worn, calloused hands, hopeful she would be strong enough, *well* enough to assist during shearing, calving, and milking seasons, and waited uncomfortably on her reassurances. Children traced her green-tinted veins, and women marveled at her hands and arms, touched her vine-tendriled hair. Two days ago, she had sat for an hour as Adelaide wove white anemones, blue scilla, and lengths of lace ribbons through her hair; the little lacemaker had recommitted herself to advocating on behalf of her son, Sturn, and his innumerable fine qualities.

Now, though, Grace dashed across the room, pausing within the backdoor's wide-open promise. Looking out over the backyard, past its bustle of scratching chickens, beyond the neatly fenced, neighboring pasture and distant swaying meadow, she glimpsed the Bright Wood's deep-green boundary.

"Thaniel's not here yet." Lettie stood at Grace's shoulder; once calm, resolute, she now fretted.

"I'll meet him on the path," Grace assured. The iron scents of damp earth and thaw lifted. Cool, budding air stroked and invited. Everything—every *thing*—vibrated, crooned, whispered.

Her mother turned and addressed Wolf and Murl and Sylvie, arranged in a half-circle about Grace. With one hand on her hip, she pointed at each of the assemblage in turn. "Take care of our girl."

Three pairs of eyes considered her—pale yellow, warm brown, clear green. She wrapped a shawl around Grace's shoulders. "I wish I were certain they understood me. . . ."

"They do." Grace smiled and kissed her mother's upturned cheek. As the telltale knock rapped the front door, she escaped through the back—down the steps, outside. Away.

Through the muddied backyard, scattering flustered hens, Grace moved—rootless—on legs still reacquainting themselves with use. Somewhere ahead, along the packed-earth road that defined the forest's undulating western border, Thaniel strode to meet her. Together, with her retinue, they would enter the Bright Wood. It was a desire—a *determination*—she knew unsettled her parents.

She empathized, but lengthened her stride anyway. With each passing day, the need within her swelled, doubled, trebled. An urgency matched by her own restoration of physical strength to return, revisit, *see* that spot where Bran and Wolf had found her months ago.

Grace fixed her gaze ahead, breathing in the forest's blue-green shadow. Her boots sucked and squelched along the spring, rain-softened path. Familiar company attended her—Sylvie prowled unheard, unseen; Wolf loped easily several paces ahead; Murl dashed back and forth, up and down, sending up screens of mud. An indiscernible thread tethered each member so that—alerted by cat and dog and wolf—she learned of Thaniel's presence before she could possibly have seen him.

"Are you certain?" He waited within a shower of green-filtered light, beneath a bow of slender, budding alders. Catching her hands in his own, he studied her face.

"Utterly." Grace smiled up at him. Her hair vined and rustled about her neck and shoulders, inched into the loose weave of her mother's shawl. Beyond the Bright Wood's edge, within the deeply forested half-light, she heard the slippery, ice-thickened gurgle of water. They would follow the stream, as she had after the storm last autumn, when she and Murl, Sylvie, Wolf, and Thrush had searched for the lost foal, Falla.

"Lead on," Thaniel said.

Grace squeezed his hands and slipped between the trees. The Bright Wood swam over her, over them, crisp and fresh and shimmering. It pulsed with the voices of creatures awakening from dormancy; with green, vegetative thoughts and complex layers of spring song. Her steps sank through snowmelt and pine needles and damp leaf mold, through seasons and a stratum of years past. The burgeoning Wood swelled about her, and she responded with each cell and mote and fiber, with each breath and heartbeat.

"Wolf says we're almost there." Murl bounded back and forth along the trail, unable to contain his excitement.

Sylvie materialized beneath a camouflaging clump of bronze ferns. "His claim is, technically, accurate." Tail tip ticking, she extended her whiskers to their full, trembling length.

Grace met Thaniel's eye and translated: "Just a little farther."

She ducked the curtain of wild roses Thaniel held aside. The forest thinned, fell back in stages. Pine needles, decayed leaves of oak and maple and beech gave way to early woodland blooms—yellow trout lilies and pale windflowers scattered among unrolling fiddleheads. Ahead, angles of tree-filtered light broke in pale gold, pollen-dusted shafts over the frantic velvet flutter of mourning cloak moths.

At the boundary, that confluence of edges where forest and meadow met, Grace paused, keenly aware of her companions. Murl emulated Wolf's posture—ears pricked, body taut—and scented the air; Sylvie switched her tail over Grace's skirts and ankles; and Thaniel stood at her left shoulder. A small exhilaration swept through her. Dog, cat, wolf, man—each a unique and individual presence; a compass point; a bastion; an affirmation to her being.

Ahead, the clearing pulsed with spring, bright and unabashed. Grace blinked against spangled light. Her breath fluttered in her throat's hollow like a leaf or feather; her pulse, like a scintillant particle of light. The Bright Wood spread itself wide, and she peered into its vibrant, meadow-filled heart.

"There . . ." She pointed toward the middle distance and reached for Thaniel's hand.

The great tree stood at the meadow's center. It both consumed and defied comprehension in a single glance. So much so that vision and conscious thought sought to diminish its scope to a more comprehensible size, as the senses might grapple with boundless sky or limitless ocean. Where at first glance, a dense copse of trees stood, the reality of a single, massive trunk grew skyward, with limbs and crown extending in width and spread and height, to dominate the meadow-scape.

"Is it really . . . *there*?"

Grace heard the catch of Thaniel's indrawn breath, his bewilderment, and she squeezed his fingers, drawing him with her, out from beneath the Bright Wood's canopy. Her feet followed her body's memory; her steps gathered up and measured the meadow's dips and swells. Sweet grasses lapped at her skirt's hem. The air hummed, and her veins rang. Each forward pace decreased distance and separation, until the tree's tumbled drift of greening shadow fell over her, over them.

Standing at its base, chin lifted as vine- and leaf-twined hair spilled down her back, Grace took in the complex warp and weft of networked branches. The tree revealed all of its incongruous nature. In full leaf and bud and fruit and bloom, pale-petaled tassels, and soft yellow-brown, pendant spheres suspended beneath broad, green-leaved limbs, while the tree's neighbors hesitated to push out tight green buds.

"It's . . . too big . . ." Thaniel stood at the tree shadow's edge, blinking.

"It's smaller than I remember." She peered up through a light-and-shadow pattern of star-shaped leaves and wondered when she had lost hold of Thaniel's hand.

"Is that possible?"

Wolf scratched at a moss-covered root. "It is neither too big, nor too small. It *is* as it *is*."

"Humans . . ." Sylvie's gaze darted about the dense canopy. "Such skeptics."

"I don't like ticks." Murl paused mid-roll among a clutch of wildflowers, white belly shining, legs kicking. "Ticks bite."

Grace scratched Murl's ribs as the dog curled head-to-haunches and chewed on his hind foot. Then, stepping carefully on and around and over thick, turf-boring roots, she circled the tree's massive trunk. Silver-, ivory-, and brown-mottled bark ran beneath her fingers' touch. Completing a full circuit, she lingered, her gaze drawn to a hollow depression of root and trunk. A tangle of slim young suckers and slender rootlets laced a shallow cavity; each tip, snapped and broken; a raw, pale, fibrous wound.

"This," Grace said. No need to speculate. No need for confirmation. "*Here* . . ."

Wolf rumbled; Murl whined; Sylvie batted at broken roots with sickle claws.

Thaniel merely nodded.

For a moment, she considered, then slid down the tree's smooth trunk. Knees bent, legs folded with feet curled beneath her, she tucked herself into the healing wound. The hollow fit perfectly, contoured to the shape of her body—skull, shoulder, hip, and legs. With her left cheek pressed to the tree's trunk, she spread her right palm and fingers over its mottled bark, warmth beneath her touch. She sensed a low, slow, steady thrum.

Grace closed her eyes. Almost, she remembered; almost, she could reimagine—the suckers and tendrils grown to embrace her form, to cocoon her in improbable warmth and safety on that now-distant, frozen night. Ear pressed to the great tree's torso, she recognized its whispered, leafy voice. Grounding. Sonorous. Shelter assured. The voice had filled her prolonged slumber's dreaming; had, implausibly, sustained her through a long winter's night and borne her into dawning spring. The voice she would carry with her always.

She understood everything and nothing. The truths she sought and found here defied comprehension. The tree would keep its secrets. Opening her eyes, she blinked up through the sap-drenched light at Thaniel.

"I thought I might remember something . . . more. Something *else*." She pressed her palm to the tree's bark, reluctant to surrender contact, and looked up again through crowded branches. A half-formed thought germinated at the back of her head; more likely, a memory half-forgotten and rapidly falling away.

Months ago, that night, she had absorbed some deep understanding through her flesh, into her bones and psyche. It now coursed through her veins like sap and vined through her hair like a careless crown. The memory, however, the *knowing*, had tumbled away when she awoke; it would endure teasingly out of reach, semi-dormant within her. She felt the weight of four pairs of eyes watching, measuring her, and pushed herself from the tree's trunk, up and to her feet.

"I still don't understand." She shook her head, hair whispering in leaves.

"Did your uncle? Who was it?" Thaniel searched her face. "The one who glowed."

"Talbin? Maybe not. I don't know." One hand grazing the tree's trunk, she stood an arm's length from him, a veritable bridge between two worlds. "He adapted. And my aunt knit nightcaps and stitched quilts."

"You'll adapt, too," he said. "Give it time."

"That," she said, considering him, "is your answer for everything."

The corner of his mouth lifted in an amused half-smile. "It's an answer I've found well-suited to a great many situations."

Sylvie yawned approval. "Indeed."

The great tree continued to drone beneath Grace's touch. Peeling her fingers from patchwork bark, she broke the direct connection and stepped backward over thick roots—roots that knuckled and knotted earth, ducked and dove and emerged from damp soil and thick, moss mats with an indecipherable pattern. In two steps, she halved the distance between herself and Thaniel, then wove her fingers through his.

"You," she said, looking up at him. Dappled light reflected in his eyes, his smooth brow, his composed features.

"What of me?" Grinning, he confirmed their enmeshed fingers with a squeeze.

Head tilted slightly to one side, she looked up at him slantwise. Returning his hand's gentle pressure, she shook her head, but did not release his gaze. She pulled herself close, into him. She laid her cheek against his chest, resting her head within the hollow of his neck and shoulder. The weight of his arms about her hips, the steady thud of his heart against her own made sense—there was no need for the wind's coy remarks.

Eyes closed, she listened beyond Thaniel, beyond herself—to the meadowlark singing his domain; the field mouse darting among the grasses' roots; the arch and yawn of wildflowers; and, of course, to the tree. The rise and fall of all those voices, each overlaid one upon another, created a singular harmony. Though rooted, snug within Thaniel's arms, she felt herself joined to that song—until a small thump and slide against her ankles interrupted.

"Why do you *leave*?" Sylvie asked, with a note of feline pique.

Grace laughed. She leaned out and down from Thaniel's arms to stroke the cat's sleek form.

"So you can call me back," she said to Sylvie. Addressing Murl and Wolf, she added, "Each of you."

Murl thumped the mossy earth with his tail, while Wolf waited with patient disinterest until Grace dug her fingers deep into his ruff.

Standing, straightening, she cast another sidelong glance at Thaniel, and returned to the weave of his arms. Before him, toe to toe, her mouth curved into a mischievous smile.

"You are remarkable," she said.

"Me?" he asked, lightly kissing her knuckles through their fingers' clasp.

"Yes. You." Her words rustled with green-toothed margins.

"Hmmm . . ." He moved his attention to her wrists. "And I thought that of *you*."

"I think," she persisted, over the race of her pulse, "I'm ready."

"Ready?" he breathed against her neck. "For what?"

"Are you really going to make me say it?"

"Yes," he said, forehead touching hers. "I think I am."

"Thaniel," she leaned into the net of his arms, looked up at him. "Will you bind yourself to me? Here? In this place?"

He gathered her up in full embrace. "I have wanted nothing more."

She welcomed his adoration—over her forehead and cheeks, the tip of nose, her mouth. Holding him close, she walked her fingers up his back to the nape of his neck, threading them through waves of nut-brown hair escaped from their binding. She inhaled the pine and cedar and sandalwood scent of him, felt his breath warm against her neck and ear.

Cheek pressed to Thaniel's breast, Grace closed her eyes, and the great tree wove around them a song of wind-rustled leaves and rasping branches, deep-anchoring roots, and pale ocher-yellow seed pods—of rescue, reunion, and renewal.

CHAPTER THIRTY-SIX

"Mom, really." Grace chose her words carefully. She watched her mother measure out thick cuts of butter, scoops of flour and sugar, spoonsful of baking powder and salt, and add each to the wide wooden bowl. "My birthday was *weeks* ago."

Lettie looked up from the kitchen table, her hair haloed in motes. "You slept through your birthday." Briskly, she combined the ingredients. Her eyes shone. "You need a birthday cake before you have a bridal cake."

"Yes, but—"

"I'll make as many cakes as I like, thank you." A small drift of flour lifted from the bowl's wide rim as she stirred. "For you or anyone else."

Grace blinked and glanced at her father. He tamped the bowl of his pipe, lifting his gray brows in mute comment, unwilling to participate. She made a face at him.

"You slept through winter." Sylvie mewed and leaned into Grace's shins, a singular voice of reason. "She wept and worried."

Grace bent and ran her thumb along the cat's jaw in silent acknowledgment. She pushed her hair behind one ear, then drew her hand away. A small, pale flower caught between her fingers—the green vines had recently broken into bloom, wreathing her in a scent evocative of honeysuckle. The bloom fell in a spiral path as Grace rose, and Sylvie swatted at it.

"Can I help?" Grace asked. Crossing the room, she wrapped her arms about her mother's waist, tucking her chin into the small curve between her neck and shoulder.

"Go collect some flowers to decorate the cake." Her mother's head swiveled toward Grace's, nested beside her, and she added quickly, "Not *those*. Cherry or plum or wild rose. Something we *know* is edible." Wooden spoon in hand, Lettie loosed herself from the hoop of Grace's arms, turned fully to face her, and added, "But don't go far."

"All right," Grace said.

"And take Murl with you."

"Yes, Mother."

"And Wolf."

"He's not here," Grace said. Silently, she noted her mother's acceptance of Wolf within their home. A year's worth of change, caught in a phrase. "He's with his family."

"Oh." Lettie's brow creased. With her free hand, she reached to adjust the battered delicate silk flower secured behind Grace's left ear. "You can barely see it there anymore, for all the other . . ." She fluttered her hand vaguely.

"I know it's there." She hugged her mother close. "*Thaniel* knows."

"Will he be joining you?"

Grace shook her head, loosed a flutter of soft petals. "He's on a call."

Her mother stepped back a pace, regarded her daughter with a stern eye, did not release her hands. Firmly, she said, "Stay out of the Wood."

"*Mom.*" Grace rolled her eyes toward the light and blue-shadow-stroked beam-and-plaster ceiling.

"And don't talk to strangers."

"Mom! I'm twenty years old!" Grace threw a pleading glance in her father's direction. "Dad!"

"Twenty, as you say," her father said. Pipe clamped between his teeth, he turned the page of a journal, made a notation. "You don't need my help. And I'm smart enough not to get involved."

"*He* could be out there," Lettie said.

Gaven blew a coil of smoke and muttered under his breath, "He *should* be in *jail.*"

"Bran is seeing to him," Grace reminded them. She tried to wriggle her fingers free of her mother's grasp, only succeeded in securing their weave.

"That," her mother sniffed, "is a very small comfort."

"Like father, like son," her father agreed.

"They're *nothing* alike. And I *trust* Bran." Exasperated, Grace looked at them both in turn. "That must count for something?" She felt her blood warm, rising like sap.

Her father thumbed the journal's pages. "She has a point, Lettie."

"Of course, we trust you, Grace," her mother said, loosening her hands' clasp.

"You," her father muttered, "without question. Him, not so much."

Murl padded between the two women, looked up, and whined, "Please don't fight."

"Stay out of it, dog," Sylvie advised, ears ticking.

Grace looked at her mother—so loved, so admired, who so loved *her*, and whose wounds remained unseen. Her thoughts collapsed in a soft ache. "I'll be fine," she said. "Really."

"Of course you will." Lettie nodded, smiled. Lifting her chin, she drew the back of her hand along the corner of her eye, leaving a pale smudge of flour. "Go on, then. Maybe you'll find some late violets."

Grace eased her way to the back door, flung wide to accept a breeze, to air the house. Spring faded, reshaped itself and rioted in a headlong dash toward summer.

Brilliant and brash, sunlight poured from the sky's clear blue expanse, past the fringe of her lashes. Her pulse quickened in response; her veins coursed verdant beneath thin skin.

"Don't forget to come home," her mother called.

"I won't," Grace promised. Looking quickly over her shoulder, she sidestepped her boots and slipped past the door, outside. "Come on, Murl."

"Where are we going?"

"Not far," she said, loud enough for her mother's benefit.

"Sylvie, too?" The dog wagged, tongue lolling.

"Yes," the tabby confirmed. She leapt down the back steps and pounced on a thatch of grass. "Invited or not, I'm coming." She smoothed, with one front paw, the dark M on her forehead, her whiskers.

"Well, then," Grace said. "Off we go."

Dog at her heels and cat sashaying beside, Grace set out across the rear yard, packed earth cool beneath her feet, past spider's woodshed and timber fence and chicken coop. Buff and marigold hens pecked her hem and toes, scolded cat and dog in equal measure and with such fury that their outrage drew the rooster's spurred attention. Reaching into her skirt's pockets, Grace tossed a handful of dried corn, leaving the hens in a competitive clamor. They safely navigated the yard's confines amid the flock's distraction.

"Hens are *pointy*," Murl barked.

"Dog," Sylvie spat—tufts of fur missing from her tail—"you have a penchant for understatement."

Daylight lounged, stretched, broad and golden. The summer solstice advanced in steady degrees—the day she and Thaniel had set to bind themselves, one to the other, beneath the great tree. Much required doing, and her mother threw herself into the doing with enthusiasm—thus, this impromptu excursion to collect flowers for her own belated birthday cake.

"Are we going to the meadow?" Murl loped ahead, loosening earth and strewing pebbles.

"We are," she confirmed.

"He'll have everything scattered before we even arrive," Sylvie said.

Grace looked down at the tabby. "I'd really prefer you didn't hunt while we're out together."

"If hopes were hedgehogs . . ." Sylvie dashed off after Murl, chasing scree loosened in the dog's wake.

Grace trailed increasingly behind both, watching them bound parallel to her father's timber fence in the meadow's general direction. Pausing, she leaned against a rail among the pinks and wild daisies and fairy-crowned grasses, and observed the goats. A half-dozen kids kicked up their heels and ran circles over the clovered ground—around and about; over, under, and between their enduring mothers.

She stroked a nanny's forehead whose cream-and-rust sides jarred with the movements of her unborn young.

"Twins?" Grace asked. "I imagine they'll be here soon."

The nanny chewed, jaws sliding laterally over a mouthful of ivy. Before she could respond, the fervid exchange of a pair of kids interfered:

". . . am not!"

"Are *so*."

"Am *not*!"

"Are *so*!"

"*Maaaaaaaaaam*!" The smaller of the two kids elongated his neck and bleated at a tired gray nanny who stood nearby. "Tell her I am *not* a sheep!"

The cream-and-rust nanny regarded Grace with a deliberate, slot-pupiled eye. "I'm in no hurry," she said, and nibbled a leaf from Grace's vine-tumbled hair.

Scratching the nanny's bearded chin, Grace continued along the fence. Ahead, the quince tree rose, a sentinel contortion of dark limbs and oblong leaves that hovered over the beehive's white gleam. A constant stream of bees zipped and hummed and spiraled back and forth through the air. Reflexively, Grace lifted her hand, receiving a fuzzy black-and-yellow individual. It danced across her palm, rear legs brushed thick with bright pollen.

"Cherry . . . honeysuckle . . . and wild rose." Grace nodded. "Perfect."

In a shimmer of wings, the tiny creature whizzed off to make her delivery and share her dancing report. By the time Grace reached the fence's end, where weathered rails and posts jogged sharply off to the right, her sleeves and hair glittered with attendant bees. She continued straight past the fence's end and cut across the wide-open pasture, through the warp and weft of calf-high grasses which Murl had parted—she saw the sweep of his brush tail and Sylvie's creep and prowl.

Beyond the pasture, with its sleek auburn and black-and-white cows, the Bright Wood's edge glittered. Grace slowed her pace. Somewhere in that borderland of dappled light and shadow, within the push and pull of wood and meadow, Wolf's mate made her den. An attentive mate and father, Wolf no longer stayed at the cottage. When he scratched at the back door, once or twice a week, she heard contentment in his voice, perceived it in his bearing. He promised introductions when the pups were weaned.

Lingering, she tilted her head, strove to hear beyond the cows' mournful lowing, hoping to hear the rapid patter of the pups' small, bright pulses stitched into the world's fabric. As she stood, listening, the grasses swished and parted, and Murl bounded toward her. Jaws fixed around a mouthful and crowded with words indecipherable, he dropped a small brown lump at her feet.

"I found a toad!" He wagged and grinned.

Grace knelt, rested a hand on Murl's shoulder. With the index finger of her other hand, she probed the toad's pale, upturned underbelly. The small creature righted itself with an awkward thrust of bowed rear legs. His throat bulged and collapsed, glistening around furious comment, before he hopped off through a screen of interwoven stems.

"Toads taste *bad*." Murl pulled up tufts of grass and chewed.

Sylvie peered through the grass. "A startling display of discrimination."

Grace, ignoring Sylvie's comment, quirked an eyebrow at Murl.

"I didn't *swallow* it." He hung his head and licked dirt from his muzzle.

With two hands, she tousled the dog's neck ruff. "Well done."

Tongue lolling, Murl hurtled off again.

Orienting herself, Grace turned edgewise to the Bright Wood, roughly facing the meadow's center. Her shadow swelled and contracted, a fluid blue-green column cast over a sea of wildflowers and grasses flecked with white and pink and lavender. Heart, thought, and senses—she opened to the meadow, to its countless inhabitants. The response struck immediately, a resounding current of intertwined voices, brilliant as stars. She swayed, slightly giddy, and curled her toes among thick mats of clover for support. Inhaling the meadow's sweet breath, she began to walk a narrowing, spiral path through the grasses toward the meadow's heart. Ladybugs and lacewings gathered along her collar, her shirt's cuffs; cabbage moths and sulfurs adorned her sleeves and shoulders. From all sides, crickets sang counterpoint to larks and swallows.

Onward she waded, slowly filling her apron with blooms, her thoughts echoing her steps' circuitous path.

When at last her bare feet found the focus of her search, she very nearly tripped over it—Thrush's great-great-great-grandfather's rock. A hulking, low-profile mass covered in moss and lichens. It protruded from the meadow's sawing, flower-sewn grasses like some fairy-tale giant's toe.

Grace considered the stone, its length and breadth, its weather-worn, undulate-humped back. Catching up her apron, she sat on her heels, pressed her knees to the earth, and knelt before the broad sweep and curve of sun-warmed stone. The color of old wine, its surface glittered with chinks of white quartz. Time and weather had scoured and polished away all roughness.

She swept the stone's surface clear, freeing it of hollow, whorled snail shells; of shards and fragments of acorn and hickory shells; of thistle and sunflower seeds; of black walnut hulls. She flattened her palms, spread and pressed her fingers to the stone's rough bulk—flesh and blood to earth's bones. Bending forward, she rested her forehead lightly against the stone's face. Closing her eyes—conscious of its solid, near-timeless presence, of her comparably fleeting self—she listened, searching for the stone's voice.

An hour. A day or night or season. A year or lifetime. She listened. And, at last, in its own time and manner, the stone spoke. It rumbled foundational imagery: of itself, of its brethren—the mountains, hills, valleys—in a voice so deep and slow, so methodical and sonorous as to be almost unintelligible to her hasty ear and to her mind's ability to fathom. She felt its kinship to peaks and foothills; perceived its strength, solidity, and endurance; felt sweeping wind, drenching rain, sun- and moon- and starlight turning and limning and passing. She understood its indulgence toward the world's young—grandfatherly and forbearing; toward all those diminutive creatures that came and went, generation upon generation—lizard, basking in two-fold warmth; chipmunk, barking the daily bulletin and forecast; countless insects alighting and crawling and skittering over its mottled surface. Of Pipit and Meadowlark and Thrush and generations of his sweet-voiced family, who trapped insects and cracked open seeds and snails upon its curved back—beaks and claws randomly applied.

"Tell ▽ Thrush . . ."

The stone's wine-red flanks rumbled in Grace's thoughts, its voice thrummed in her bones.

"A ▽ little ▽ to ▽ the ▽ left . . ."

She sat back on her heels—surprised at her own surprise—simultaneously aware that, somewhere along the Bright Wood's fringe, a liquid, golden song darted through the green-leafed canopy. It was a song that recalled one of her earliest conversations—with Thrush. Setting her hands against the stone, she felt its bones-deep humor drum through every cell and fiber of her being—a delighted, earthen roll.

Grace's laughter pattered: small, smooth pebbles of sound cast alongside the stone's deep chortle. If anything truly chortled, she thought, it was stone. She caught her breath and said, "I will. I'll let him know."

Rising, she struck out across the meadow and followed the liquid song to its source, perched on a limb in the Bright Wood.

WITH GRATITUDE

A first book must always be written with heaps of gratitude, and *Grace* is, too. For Adam, who since the day we met, saw magic in me that I'd forgotten, and who has walked beside me in unwavering support and confidence as I began to remember—you are my Thaniel. For Aaron, who helped me develop a logical foundation for the Bright Wood's magic—maybe, now, you'll read *Grace*! For Caprice Garvin and Tess Callahan, who quietly, repeatedly, and firmly insisted I belonged at the writers' table and then made me comfortable there. For Andrew Alford, Holly Obernauer, and Sasha Troyhan, for listening with hearts, senses, literary expertise, and for demystified on-the-spot feedback. For Elizabeth Dee and Allysa McPherson, for their encouraging and enthusiastic critiques and hawk-eyed line editing skills. For Jeremy Brooks and Holly Petti, who created an incredibly beautiful website, even though I struggled to articulate specifics. For Lisa Schroeder, who designed my book's cover—your abilities to translate a dream into reality is astounding. For Nancy Sulla, who connected me with my incredible editor/agent, Tara Tomczyk of Blydyn Square Books—Tara is one of the hardest working, most dedicated individuals I know. I'm exceptionally grateful she believed in *Grace* when others wouldn't glance her way, and I'm thrilled to be part of the growing BSB family. Finally, although to my heartbreak, they will never read it, I think both my dear friend Lydia Lefkowitz and my mother-in-law Barbara Jewell would have loved *Grace*, simply because I know they loved me. I also have immense gratitude for all the furred, feathered, and scaled creatures I've known throughout my life—too many to name here, but most recently Cassiapurra and Philomena Marigold. They—and all of Nature—have so much to share with us, if we only take time to pause, observe, and gently engage. As Khalil Gibran said: "*And forget not that the earth delights to feel your bare feet and the winds long to play with your hair.*" Thank you.

ABOUT THE AUTHOR

Carrie Birde was born with a foot in two worlds—the real and the imaginary—and currently maintains citizenship in both. Although recent events challenge her ambitions of invisibility, she believes she can easily resume those studies in the future. When she isn't writing, collaging, and dreaming, she can generally be found outside seeking active fairy rings, concealed doors in hedges, and those fabled thresholds where the veil between worlds thins. She lives contentedly in the Beautiful Boonton Bubble with her husband, son, a singing calico cat, and a small fey creature currently disguised as a dog. If this doesn't satisfy your curiosity, please visit CarrieBirde.com.

Thank You

FOR READING

A Small Tale of Uncommon Grace!

WE HOPE YOU'VE ENJOYED IT! HERE AT BLYDYN SQUARE BOOKS, WE TAKE SPECIAL CARE IN PRODUCING BOOKS OF THE HIGHEST QUALITY FOR YOUR ENTERTAINMENT AND EDUCATION. WE DO OUR BEST TO CREATE "BOOKS THAT MAKE YOU THINK!"

TO FIND OUT MORE ABOUT US OR TO SEE WHAT OTHER TITLES WE OFFER, PLEASE VISIT BLYDYNSQUAREBOOKS.COM.

STAY UP TO DATE WITH OUR LATEST NEWS (AND BE ELIGIBLE TO WIN PRIZES) BY SUBSCRIBING TO OUR NEWSLETTER:

www.ingramcontent.com/pod-product-compliance
Lightning Source LLC
LaVergne TN
LVHW010308070526
838199LV00065B/5480